Beautiful
REDEMPTION

ALSO BY JAMIE MCGUIRE

Providence (Providence Trilogy: Book One)
Requiem (Providence Trilogy: Book Two)
Eden (Providence Trilogy: Book Three)

Beautiful Disaster
Walking Disaster
A Beautiful Wedding (A Beautiful Disaster Novella)
Beautiful Oblivion

Red Hill
Among Monsters

Happenstance: A Novella Series
Happenstance: A Novella Series (Part Two)
Happenstance: A Novella Series (Part Three)

Apolonia

Beautiful
REDEMPTION

JAMIE McGUIRE

For Autumn Hull,
Your friendship is invaluable.

And for Kelli Spear,
I'm so thankful to have you in my corner.

CONTENTS

CHAPTER ONE

CONTROL WAS ALL THAT WAS REAL. I had learned from a young age that planning, calculation, and observation could avoid most unpleasant things—unnecessary risk, disappointment, and most importantly, heartache.

Planning to avoid the unpleasant though wasn't always easy, a fact that had become glaringly apparent in the dim lights of Cutter's Pub.

The dozen or so neon signs hanging on the walls and the weak track lighting from the ceiling, highlighting the bottles of liquor behind the bar, were only slightly comforting. Everything else made it evident just how far I was from home.

The reclaimed barn wood made up the walls, and the blond pine smudged with black stain had been designed specifically to make the Midtown space look like a hole-in-the-wall bar, but it was too clean. A hundred years of smoke hadn't saturated the paint. The walls didn't whisper about Capone or Dillinger.

I'd been sitting on the same stool for two hours since I'd quit unpacking the boxes in my new condo. For as long as I could stand, I'd put away my items that made up who I was. Exploring my new neighborhood was much more appealing, especially in the amazingly mild night air even though it was the last day in February. I was experiencing my new independence with the added freedom of having no one at home who expected a report of my whereabouts.

The seat cushion that I was keeping warm was covered in orange substitute leather, and after drinking a respectful percentage of my relocation incentive that the Federal Bureau of Investigation had so generously deposited into my account that afternoon, I was doing well to keep from falling off of it.

The last of my fifth Manhattan of the evening slid from inside the fancy glass into my mouth, sizzling down my throat. The bourbon and sweet vermouth tasted like loneliness. That at least made me feel at home. *Home* though was thousands of miles away, and it felt even farther the longer I sat on one of the twelve stools lining the curved bar.

I wasn't lost though. I was a runaway. Stacks of boxes sat in my new fifth-floor condo, boxes that I had packed with enthusiasm while my former fiancé, Jackson, stood and sulked in the corner of our tiny shared Chicago apartment.

Moving on was key to climbing the ranks in the Bureau, and I had gotten very good at it in a small amount of time. Jackson had been unfazed when I first told him I was being transferred to San Diego. Even at the airport, right before I'd left, he'd promised that we could still make it work. Jackson wasn't good at letting go at all. He had threatened to love me forever.

I dangled the cocktail glass in front of me with an expectant smile. The bartender helped me set it soundly on the wood, and then he poured another. The orange peel and cherry were in a slow dance somewhere between the surface and the bottom—like me.

"This is your last one, honey," he said, wiping the bar on each side of me.

"Stop working so hard. I don't tip that well."

"The Feds never do," he said without judgment.

"Is it that obvious?" I said.

"A lot of you live around here. You all talk the same and get drunk the first night away from home. Don't worry. You don't scream Bureau."

"Thank God for that," I said, holding up my glass. I didn't mean it. I loved the Bureau and everything about it. I'd even loved Jackson, who was an agent, too.

"Where did you transfer from?" he asked. His too-tight black V-neck, manicured cuticles, and perfectly gelled coif betrayed his flirtatious smile.

"Chicago," I said.

His lips pulled back and puckered until he somewhat resembled a fish, and his eyes widened. "You should be celebrating."

"I guess I shouldn't be upset unless I run out of places to run to." I took a gulp and licked the smoky burn of bourbon from my lips.

"Oh. Getting away from your ex?"

"In my line of work, you never really get away."

"Oh, hell. He's a fed, too? Don't shit where you sleep, sweetie."

I traced the rim of my glass. "They don't actually train you for that."

"I know. It happens a lot. See it all the time," he said, shaking his head, while he washed something in a suds-filled sink behind the bar. "You live close?"

I eyed him, wary of anyone who could sniff out an agent and asked too many questions.

"Will you be frequenting here?" he clarified.

Seeing where he was going with his inquisition, I nodded. "Likely."

"Don't worry about the tip. Moving is expensive, and so is drinking away what you left behind. You can make it up to me later."

His words made my lips curve up in a way they hadn't in months even though it probably wasn't noticeable to anyone but me.

"What's your name?" I asked.

"Anthony."

"Does anyone call you Tony?"

"Not if they want to drink here."

"Noted."

Anthony tended to the only other patron at the bar on this late Monday night—or some might call it an early Tuesday morning. The pudgy middle-aged woman with swollen red eyes wore a black dress. As he did so, the door swung open, and a man around my age breezed in, sitting two stools down. He loosened his tie and unfastened the top button of his perfectly pressed white oxford. He glanced in my direction, and in that half second, his hazel-green eyes registered everything about me he wanted to know. Then, he looked away.

My cell phone buzzed in my blazer pocket, and I pulled it out to check the display. It was another text message from Jackson. Beside his name, a small six fit snuggly between parentheses, noting the number of messages he'd sent. That trapped number reminded me of the last time he'd touched me—during a hug I'd had to coax him out of.

I was two thousand one hundred and fifty miles from Jackson, and he was still able to make me feel guilty—but not guilty enough.

I clicked the side button on my cell phone, darkening the screen, without replying to Jackson's message. Then, I lifted my finger to the bartender while gulping down the remainder of my sixth glass.

I'd found Cutter's Pub right around the corner from my new condo in Midtown, an area in San Diego nestled between the International Airport and the zoo. My Chicago colleagues were wearing FBI-standard parkas over their bulletproof vests while I was enjoying the warmer than usual San Diego weather in a tube top and blazer with skinny jeans. I felt a little overdressed and a tad sweaty. Granted, that could be from the amount of liquor in my system.

"You're awfully little to be in a place like this," the man two stools down said.

"A place like what?" Anthony said, raising a brow while practically fisting a tumbler.

The man ignored him.

"I'm not little," I said before taking a drink. "I'm petite."

"Isn't that the same thing?"

"I also have a Taser in my purse and a mean left hook, so don't bite off more than you can chew."

"Your kung fu is strong."

I didn't give the man the gratification of attention. Instead, I stared forward. "Was that a racist remark?"

"Absolutely not. You just seem a little violent to me."

"I'm not *violent*," I said although it was preferable to coming off as a vapid, easy target.

"Oh, really?" He wasn't asking. He was antagonizing. "I just recently read about female Asian peace leaders being honored. I'm guessing you weren't one of them."

"I'm also Irish," I grumbled.

He chuckled once. There was something in his voice—not just ego but more than confidence. Something made me want to turn and get a good look at him, but I kept my eyes on the line of liquor bottles on the other side of the bar.

After the man realized he wasn't going to get a better response, he moved to the empty stool next to me. I sighed.

"What are you drinking?" he asked.

I rolled my eyes and then decided to look over at him. He was as beautiful as the Southern California weather, and he couldn't have looked less like Jackson. Even sitting down, I could tell that he was tall—at least six foot three. His pear-colored eyes glowed against his beach-bronzed skin. Although he might be intimidating to the average male, I didn't get the sense that he was dangerous—at least not to me—even if he was twice my size.

"Whatever I'm buying," I said, not trying to hide my best flirtatious smile.

Letting my guard down for a beautiful stranger for an hour was justifiable, especially after a sixth glass. We would flirt, I would forget about any residual guilt, and I would go home. I'd possibly even get a free drink. That was a respectable plan.

He grinned back. "Anthony," he said, holding up a finger.

"The usual?" Anthony asked from the end of the bar.

The man nodded. He was a regular. He must live or work close by.

I frowned when Anthony took my glass instead of refilling it.

He shrugged, no apology in his eyes. "Told you it was your last one."

In half a dozen pulls, the stranger knocked back enough cheap beer to be at least close to my level of intoxication. I was glad. I wouldn't have to pretend to be sober, and his drink of choice told me he wasn't fussy or trying to impress me. Or maybe he was just broke.

"Did you say I couldn't buy you a drink because Anthony capped you or because you really wouldn't let me?" he asked.

"Because I can buy my own drinks," I said, albeit a bit slurred.

"Do you live around here?" he asked.

I peeked over at him. "Your stunted conversational skills are disappointing me by the second."

He laughed out loud, throwing his head back. "Christ, woman. Where are you from? Not here."

"Chicago. Just blew in. Boxes are still stacked in my living room."

"I can relate," he said, nodding in understanding while holding up his drink with respect. "I've made two cross-country moves in the last three years."

"To where?"

"Here. Then, DC. Then, back."

"Are you a politician or a lobbyist?" I asked with a smirk.

"Neither," he said, his expression twisting into disgust. He took a swig of his beer. "What's your name?" he asked.

"Not interested."

"That's a terrible name."

I made a face.

He continued, "That explains the move. You're running from a guy."

I glared at him. He was beautiful, but he was also presumptuous—even if he was right. "And not looking for another one. Not a one-night stand, not a revenge screw, nothing. So, don't waste your time or your money. I'm sure you can find a nice West Coast girl who would be more than happy to accept a drink from you."

"Where's the fun in that?" he said, leaning in.

My God, even if I were sober, he would be intoxicating.

I looked down at the way his lips touched the rim of his beer bottle, and I felt a twinge between my thighs. I was lying, and he knew it.

"Did I piss you off?" he asked with the most charming smile I'd ever seen.

Clean shaven with just a couple of inches of light-brown hair, that man and his smile had conquered far more daunting challenges than me.

"Are you trying to piss me off?" I asked.

"Maybe. The way you hold your mouth when you're angry is...pretty fucking amazing. I might be a dick to you all night just so I can stare at your lips."

I swallowed.

My little game was over. He'd won, and he knew it.

"You want to get out of here?" he asked.

I signaled to Anthony, but the stranger shook his head and put a large bill on the counter. Free drink—at least that part of my plan had worked out. The man walked over to the door, gesturing for me to lead the way.

"A week's worth of tips says he doesn't go through with it," Anthony said loud enough for the beautiful stranger to hear.

"To hell with it," I said, walking quickly through the door.

I passed my new friend and walked out onto the sidewalk, the door sweeping slowly closed. He grabbed my hand, playful but firm, and pulled me against him.

"Anthony seems to think you'll back out," I said, looking up at him.

He was so much taller than me. Standing that close to him felt like sitting in the front row at the movie theater. I had to lift my chin and lean back a bit to look him in the eyes.

I leaned in, daring him to kiss me.

He hesitated while he scanned my face, and then his eyes softened. "Something tells me, this time, I won't."

He leaned down, and what began as an almost experimental soft kiss turned both lustful and romantic. His lips moved with mine as if he'd remembered them, even missed the way they'd felt. Unlike anything I'd experienced before, a strange electrical current crackled through me, melting my nerves away. We had done this so many times before—in a fantasy or maybe a dream. It was the best kind of déjà vu.

For less than a second after he pulled away, his eyes were still closed as if he were savoring the moment. When he looked down at me, he shook his head. "Definitely not backing out."

We rounded the corner, walked quickly across the street, and then went up the stoop of my building. I fished inside of my purse for my keys, and then we walked inside, waiting in the elevator bay. His fingers grazed mine, and once they intertwined, he yanked me against him. The elevator opened, and we stumbled inside.

He gripped my hips and pulled me against him as my fingertips searched for the correct button. He touched his silken lips to my neck, and every nerve sparked and danced under my skin. The tiny kisses he peppered along my jawline, from ear to collarbone, were purposeful and experienced. His hands begged me to be closer to him with each touch as if he'd been waiting for me his entire life. Even though I had that same irrational feeling, I knew it was all part of the appeal, a part of the ruse, but the way he noticeably restrained himself from tugging too hard at my clothes made tiny shock waves careen through my body.

When we reached the fifth floor, he had my hair pulled to the side and one shoulder exposed while he skimmed his lips over my skin.

"You are so soft," he whispered.

Ironically, his words made thousands of tiny bumps rise all over my skin.

My keys jingled while I fumbled with the lock. The man twisted the knob, and we nearly fell inside. He leaned away from me, pushing the door closed with his back, and pulled me against him by my hands. He smelled like beer and a hint of saffron and wood from his cologne, but his mouth still tasted of mint toothpaste. When our mouths met again, I willingly let his tongue slip inside as I laced my fingers behind his neck.

He slid my blazer off my shoulders and let it fall to the floor. Then, he loosened his tie and pulled it over his head. As he unbuttoned his shirt, I pulled my tube top up and over my head. My bare breasts were exposed for only a moment before my long black hair cascaded back down to cover them.

The stranger's shirt was off, his torso a combination of impressive genes and several years of an intensive daily workout regimen that had sculpted the perfection in front of me. I kicked off my heels, and he did the same with his shoes. I ran my fingers over each of his protruding muscles and the ripples of his abdomen. One hand settled on the button of his pants while the other gripped the thick hardness under them.

Holy. Giant. Cock.

The sharp sound of his zipper made the warmth between my legs throb, practically begging to be caressed. I pressed my fingers into the backs of his arms while his kisses left my neck for my shoulders and then my chest. All the while, he slowly slipped off my jeans.

He stood and paused for a few seconds, taking a moment to appreciate that I was standing completely naked before him. He also seemed a bit surprised. "No panties?"

I shrugged. "Never."

"Never?" he asked, his eyes begging me to say no.

I loved the way he was looking at me—part amazed, part amused, part overwhelmingly aroused. My girlfriends in Chicago had always lauded the benefits of the strings-free one-night stand. This guy seemed like the perfect one to try it with.

I arched an eyebrow, relishing how sexy this total stranger made me feel. "Don't own a single pair."

He lifted me up, and I hooked my ankles around his backside. The only fabric still left between us was his dark gray boxer briefs.

He kissed me as he carried me to the couch, and then he gently laid me onto the cushions. "Comfortable?" he asked, nearly breathing the words.

When I nodded, he kissed me once and then left quickly to fish a square package from his wallet. When he returned, he ripped it open with his teeth. I was glad he'd brought his own. Even if I had thought to purchase condoms, I wouldn't have had the foresight or optimism to buy any in his size.

He quickly unrolled the thin latex over his length and then touched his tip to the delicate pink skin between my legs. He leaned down to whisper in my ear, but he only let out a faltering breath.

I reached around to his tight backside and pressed my fingers into his skin, guiding him, as he slid himself inside me. It was my turn to let out a sigh.

He groaned and then put his mouth on mine again.

After ten minutes of maneuvering on the couch, sweaty and red-faced, the stranger looked at me with a frustrated and apologetic smile. "Where's your bedroom?"

I pointed to the hallway. "Second door on the right."

He lifted me, holding my thighs, and I tightened them around his middle. He padded down the hall in his bare feet, passing boxes and plastic bags along with stacks of plates and linens. I wasn't sure how he kept from tripping in the dim light of an unfamiliar condo with his mouth on mine.

As he walked while still inside me, I couldn't help but cry out the only name I could, "Jesus Christ!"

He smiled against my mouth and pushed open the door before lowering me to my mattress.

He didn't take his eyes from mine as he positioned himself over me. His knees were a little wider apart than they had been while we were on the couch, allowing him to go deeper and to move his hips so that he touched me in a spot that made my knees quiver with each thrust. His mouth was on mine again as if the wait had been killing him. If I hadn't just met him half an hour before, I would have mistaken the way he touched me, kissed me, moved against me for love.

He touched his cheek to mine and held his breath as he concentrated, building up to an end. At the same time, he was trying to prolong the senseless, foolish, and irresponsible but amazing ride we were both on. He pushed against the mattress with one hand and held my knee against his shoulder with the other.

I white-knuckled the comforter as he thrust himself inside me, over and over. Jackson hadn't been unfortunate in size, but without a doubt, this stranger filled every inch of me. Every time he buried himself, it would send a rush of fantastic pain throughout my entire body, and every time he pulled back, I'd nearly panic, hoping it wasn't over.

With my arms and legs wrapped around him, I cried out again for the dozenth time since he had climbed the stairs. His tongue was so forceful and commanding in my mouth that I knew he'd done this many, many times before. That made it easier. He didn't care enough to pass judgment on me later, so I wouldn't have to either. Once I'd seen what kind of body was under that button-down oxford, I couldn't really blame myself, even if I were sober.

He rocked into me again, his sweat mixing with mine, making our skin feel like we were melting together. My eyes nearly rolled back into my head with the devastating mixture of ache and pleasure surging through my body with every movement.

His mouth returned to mine, and I was easily lost in thoughts of how eager yet smooth and amazing his lips were. Every flick of his tongue was calculated, practiced, and seemed like it was all in pursuit of my pleasure. Jackson hadn't been a particularly good kisser, and even though I'd only just met this man above me, I would miss those longing kisses once he ducked out of my condo in the early hours of the morning—if he even waited that long.

While he wonderfully and mercilessly fucked me, he gripped my thigh with one hand, spreading my legs further apart, and then he slid his other hand between my legs, tenderly rubbing his thumb in tiny circles over my swollen, sensitive pink skin.

A few seconds later, I was crying out, raising my hips to meet his and then squeezing his waist with my trembling knees. He leaned down and covered my mouth with his while I moaned. I could feel his lips turn up into a smile.

After a few slow movements and tender kisses, his restraint was gone. His muscles tensed as he thrust himself inside me, each time more powerful than the one before. With my climax impressively achieved, he concentrated only on himself as he thrust harder and ruthlessly against me.

His groan was muffled inside my mouth, and then he pressed his cheek against mine while he rode the wave of his orgasm. Gradually, he lay still above me. He took a moment to catch his breath, and then he turned to kiss my cheek, his lips lingering for a while.

Our encounter had gone from a spontaneous adventure to painfully awkward in less than a minute.

The silence and stillness in the room made the alcohol disappear, and the reality of what we'd done weighed down on me. I'd gone from feeling sexy and desired to an embarrassingly eager, cheap score.

The stranger leaned down to kiss my lips, but I lowered my chin, pulling back, which felt ridiculous since he was still engaged.

"I," I began, "have to be at work early."

He kissed me anyway, ignoring my shamed expression. His tongue danced with mine, caressing it, memorizing it. He deeply breathed in through his nose, not at all in a hurry, and then he pulled back, smiling.

Damn it, I would miss his mouth, and I suddenly felt really pathetic for that. I wasn't sure if I'd ever find someone who could kiss me that way.

"Me, too. I'm…Thomas, by the way," he said softly. He rolled over and relaxed beside me, his head propped by his hand. Instead of getting dressed, he looked as if he were ready for conversation.

My independence was slipping away from me every second the stranger became something more. Thoughts of reporting my every move to Jackson flipped like television channels in my mind. I hadn't transferred thousands of miles away to be chained to another relationship.

I pressed my lips together. "I'm"—*Do it. Do it, or you'll just kick yourself later.*—"emotionally unavailable."

Thomas nodded, stood up, and then walked into the living room to dress in silence. He stood in the doorway of my bedroom with his shoes in one hand, his keys in the other, his tie hanging askew from his neck. I tried not to stare, but I did, so I could study every inch of him to remember and fantasize over for the rest of my life.

He looked down and then chuckled, judgment still absent from his expression. "Thanks for a great and unexpected end to a shitty Monday." He began to turn around.

I pulled the blanket across me and sat up. "It's not you. You were great."

He turned back to face me, a smirk on his shadowed face. "Don't worry about me. I'm not walking out of here, doubting myself. You gave me fair warning. I wasn't expecting anything more."

"If you wait a second, I'll walk you out."

"I know the way. This is my building. I'm sure we'll run into each other again."

My cheeks paled. "You live in *this* building?"

He peered up at the ceiling. "Just above you."

I pointed up. "The next floor up, you mean?"

"Yes, but," he said with a sheepish grin, "my place is right above yours. But I'm rarely home."

I swallowed, horrified. *So much for a strings-free one-night stand.* I began nibbling at my thumbnail, trying to think of what to say next. "Okay…well, I guess good night then?"

Thomas flashed an arrogant, seductive smile. "Night."

CHAPTER TWO

DRINKING AWAY JACKSON'S GUILT TRIP the night before my first day in the San Diego field office proved not to be the most intelligent thing I'd done.

I arrived with only my vest, and I was given a sidearm, credentials, and a cell phone once I'd checked in. Assigned to Squad Five, I found the only empty desk, vacated by the last agent who hadn't meshed with the infamous Assistant Special Agent in Charge, who we referred to as the ASAC. I had heard about him all the way in Chicago, but it would take more than a bad temper to scare me away from a chance at a promotion.

Only a few sections of the desk's surface didn't have a light film of dust, probably from where his or her computer and belongings had been set. My headphones case sat next to my laptop, and a lack of picture frames or miscellaneous decor looked rather pathetic compared with the other desks in the squad room.

"That's pathetic," a female voice said, making me wonder if I'd spoken my thoughts aloud.

A woman, young but slightly intimidating, stood with her arms crossed and resting on the ledge of the four-by-five fabric-covered wall that separated my cubicle from the main hallway that was used to get from one end of the squad room to the other. Her shiny but otherwise ordinary brown hair was pulled into a low bun at the nape of her neck.

"I can't disagree," I said, wiping the dust away with a paper towel.

I had already put my vest in my locker. It was the only thing I had brought from the Chicago office. I had moved to San Diego to start over, so it didn't make much sense to put my old life on display.

"I don't mean the dust," she said, watching me with her hooded green eyes. Her cheeks were a bit chubby, but that only gave away her youth. She was certainly fit everywhere else.

"I know."

"I'm Val Taber. Don't call me Agent Taber, or we can't be friends."

"Shall I call you Val then?"

She made a face. "What else would you call me?"

"Agent Taber," a tall, slender man said as he walked by. He smirked as if he knew what would follow.

"Fuck off," she said, pulling a file from his hands. She glanced at it and then looked back to me. "You're the intelligence analyst? Lisa Lindy?"

"Liis," I said, cringing. I had never gotten used to correcting people. "Like geese but with an L."

"Liis. Sorry. I hear you got fast-tracked." Her voice was laced with sarcasm. "I call bullshit, but it's not really any of my business."

She was right. Being a female federal agent who specialized in languages had all but rolled out the red carpet for my transfer, but I had been instructed not to mention my specialization to anyone unless I had approval from my supervisor.

I looked over at the office of the supervisor. It was even more barren than my desk. Getting any approval from an empty office would prove to be difficult.

"You're correct," I said, not wanting to get into specifics.

It was pure luck that Squad Five had needed a language expert the moment I'd decided to leave Chicago. The stressed discretion meant there was likely an issue within the Bureau, but assuming wouldn't have helped score a transfer, so I'd filled out my paperwork and packed my bags.

"Great." She handed me the file. "Title Three for you to transcribe here. Maddox also wants a FD-three-oh-two. The first email in your inbox should be from the welcome wagon, and the next should be an audio file from Maddox. I went ahead and brought you copies of the FD-three-oh-twos and a CD until you get used to our system. He wants you to get started right away."

"Thank you."

Title Threes, known to Hollywood and the general public as phone or wire taps, made up a large portion of my function at the Bureau. Recordings were created, and then I would listen, translate, and write a report—also known as the infamous FD-302. But the Title Threes typically given to me were in Italian, Spanish, or my mother's language, Japanese. If the recording were in English, the OST—the squad secretary—would transcribe it.

Something told me that Val thought something was off about an analyst interpreting a Title Three, because curiosity—or maybe suspicion—was flickering in her eyes. But she didn't ask, and I didn't tell. As far as I knew, Maddox was the only agent who knew about my true purpose in San Diego.

"On it," I said.

She winked at me and smiled. "Want me to show you around later? Anything you didn't get to during the orientation tour?"

I thought about that for half a second. "The fitness room?"

"I know that one. I frequent there after work—right before I frequent the bar," she said.

"Agent Taber," a woman with a tight bun said as she walked by.

"Fuck off," she said again.

I arched an eyebrow.

She shrugged. "They must love it, or they wouldn't talk to me."

My mouth pulled to the side while I tried to suppress a laugh. Val Taber was refreshing.

"We have a squad meeting first thing in the a.m." She pondered that for a moment. "I'll show you the fitness room after lunch. It's sort of off-limits between eleven and noon. The boss likes to focus," she said, whispering the last bit and making a show of putting her fingers to one side of her mouth.

"Twelve thirty," I said with a nod.

"My desk," Val said, pointing to the next cubicle over. "We're neighbors."

"What's with the stuffed bunny?" I asked, referring to the gangly white rabbit with Xs sewn on for eyes, sitting on the corner of her desk.

Her slight triangle of a nose wrinkled. "It was my birthday last week." When I didn't reply, her face screwed into disgust. "Fuck off." A grin slowly stretched across her face, and then she winked at me before rounding the corner to return to her desk. She sat in her chair and turned her back to me, opening her email on her laptop.

I shook my head and then unzipped my headphones case before placing them over my ears. After connecting them to my laptop, I opened the unlabeled white binder and pulled a CD from a plastic sheath before slipping it into the drive.

As the CD loaded, I clicked *New Document*. My pulse fluttered as my fingers curved over the keyboard, ready to type. There was something about a new project, a blank page, that gave me a particular enjoyment that nothing else could.

The file indicated the two voices speaking, their background, and why we'd sought a Title Three in the first place. San Diego's Squad Five was heavy in organized crime, and although it wasn't my preferred field of violent crime, it was close enough. When desperate to leave, any door would do.

Two distinct deep voices speaking Italian filled my ears cupped by the headphones. I kept the volume low. Ironically, inside the government agency that had been founded to unveil secrets, the four-by-four cubicles weren't conducive to keeping them.

I began to type. Translating and transcribing the conversation were only the first steps. Then, my favorite part came. It was what I had become well-known for and what would get me to Virginia—analysis. Violent crime was what I loved, and the National Center for Analysis of Violent Crime in Quantico, Virginia—also known as NCAVC—was where I wanted to be.

At first, the two men in the recording stroked each other's egos, talking about how much pussy they had each procured over the weekend, but the conversation quickly turned serious as they discussed a man who seemed to be their boss—Benny.

I glanced at the file Val had given me while I typed, getting only a quick glimpse into how many points Benny had made in the mafia game while being a decent player in Las Vegas. I wondered how San Diego had stumbled onto this case, and I wondered who was doing the groundwork in Nevada. Chicago wouldn't have much luck whenever we had to make a call to that office. Whether gamblers, criminals, or law enforcement, Vegas kept everyone very busy.

Seven pages later, my fingers were itching to start my report, but I went over the audio again to check for accuracy. This was my first assignment for San Diego, and I also had the added pressure of being known as an accomplished agent in this specific area. The report had to be impressive—at least in my own mind.

Time had gotten away from me. It seemed like just half an hour had passed before Val was eyeing me over the short partition between our cubicles, this time tapping her nails on the ledge.

She mouthed words I couldn't hear, so I pulled off my headphones.

"You're not turning out to be a very good friend. Late for our first lunch date," she said.

I couldn't tell if she was joking or not.

"I was just…I lost track of time. I'm sorry."

"Sorry doesn't put a greasy cheeseburger in my gut. Let's get moving."

I walked with her to the elevator, and Val pushed the button for the ground floor. Once in the parking garage, I followed her to her two-door black Lexus and settled in while watching her push the Start button. The seat and steering wheel adjusted to her specifications.

"Nice," I said. "You must get paid a lot more than I do."

"It's used. I bought it from my brother. He's a cardiologist. Asshole."

I chuckled as she navigated out of the property. After passing the building next to the entrance gate, she waved to the guard, and then drove to the closest burger joint.

"Don't they have burgers at the office?"

Her face twisted into disgust. "Yes, but Fuzzy's Burgers are the best."

"Fuzzy burgers? That doesn't sound appetizing at all."

"Not *fuzzy* burgers. Fuzzy's Burgers. Trust me," she said, turning right.

Then, she made a left before jerking her wheel into the parking lot of a quaint burger joint with a homemade sign.

"Val!" a man called from behind the counter as soon as we'd walked in. "Val's here!" he yelled.

"Val's here!" a woman echoed.

We barely made it to the counter when the man tossed a small round object wrapped in white paper to the woman in a pristine white apron standing at the register.

"BLT with cheese, mustard, and mayo," the woman said with a knowing smile.

Val turned to me. "Disgusting, right?"

"I'll have the same," I said.

We took our trays of food and found an empty table in the corner, near the window.

I closed my eyes and let the sunshine pour down on me. "It's weird that the weather is so beautiful, and it's barely March."

"It's not weird. It's glorious. The temp has been higher than average for this time of year, but even when it's not, it's perfect. Everyone would be happier if the world had San Diego's weather." Val dipped her golden curly fry into a small cup of ketchup. "Try the fries. Dear God, try the fries. They are so good. I crave them at night sometimes when I'm alone, which is more often than you'd think."

"I don't think anything," I said, dipping a fry into my own small cup. I popped it into my mouth.

She was right. I quickly grabbed another.

"Speaking of, do you have a guy? Or girl? I'm just asking."

I shook my head.

"Did you? Have you ever?"

"Kissed a girl?"

Val cackled. "No! Have you been in a relationship?"

"Why do you ask?"

"Oh. It's complicated. I gotcha."

"It's not complicated at all actually."

"Listen," Val said while chewing the first bite of her burger, "I'm a great friend, but you're going to have to open up more. I don't care to hang out with strangers."

"Everyone is a stranger at first," I said, thinking of my stranger.

"No, not in the Bureau."

"Why don't you just open my file?"

"That's no fun! C'mon. Just the basics. Did you transfer to move up or move on?"

"Both."

"Perfect. Keep going. Do your parents suck?" She covered her mouth. "Oh my hell, they're not dead, are they?"

I squirmed in my seat. "Um…no. I had a normal childhood. My parents love me and each other. I'm an only child."

Val sighed. "Thank Christ. I might as well ask the next offensive question."

"No, I wasn't adopted," I droned. "Lindy is Irish. My mother is Japanese."

"Is your dad a ginger?" She smirked.

I glared at her. "You only get two offensive questions on the first day."

"Continue," she conceded.

"I graduated with honors. I was dating a guy. It didn't work out," I said, tired of my own story. "No drama. Our breakup was just as boring as our relationship."

"How long?"

"Was I with Jackson? Seven years."

"Seven years. No ring?"

"Kind of," I said, making a face.

"Ah. You're married to the job. Betty Bureau."

"So was he."

Val puffed out a laugh. "You were dating an agent?"

"Yes. He was SWAT."

"Even worse. How did you live with him for that long? How did he handle coming in second place for that long?"

I shrugged. "He loved me."

"But you gave back the ring. You didn't love him?"

I shrugged again, taking a bite. "Anything I should know about the office?" I asked.

Val smirked. "Changing the subject. Classic. Hmm…what you need to know about the office. Don't piss off Maddox. He's the Assistant Special Agent in Charge."

"So I've heard," I said, brushing my hands against each other to wipe off the salt.

"All the way in Chicago?"

I nodded.

"It's justifiable gossip. He is a huge, gigantic, enormous asshole. You'll see tomorrow morning at the meeting."

"He'll be there?" I asked.

She nodded. "He will tell you that you're worthless as an agent even if you're the best of the best just so he can observe your performance when your confidence has been crushed."

"I can handle it. What else?"

"Agent Sawyer is a slut. Stay away from him. And Agent Davies is, too. Stay away from her."

"Oh," I said, processing her words. "I don't see myself engaging in interoffice relations after the debacle that was Jackson."

Val smiled. "I have firsthand knowledge of both...so you should stay away from me, too."

I frowned. "Is anyone here safe to hang out with?"

"Maddox," she said. "He has mommy issues, and he was burned bad a while ago. He wouldn't look at your tits if you flashed him."

"So, he hates women."

"No," she said, looking off in thought. "He's just sworn them off. Doesn't want to get hurt again, I imagine."

"I don't care what is wrong with him. If what you say is true, I definitely don't want to hang out with him."

"You'll do fine. Just do your job, and go on with your life."

"The job is my life," I said.

Val lifted her chin, not trying to hide that she was impressed with my answer. "You're already one of us. Maddox is a hard ass, but he'll see it, too."

"What's his story?" I asked.

She took a sip of water. "He was focused but tolerable when I came to San Diego until a little over a year ago. Like I said, he was burned by some girl in his hometown—*Camille*," she said the name as if it were poison in her mouth. "I don't know the details. No one talks about it."

"Weird."

"Will you feel like having a drink or five later?" she asked, losing interest now that the conversation wasn't centered on my personal life. "There's a cool little pub in Midtown."

"I live in Midtown," I said, wondering if I would see my neighbor again.

She grinned. "Me, too. A lot of us do. We can drown your sorrows together."

"I don't have sorrows. Just memories. They'll go away on their own."

Val's eyes were bright again with interest, but I wasn't enjoying the interrogation. I wasn't that hard up for friends. Well, I was, but I had boundaries.

"What about you?" I asked.

"That is a Friday night conversation, told over stiff drinks and loud music. So, are you here to swear off men? Are you finding yourself?" she asked the questions without an ounce of seriousness.

If my answers were yes, I wouldn't admit it. She was clearly hoping to ridicule me.

"If I were, I have already failed miserably," I said, thinking of the night before.

Val leaned forward. "Are you serious? You just got here. Someone you know? Old high school classmate?"

I shook my head, feeling my cheeks flush. The memories came quickly but in flashes—Thomas's hazel-green eyes glancing over at me from where he'd sat at the bar, the sound of my door from him pushing back against it, how easily he'd slid inside me, and my ankles high in the air, jerking with each amazing thrust. I pressed my knees together in reaction.

A wide grin spread across Val's face. "One-night stand?"

"Not that it's any of your business, but yes."

"Complete stranger?"

I nodded. "Sort of. He lives in my building, but I didn't know that until after."

Val gasped and then sat back against her wooden chair. "I knew it," she said.

"You knew what?"

She leaned forward and crossed her arms, resting them on the table. "That we are going to be great friends."

CHAPTER THREE

"WHO THE HELL IS LISA?" A loud voice bounced off the four walls of the squad room. "Lisa Lindy."

On just my second day in the San Diego office, I was one of dozens of agents waiting for the early meeting to begin. Everyone had seemed nervous before the outburst, but now, they all seemed to relax.

I looked up into the eyes of the young Assistant Special Agent in Charge and nearly swallowed my tongue. It was him—my one-night stand, the lips I missed, my neighbor.

Panic and bile instantly rose in my throat, but I swallowed it back.

"It's Liis," Val said. "Like geese but with an L, sir."

My heart was pounding against my chest. He was waiting for someone to come forward. Life was going to go from fresh start to complicated in three, two—

"I'm Liis Lindy, sir. Is there a problem?"

When our eyes met, he paused, and utter horror washed over me in waves. Recognition lit his face, too, and for just a moment, he blanched. The strings-free one-night stand was now so tangled that I wanted to hang myself.

He quickly recovered. Whatever had made him so angry melted away for a moment, but then his face tightened, and he was back to hating everything.

Special Agent Maddox's ferocious reputation had preceded him. Agents from all over the country knew of his tight rein and impossible expectations. I had been prepared to suffer under his supervision. I hadn't been prepared to do so after actually being under him.

Damn it, damn it, damn it.

He blinked and then held out the file. "This FD-three-oh-two is unacceptable. I don't know how you did things in Chicago, but in San Diego, we don't just slap shit on paper and call it good."

His harsh and very public criticism made me snap out of my shame spiral and back into the role of Betty Bureau.

"The report is thorough," I said with confidence.

Despite my anger, my mind toyed with the memories of the night before—what my boss's body had looked like under that suit, the way his biceps had flexed when he rammed himself inside me, how good his lips had felt on mine. The severity of the shitstorm I had created for myself hit me. I had no idea how I could form a sentence, much less sound confident.

"Sir," Val began, "I would be happy to take a look at the report and—"

"Agent Taber?" Maddox said.

I half-expected her to say, *Fuck off.*

"Yes, sir?"

"I am perfectly capable of discerning whether I'll accept a report or not."

"Yes, sir," she said again, unfazed, lacing her fingers on the table.

"Are you able to perform the job assigned to you, Agent Lindy?" Maddox asked.

I didn't like the way he'd said my name as if it left a bad taste in his mouth.

"Yes, sir." It felt so damn bizarre to call him sir. It made me feel too submissive. My father's blood raged in my veins.

"Then, do it."

I wanted to be in San Diego even if it put me directly in the crosshairs of a renowned asshole of an ASAC like Maddox. It was better than being in Chicago, having the same seven-year-long conversation with Jackson Schultz. That name definitely left a bad taste in my mouth.

Still, I couldn't stop myself from what I was about to say. "I would be happy to, sir, if you'll let me."

I was sure I heard maybe one or two barely audible gasps in the room. Agent Maddox's eyes flickered. He took a step in my direction. He was tall and nothing less than menacing, even in a tailored suit. Even though he was more than a foot taller than me and rumored to be lethal with a gun and his fists, my Irish side lured me to narrow my eyes and cock my head, daring my superior to take one more step, even on my first day.

"Sir," another agent said, requesting Maddox's attention.

Maddox turned, allowing the man to whisper in his ear.

Val leaned over, talking so quiet she nearly breathed the words, "That's Marks. He's closest to Maddox here."

Maddox had to lean down as Marks was not much taller than me, but he was broad-shouldered and appeared almost as dangerous as the ASAC.

Maddox nodded, and then his cold hazel eyes skimmed over everyone in the room. "We've had a few leads with Abernathy. Marks will meet with the contact agent in Vegas tonight. Taber, where are we with Benny's guy, Arturo?"

Val began to give her report just as Maddox tossed my FD-302 on the table.

He let her finish, and then he glared down at me. "Send me something when you have some actual intelligence. I brought you on board based on Carter's commendation. Don't make an ass out of him."

"Agent Carter doesn't extend his praises lightly," I said, unamused. "I take that very seriously."

Maddox raised an eyebrow, waiting.

"Sir. I take his commendation very seriously, sir."

"Then, give me something I can use by the end of the day."

"Yes, sir," I said through my teeth.

Everyone stood and dispersed, and I snatched my report off the table, glaring at Maddox, as he left with Agent Marks trailing behind.

Someone handed me a Styrofoam cup full of water, and I took it before plodding to my desk and falling less than gracefully into my chair.

"Thank you, Agent Taber."

"Fuck off," she said. "And you're toast. He hates your guts."

"The feeling is mutual," I said before taking another sip. "This is just a pit stop. My end game is to become an analyst at Quantico."

Val pulled back her long russet tresses, twisting and wrapping them into a low bun at the base of her neck. My sad thin black hair was teeming with jealousy as Val struggled with four bobby pins to keep the sheer weight of her hair from pulling the bun out of place. Her sideswept bangs were pulled across her forehead and tucked behind her left ear.

Val appeared young, but she didn't seem inexperienced. The day before, she'd mentioned several closed cases that she had under her belt already.

"I said San Diego was temporary, too, and here I am, four years later."

She followed me to the wall with the built-in coffee nook and Keurig.

Squad Five was back to the grind, typing on their computers or talking on the phone. When my mug was full, I grabbed packets of sugar and creamer and then returned to my high-backed black chair. I tried not to compare everything with my cubicle in Chicago, but San Diego had had new offices built just two years before. In certain areas, I could still smell the fresh paint. Chicago was well-worn. It had been home for six and a half years before I'd transferred. My chair there was practically molded to my backside, the files in my desk organized just the way I wanted, the cubicle walls between agents were tall enough for at least a little privacy, and the ASAC hadn't ripped me to shreds in front of the entire squad on my second day.

Val watched me set the steaming mug on my desk, and then sat in her chair.

I fingered the package of creamer, frowning.

"I'm out of half-and-half, but I do have two-percent in the refrigerator," she said, a tinge of sympathy in her voice.

I made a face. "No. I hate milk."

Val's eyebrows shot up, and then her eyes fell to the floor, surprised at my tone. "Okay then. You're not a fan of milk. Won't ask again."

"No. I hate milk—as in, my *soul* hates milk."

Val chuckled. "Well then, I won't make the trip." She eyed my empty desk, devoid of family pictures or even a penholder. "The guy who used to be at this cubicle...his name was Trex."

"Trex?" I asked.

"Scottie Trexler. God, he was cute. He transferred out, too—all the way out. I think he's with a different agency now." She sighed, her eyes seeing something I couldn't. "I liked him."

"I'm sorry," I said, not sure what else to say.

She shrugged. "I've learned not to get attached around here. Maddox runs a tight ship, and not a lot of agents can take it."

"He doesn't scare me," I said.

"I won't tell him you said that, or he really won't stay off your tail."

I felt my face get hot, enough that Val noticed, and she narrowed her eyes.

"You're blushing."

"No, I'm not."

"And now, you're lying."

"It's the coffee."

Val stared deep into my eyes. "You haven't even taken a sip. Something I said embarrassed you. Maddox…tail…"

I shifted under her intense stare.

"You live in Midtown."

"No," I said, shaking my head. I wasn't denying my residence but what I knew she would soon discover. *Damn having friends who are federal investigators for a living.*

"Maddox is your neighbor, isn't he?"

I shook my head faster, looking around. "Val, no…stop…"

"Fuckity. You're joking. Maddox is your one-night stand!" she hissed, thankfully keeping her voice to a whisper.

I covered my face and then let my forehead fall to my desk. I could hear her leaning over the cubicle.

"Oh my God, Liis. Did you just die when you saw him? How could you not know? How did he not know? He hired you, for Christ's sake!"

"I don't know," I said, rocking my head from side to side, my fingers digging into the edge of my desk. I sat up, pulling down the thin skin beneath my eyelids as I did so. "I'm fucked, aren't I?"

"At least once that I know of." Val stood, her badge wagging as she did so. She smirked at me, sliding her slender long fingers into her pockets.

I looked up at her, desperate. "Just kill me now. Put me out of my misery. You have a gun. You can do it."

"Why would I do that? This is the best thing to happen to this squad in years. Maddox got laid."

"You're not going to tell anyone, right? Promise me."

Val grimaced. "We're friends. I wouldn't do that."

"That's right. We're friends."

She craned her neck toward me. "Why are you talking to me like I'm a mental patient?"

I blinked and shook my head. "I'm sorry. I'm quite possibly having the worst day of my life."

"Well, you look hot." She walked away.

"Thanks," I said to myself as I scanned the room.

No one had heard our discussion, but it still felt like the secret was out. I sank back into my chair and slipped on my headphones as Val left the squad room for the security doors leading into the hallway.

I covered my mouth for a moment and sighed, feeling lost. *How had I messed up my fresh start so thoroughly and before it even started?*

Not only had I screwed my boss, but if the other agents also found out, it could jeopardize any chances I would have at promotions while under Maddox's supervision. If he had any integrity at all, he would continually pass me over in fear that the truth would come out. A promotion would look bad for both of us—not that it mattered. Maddox had made a point to let everyone know that he wasn't impressed with my work—a report that I had given one-hundred percent, and my best was damn good.

I looked over my transcript and shook my head. The translation was spot-on. The report was comprehensive. I hovered the mouse over the right-facing arrow and clicked it, playing the audio again.

The longer the two Italian men's voices bantered about a job and the hooker one of them had had relations with the night before, the more my cheeks reddened with anger. I took pride in my reports. It was my first assignment at the San Diego field office, and Maddox calling me out in front of everyone had just been poor form.

Then, I thought about lunch with Val the day before and the warnings she'd given me about Maddox.

"He will tell you that you're worthless as an agent even if you're the best of the best just so he can observe your performance when your confidence has been crushed."

I ripped the headphones from my head and gripped the report in my hands. I rushed toward the ASAC's office at the far end of the squad room.

I paused upon seeing the stunningly beautiful woman who served as a checkpoint before one could enter Maddox's office suite. The nameplate on her desk read CONSTANCE ASHLEY, a name that suited her with her white-blonde hair falling in soft waves, cascading just a bit over her shoulders, nearly matching her porcelain skin. She peered up at me from under thick lashes, and she practically batted her eyes at me.

"Agent Lindy," she said with just a hint of a Southern twang. Constance's rosy cheeks, poise, and down-home disposition were all a ruse. Her steely blue eyes betrayed her.

"Miss Ashley," I said, nodding.

She offered a sweet smile. "Just Constance."

"Just Liis." I tried not to sound as impatient as I felt. She was nice, but I was rather anxious to speak with Maddox.

She touched the tiny apparatus in her ear and then nodded. "Agent Lindy, I'm afraid Special Agent Maddox is away from his desk. May I set up an appointment?"

"Where is he?" I asked.

"That's classified," she said, her sweet smile unwavering.

I flicked my badge. "Thankfully, I have top-secret clearance."

Constance wasn't amused.

"I need to speak with him," I said, trying not to beg. "He is expecting my report."

She touched the small plastic device again and nodded. "He'll return after lunch."

"Thank you," I said, turning on my heels and heading back the way I'd come.

Instead of retreating to my cubicle, I went into the hall and poked around until I found Val. She was in Agent Marks's office.

"Can I speak with you for a minute?" I asked.

She looked at Marks and then stood. "Sure."

She shut the door behind her, biting her lip.

"Sorry to interrupt."

She made a face. "He's been chasing me for six months. Now that Trex is out of the way, he is under the misapprehension that he has a chance."

My face compressed. "Did I transfer to a singles bar?" I shook my head. "Don't answer that. I need a favor."

"Already?"

"Where does Maddox frequent around lunchtime? Does he have a favorite eatery? Does he stay here?"

"The fitness room. He's there every day at this time."

"That's right. You've mentioned that. Thanks," I said.

She called after me, "He hates being interrupted! As in, his *soul* hates being interrupted!"

"He hates everything," I grumbled under my breath, pressing the button for the elevator.

I went down two levels and then took the skywalk to the west offices.

The newly built San Diego office was comprised of three large buildings, and it would likely be a maze to me for a week or two at least. It was a stroke of luck that Val had shown me the way to the fitness room the day before.

The closer I came to the fitness room, the faster I walked. I held my badge against the black square protruding from the wall. After a beep and the sound of the lock opening, I pulled open the door to see Maddox's feet dangling in the air, his face red and glistening with perspiration, while he bobbed quickly on a chin-up bar. He barely acknowledged me, still carrying on with his workout.

"We need to talk," I said, holding up my report, which was now crinkled from my grip. That made me even angrier.

He let go of the bar, his sneakers landing on the floor with a thud. He was breathing hard, and he used the collar of his heather-gray FBI T-shirt to wipe the dripping sweat from his face. The bottom hem pulled up, revealing just a sliver of his perfectly cut lower abs and one side of the V that I had fantasized about at least a dozen times since the first time I'd seen it.

His answer brought me back to the present. "Get out."

"This is for all employees of the facility, is it not?"

"Not between eleven and noon."

"Says who?"

"Me." His jaw flitted under his skin, and then he eyed the papers in my hand. "Did you rework that FD-three-oh-two?"

"No."

"No?"

"No," I seethed. "The transcription and translation are accurate, and the FD-three-oh-two, like I've said, is thorough."

"You're incorrect," he said, glaring down at me.

Behind the irritation was something else although I couldn't quite decipher it.

"Can you explain to me what is missing?" I asked.

Maddox walked away from me, the fabric under both of his arms and his lower back dark with perspiration.

"Excuse me, sir, but I asked you a question."

He flipped around. "You don't come to me, asking questions. You take orders, and I told you to modify that report to my satisfaction."

"How exactly would you like me to do that, sir?"

He laughed once, unamused. "Did your superior do your job for you in Chicago? Because in—"

"I'm in San Diego. I know."

He narrowed his eyes. "Are you insubordinate, Agent Lindy? Is that why you were sent here—to be under my command?"

"You requested *me*, remember?"

His expression was still one I couldn't read, and it was driving me mad.

"I didn't request you," he said. "I requested the best language expert we had."

"That would be me, sir."

"Forgive me, Agent Lindy, but after reading that report, I'm having a hard time believing you're as good as you think you are."

"I can't give you intelligence that isn't there. Maybe you should tell me what you want to hear from that Title Three."

"Are you suggesting that I'm asking you to lie in your report?"

"No, sir. I am suggesting you tell me what you expect of me."

"I want you to do your job."

I clenched my teeth, trying to keep my Irish side from getting me fired. "I would love to accomplish my responsibilities, sir, and do it to your satisfaction. What about my report do you find lacking?"

"All of it."

"That's unhelpful."

"Too bad," he said in a smug tone, walking away again.

My patience had run out. "How in the hell did you get promoted to ASAC?"

He stopped and turned on his heels, leaning down a bit, looking incredulous. "What did you say?"

"Forgive me, sir, but you heard me."

"This is day two for you, Agent Lindy. You think you can—"

"And it very well be my last after this, but I'm here to do a job, and you're in my way."

Maddox eyed me for the longest time. "You think you could do better?"

"You're damn right I could."

"Great. You're now the supervisor of Squad Five. Give your report to Constance to digitize and then get your shit in your office."

My eyes danced around the room, trying to process what had just happened. He'd just given me a promotion that I'd thought would take at least four more years.

Maddox walked away from me and pushed through the door to the men's locker room. I was breathing hard, maybe harder than he was after his workout.

I turned around, seeing a dozen people standing at the glass door. They stiffened and walked away when they realized they had been caught. I pulled open the door and walked back down the hall and across the skywalk in a daze.

I remembered seeing an empty box next to the Keurig, so I retrieved it and sat it atop my desk, filling it with my laptop, sidearm, and the few files I had in my drawers.

"It went that bad, did it?" Val said, genuine concern in her voice.

"No," I said, still dazed. "He promoted me to squad supervisor."

"I'm sorry." She chuckled. "I thought you said you're the supervisor."

I looked up at her. "I did."

Her eyebrows shot up. "He looks at you with more hate than he does Agent Sawyer, and that's saying something. You're telling me you stood up to him once, and he gave you a promotion?"

I looked around the room, trying to think of a plausible reason as well.

Val shrugged. "He's lost it, gone off the deep end." She pointed at me. "If I had known being insubordinate and doing something as taboo as telling another agent how to run a case meant a promotion, I would have told him off a long time ago."

I took in a deep breath and picked up the box before walking into the empty supervisor's office. Val followed me in.

"This has been empty since Maddox's promotion to ASAC. He's one of the youngest ASACs in the Bureau. Did you know that?"

I shook my head as I set the box on my new desk.

"If anyone can get away with this, it's Maddox. He's so far up the director's ass that I bet he'll make S.A.C. early, too."

"He knows the director?" I asked.

Val laughed once. "He has dinner with the director. He spent Thanksgiving at the director's house last year. He's the director's favorite, and I don't mean out of the San Diego office, or even out of the offices in California. I mean, in the *Bureau*. Thomas Maddox is the golden boy. He can have whatever he wants, and he knows it. Everyone does."

I made a face. "Doesn't he have a family? Why didn't he go home for Thanksgiving?"

"Something to do with the ex, or so I hear."

"How does rubbing elbows with the director even happen for someone like Maddox? He's got the personality of a badger."

"Maybe. But he's loyal to those in his circle, and they're loyal to him. So, be careful what you say about him and to whom. You could go from surprise promotion to surprise transfer."

That gave me pause. "I'll just, uh...get set up."

Val walked toward the hall, pausing in the doorway. "Drinks tonight?"

"Again? I thought you said I should stay away from you?"

She smiled. "Don't listen to me. I am known for giving horrible advice."

I pressed my lips together, trying to suppress a smile.

Even with my monumental fuck-up, maybe it wouldn't be so bad here after all.

CHAPTER FOUR

"Look who it is," Anthony said, setting a pair of napkins in front of two empty stools.

"Thanks for the warning the other night," I said. "You could have told me I was leaving with my boss."

Val puffed out a laugh. "You let her walk out of here with him? Not even a hint? That's just cruel."

Anthony pulled his mouth to the side. "He wasn't your boss…yet. Besides, I knew nothing was going to happen."

I narrowed my eyes. "But you knew he was going to be, and you lost that bet."

Anthony was stunned. "Maddox? Oh no, honey, you must have hallucinated."

"Don't look so shocked," I said. "It's rude."

"It's not that…it's just…" Anthony looked to Val. "I've just seen him shoot so many women down. It was enough of a surprise that he asked you to leave with him."

Val shook her head and chuckled. "I told you. He's sworn off women."

"Well, Saint Thomas has broken his vow," I said.

Anthony pointed his finger, swirling tiny invisible circles in the air. "You must have voodoo in your hoohoo."

Val cackled.

"Maybe I do!" I said, feigning insult.

Anthony seemed remorseful in a don't-shoot-me sort of way. "You're right. I should have given you a heads-up. First round is on me. Friends?"

"That's a start," I said, sitting.

"Oh," Anthony said, looking to Val, "she's feisty."

"Just wait until Maddox finds out you knew she was an agent."

Anthony held his hand to his chest, looking genuinely concerned. "Christ on the cross, you're not going to tell him, are you?"

"I just might," I said, chewing on my thumbnail. "You'd better have my back from now on."

"Swear," Anthony said, holding up three fingers.

"Quit that shit. You were never a Boy Scout," Val said.

"Hey," a male voice said before bending down to kiss Val's cheek and sitting in the empty stool next to her.

"Hey, Marks. You know Lindy."

Marks leaned forward, took one look at me, and then leaned back. "Yep."

Val made a face. "What's that about?" He was focused on the large television screen above us, and when he didn't answer, she backhanded his arm. "Joel! What's with the douchebaggery?"

"What the…why are you hitting me?" he said, rubbing his arm. "I just choose to keep my distance from trouble."

I rolled my eyes and looked to Anthony.

"The usual?" Anthony asked.

I nodded.

"You already have a usual?" Val said. "How often do you come here?"

I sighed. "This is just my third time."

"In as many days," Anthony added. He set a Manhattan on the napkin in front of me. "Are you going to speak to me this time?"

"You're lucky I'm speaking to you now," I said.

Anthony nodded, conceding, and then looked to Val. "If she'd ordered only one drink, I still would have remembered. Whose bar do you think this is?"

Val cocked an eyebrow. "This is not your bar, Anthony."

"It's my bar," he said, sitting a short tumbler in front of her. "Do you see anyone else running this shit?" He motioned all around him. "Okay."

Val chuckled, and Anthony took Marks's order. I was used to more pleasantries, more courtesy. I liked the sharp wit and jagged edges of their banter—no hurt feelings, no seriousness. After a day at the office, it was refreshing.

The door chimed, and a quick glance turned into a long stare while Maddox made his way to the stool next to Marks. Maddox's eyes caught mine for a fraction of a second, and then he greeted his friend. Before Maddox could settle into his seat and loosen his tie, Anthony had already set a beer bottle on the counter in front of him.

"Relax," Val whispered. "He won't stay long. Maybe one drink."

"I'm glad I never tried undercover work. I'm beginning to think my thoughts and feelings are surrounded by glass walls and subtitled just in case I'm not obvious enough."

Val helped me to carry on a semi-normal conversation, but then Maddox ordered another drink.

Val's face compressed. "That's not like him."

I tried to remember if he'd had more than one drink the first time we met.

"Hell," I whispered, "I should probably head home anyway."

I gestured to Anthony for my check, and Marks leaned forward.

"You leaving?" he asked.

I simply nodded.

He seemed miffed by my silence. "You don't talk now?"

"Just trying to help you stay out of trouble." I signed the small strip of paper for Anthony, leaving behind a tip that covered all three nights, and then I slipped the strap of my purse over my arm.

The night air begged me to take a stroll in a different direction than my condo, but I rounded the corner and crossed the street, climbing the stoop of my building. Once inside, my heels clicked against the tile floor until I stopped in front of the elevator bay.

The entrance door opened and closed, and then Maddox slowed to a stop when he saw me.

"Going up?" he asked.

I stared at him with a blank expression, and he looked around as if he were lost, or maybe he couldn't believe he'd said something so stupid. We were on the ground floor.

The doors slid open with a cheerful chime, and I stepped inside. Maddox followed. I pressed the buttons for the fifth and sixth floors, unable to forget that Maddox lived directly above me.

"Thank you," he said.

I thought I caught his attempt to soften his gruff I'm-the-boss voice.

While the elevator climbed five floors, the tension swirled around my supervisor and me, increasing just like the illuminated numbers above the door.

Finally, as my floor came into view, I stepped out and let out the breath I'd been holding. I turned to nod to Maddox, and just before the doors slid closed, he stepped out.

As soon as his feet hit the fifth-floor carpet, he seemed to regret it.

"Isn't your place—"

"The next floor up. Yes," he said. He looked over at my door and swallowed.

Upon seeing the scuffed blue paint on my door, I wondered if the memories came as fast and as hard for him as they did for me.

"Liis…" He paused, seeming to choose his words carefully. He sighed. "I owe you an apology for the first night we met. If I had known…if I had done my job and thoroughly reviewed your file, neither of us would be in this position."

"I'm a big girl, Maddox. I can shoulder the responsibility just as well as you can."

"I didn't give you the promotion because of that night."

"I certainly hope not."

"You know as well as I do that your report was exceptional, and you have a bigger set of balls than most of the men in our unit. No one has stood up to me the way you have. I need an agent like that as supervisor."

"You questioned me in front of everyone just to see if I would stand up to you?" I asked, both incensed and dubious.

He thought about that, and then he put his hands in his pockets and shrugged. "Yeah."

"You're an asshole."

"I know."

My gaze involuntarily fell to his lips. I was lost for a moment in the memories and how amazing it'd felt when he held me. "Now that we've established that, I think we got off on the wrong foot. We don't have to be enemies. We work together, and I think it's in the best interest of the squad to be cordial."

"I think, given our history, trying to be friends would be a particularly bad idea."

"Not friends," I said quickly. "A…mutual respect—as colleagues."

"Colleagues," he deadpanned.

"Professionals," I said. "Don't you agree?"

"Agent Lindy, I just wanted to clarify that what happened between us was a mistake, and although it was quite possibly one of the best nights I've had since being back in San Diego…we…we can't make that mistake again."

"I'm aware," I said simply. I was trying very hard to ignore his remark about what a great night it was because it had been great, more than great, and I would never have it again.

"Thank you," he said, relieved. "I wasn't looking forward to this conversation."

I looked everywhere but at Maddox and then pulled my keys from my purse. "Have a good night, sir."

"Just…Maddox is fine when we're not at the office. Or…Thom—Maddox is fine."

"Good night," I said, pushing the key into the knob and twisting it.

As I closed the door, I saw Maddox turn for the stairs with an angry expression.

My couch was being held hostage, surrounded by cardboard. The white walls with no drapes felt uncomfortably cold, even with the mild temperature outside. I went straight to the bedroom and fell onto my back, staring up at the ceiling.

The next day would be long, organizing my office and figuring out where we were on the Vegas case. I would have to develop my own system for tracking everyone's progress, nailing down where they were in their current assignments and what they would be working on next. This was my first assignment as supervisor, and I was working under an ASAC who expected perfection.

I huffed.

In the corner, the ceiling had a small water stain, and I wondered if Maddox had once let his tub run over or if there was just a leak somewhere in the walls. A faint knock filtered through the drywall that separated our condos. He was up there, probably getting in the shower, which meant he was getting undressed.

Damn it.

I had known him as something other than my boss, and now, it was hard not to remember the intoxicating man I'd met at the bar, the man who belonged to the pair of lips I'd lamented before he'd even left my bed.

Anger and hate were the only ways I was going to get through my time in San Diego. I would have to learn to hate Thomas Maddox, and I had a feeling he wasn't going to make that hard for me.

The shelves were empty but dust free. A space bigger than I could ever hope to fill, the office of the supervisor was everything I had strived for, and at the same time, the next step felt like just another broken rung on my climb up the Bureau's ladder.

What might look to the average person like a mess of photos, maps, and Xerox copies was my way of keeping straight what agent was assigned to which task, which leads were promising, and which person of interest was more interesting than others. One name in particular caught my eye and came up over and over again—a washed-up poker legend by the name of Abernathy. His daughter, Abby, was also in a few black-and-white surveillance photos although I hadn't gotten to the reports on her involvement yet.

Val came in and watched in awe as I tacked the final pin into the last frayed edge of red yarn. "Whoa, Liis. How long have you been at this?"

"All morning," I said, admiring my masterpiece while climbing down off my chair. I put my hands on my hips and puffed. "Fantastic, isn't it?"

Val took a deep breath, seeming overwhelmed.

Someone knocked on the door. I turned to see Agent Sawyer leaning against the doorway.

"Morning, Lindy. I had a few things I'd like to discuss with you, if you're not busy."

Sawyer didn't look like the creep Val had made him out to be. His hair was freshly trimmed, long enough to run his fingers through but still professional. Maybe he used a bit too much hair spray, but the James Dean coif flattered him. His squared jaw and straight white teeth set off his bright blue eyes. He was kind of beautiful, but something behind his eyes was ugly.

Val made a face. "I'll let the janitor know you have trash in your office," she said, shouldering past him.

"I'm Agent Sawyer," he said, taking the few steps to shake my hand. "I meant to introduce myself yesterday, but I got caught at the courthouse. Late day."

I walked behind my desk and attempted to organize the stacks of papers and files. "I know. How can I help you, Sawyer?"

Sawyer sat in one of the twin tufted leather club chairs set in front of my large oak desk.

"Have a seat," I said, making a show of gesturing toward the seat he'd sat in.

"I'd planned on it," he said.

Slow and without looking away from the pair of ocean-blue eyes across from me, I lowered myself into my oversized office chair, the tall back making me feel like I was sitting in a throne—my throne, and this joker was trying to piss in my court. I stared him down like he was a mangy dog.

Sawyer placed a file on my desk and opened it, pointing to a paragraph highlighted in bright orange. "I've previously brought this up before to Maddox, but now that we have a pair of fresh eyes—"

Maddox stomped into my office.

Sawyer stood up like he'd been shot at. "Morning, sir."

Maddox simply nodded toward the door, and Sawyer scurried off without a word. Maddox slammed the door shut, and the glass wall shuddered, so I didn't have to.

I leaned back into my throne and crossed my arms, both anticipating and hoping for a dick comment to come out of his perfect mouth.

"How do you like your office?" he asked.

"Excuse me?"

"Your office," he said, pacing and throwing his hand out at the empty shelves. "Is it to your satisfaction?"

"Yes?"

Maddox's eyes targeted me. "Is that a question?"

"No. The office is satisfactory, sir."

"Good. If you need anything, let me know. And"—he pointed to the glass wall—"if that slimy piece of shit bothers you, you come directly to me, understand?"

"I am capable of handling Sawyer, sir."

"The moment," he seethed, "he makes a snide remark, questions your authority, or makes a pass at you, you come straight to my office."

Makes a pass at me? Who does he think he's fooling? "Why did you assign him to this case if you dislike him so much?"

"He's good at what he does."

"Yet you don't listen to him."

He rubbed his eyes with his thumb and forefinger, frustrated. "Just because I have to put up with his bullshit to use his talent doesn't mean you have to."

"Do I seem weak to you?"

His brows pulled in. "Pardon?"

"Are you trying to undermine me?" I sat up. "Is that what your game is? I've been trying to figure all of this out. I guess it would look much better to make me seem whiny and incompetent than for you to just run me out on the rails."

"What? No," he said, looking genuinely confused.

"I can handle Sawyer. I can handle my newly appointed position. I am capable of running this squad. Is there anything else, sir?"

Maddox realized his mouth was hanging open, and he snapped it shut. "That will be all, Agent Lindy."

"Fantastic. I have work to do."

Maddox opened the door, slipped both of his hands into his pants pockets, nodded, and then left, walking toward the security door. I looked up at the clock and knew exactly where he was headed.

Val scampered in, eyes wide. "Holy shit, what was that?"

"I have no idea, but I'm going to find out."

"He was in a hurry to leave the pub last night. Did he walk you home?"

"No," I said, standing up.

"Lie."

I ignored her. "I need to burn off some steam. Care to join me?"

"The fitness room during the ASAC's time? Hell no. You shouldn't push him, Liis. I get that you two have some weird competition going on, but he is famous for his temper."

I picked up my gym bag off the floor and jerked it over my shoulder. "If he wants me to push back, I'll push."

"To where? Over the edge?"

I thought about that for a moment. "He just came in here all pissy about Sawyer."

Val shrugged. "Sawyer is a jackass. He makes everyone pissy."

"No, I got the distinct feeling Maddox was…I realize how this sounds, but he was behaving like a jealous ex-boyfriend. If that's not it, then I think he gave me this promotion to make me look incompetent. It falls in line with what you've said about him before and what he did to me before I got the promotion."

Val reached into her pocket and opened a small bag of pretzels. She held one to her mouth and chewed on it in small bites like a chipmunk. "I'm leaning more toward your theory that Maddox is jealous, but that's impossible. First of all, he would never be jealous of Sawyer." Her face twisted. "Second, he just isn't wired that way anymore, not since that girl made him hate anything with a vagina."

I wanted to remind her that he hadn't slept with anyone before me either, but that would imply that I wanted him to be jealous, and I didn't. "What makes you think it was her fault?" I asked.

That made her pause. "He was in love with that girl. Have you been in his office?"

I shook my head.

"Those empty shelves used to hold several frames with pictures of her. Everyone knew how much he struggled to do the job and love her the way he thought she deserved. Now, no one talks about it—not because he did something wrong, but because she broke his heart, and no one wants to make him more miserable than he already is."

I ignored her. "I'm an intelligence analyst, Val. It's in my nature to piece together bits of information and form a theory."

Her nose wrinkled. "What does that have to do with anything? I'm trying to argue the point that he's not jealous of Sawyer."

"I never said he was."

"But you want him to be." Val was confident she was right. It was maddening.

"I want to know if I'm right about him. I want to know if he's trying to sink me. I want to peel back that top layer and see what's underneath."

"Nothing you'll like."

"We'll see," I said, walking past her toward the door.

CHAPTER FIVE

MADDOX STOPPED MIDWAY in an inverted sit-up and sighed. "You're joking."

"Nope," I said, heading straight for the women's locker room.

He let his back fall flat against the bench he was sitting on, his legs bent and his feet firmly planted on the floor. "Do you want us to hate each other?" he said, looking at the ceiling. "I'm getting the feeling that you do."

"You're not far off," I said, pushing through the swinging door.

After removing my workout clothes from my small duffel bag, I shimmied my navy pencil skirt over my hips and unbuttoned my light-blue blouse, and then I switched out my C-cup for a sports bra. It was amazing how one piece of fabric could take me from modest curves to the build of a twelve-year-old boy.

The room lined with lockers and motivational posters didn't smell like the mildew and dirty sneakers I'd expected. Bleach and fresh paint dominated the air.

Maddox was finishing his sit-ups while I made my way to the closest treadmill, my Adidas making squish noises as each foot pressed and lifted from the rubber floor. I stepped up onto the belt of the machine and threaded the bottom of my white FBI T-shirt through the safety clasp.

"Why now?" he said from across the room. "Why do you have to be here during my lunch hour? You can't work out in the mornings or the evenings?"

"Have you seen this room before and after hours? The equipment is full. The best time of day to get a full workout without dodging sweaty bodies is at your lunch hour because no one wants to come in here while you're here."

"Because I don't let them."

"Are you going to ask me to leave?" I asked, looking at him over my shoulder.

"You mean, tell you to leave?"

I shrugged. "Semantics."

His eyes poured over my tight leggings as he thought about that, and then he left the bench for the double bars before lifting both of his legs nearly chest-high. If he worked out like that five times a week, it was no wonder he had an eight-pack. Sweat was dripping from his hair, and his entire torso glistened.

I pretended not to notice as I pressed the button to start the treadmill. The belt moved smoothly forward, the gears causing a familiar shudder beneath my feet. Placing earbuds in my ears, I used the music to help me forget that Maddox was behind me, perfecting perfection, and increasing the speed and incline of the treadmill helped, too.

After a few laps, I pulled one earbud out and let it hang down over my shoulder. I turned to look at the wall of mirrors on my left and spoke to Maddox's reflection, "By the way, I'm onto you."

"Oh, yeah?" Maddox said, puffing in the background.

"You're damn straight I am."

"What the hell is that supposed to mean?"

"I'm not going to let you do it."

"Do you really think I'm trying to sabotage you?" He seemed amused.

"Aren't you?"

"I already told you no." After a short pause, he was standing next to the treadmill, his hand resting on the safety handles. "I know I made a negative impression on you, Lindy. Admittedly, it wasn't unintentional. But I'm motivated to make agents better, not tank their careers."

"Does that include Sawyer?"

"Agent Sawyer has a history in our squad that you know nothing about."

"So, educate me."

"It's not my story to tell."

"That's it?" I smirked.

"I don't get your meaning."

"You're not allowing him to speak to me because of someone else's story?"

Maddox shrugged. "I just like to get in his way."

"Your tantrum in my office *after* Agent Sawyer left was you getting in his way. Right."

Maddox shook his head and then walked away. I started to put my earbud back into my ear, but he appeared at my side once again.

"Why am I the asshole for keeping a fuckstick like Sawyer away from you?"

I pushed a button, and the treadmill came to a stop. "I don't need your protection," I puffed.

Maddox began to speak, but then he walked away again. This time, he pushed through the door of the men's locker room.

After eight minutes' worth of stewing over his attitude, I hopped off the treadmill and stomped into the men's locker room.

Maddox had one hand on the sink, the other holding a toothbrush. His hair was wet, and he was covered only in a towel.

He spit, rinsed, and then tapped his toothbrush on the sink. "Can I help you?"

I shifted my weight. "You might be able to charm the brass all the way up to the director, but I'm onto you. Don't think for a second that I don't see through your bullshit. I'm not going anywhere, so you can stop whatever game you're playing."

He dropped his toothbrush in the sink and walked toward me. I stepped backward, quickening my pace as he did. My back hit the wall, and I gasped. Maddox slammed his palms against the wall on each side of me just above my head. He was inches from my face, his skin still dripping from his recent shower.

"I promoted you to supervisor, Agent Lindy. What makes you think I want you gone?"

I lifted my chin. "Your bullshit story about Sawyer doesn't add up."

"What do you want me to say?" he said.

I could smell the mint on his breath and the bodywash on his skin. "I want the truth."

Maddox leaned in, his nose tracing my jaw. My knees nearly gave way as his lips touched my ear.

"You can have whatever you want." He leaned back, his eyes falling to my lips.

My breath caught, and I braced myself as he moved closer, closing his eyes.

He stopped just short of my mouth. "Say it," he whispered. "Say you want me to kiss you."

I reached up with my fingers, sliding them down his rippled abdomen, smearing the beads of water until I touched the top of his towel. Every nerve in my body begged me to say yes.

"No." I pushed past him and walked out the door.

I climbed back onto the treadmill, chose the fastest setting, and replaced my earbuds in my ear, changing songs until something screamy began to play.

Forty-five minutes later, breathless and sweating, I slowed my pace, walking with my hands on my hips. After my five-minute cooldown, I showered and then dressed before pinning my hair into a damp bun.

Val was waiting for me on the other side of the skywalk. "How did it go?" she asked, genuinely concerned.

I continued to walk toward the elevators, and she kept pace.

I tried my best to keep my shoulders and expression relaxed. "I ran. It was great."

"Lie."

"Let it go, Val."

"You just...ran?" She seemed confused.

"Yes. How was your lunch?"

"I brought a sack—PB and J. Did he yell at you?"

"No."

"Try to kick you out?"

"No."

"I don't...understand."

I chuckled. "What's to understand? He's not an ogre. Actually, at this point, he might think *I'm* the ogre."

We entered the elevator together, and I pressed the button for our floor. Val took a step toward me, getting close enough that I leaned back.

"But he is—an ogre. He's mean and ruthless and yells at people when they walk into the fitness room during his hour even if it's just to retrieve a left sneaker. I know. I was that agent. He screamed at me, totally lost his shit, over me trying to retrieve a fucking forgotten sneaker," she said the last few words slow and emphatic as if she were standing in front of a snapping audience, sharing her slam poetry.

"Maybe he's changed."

"Since you got here? In three days? No."

Her dismissive tone annoyed me.

"You're being a tad excessive."

"Dramatic?"

"Yes."

"That's just how I talk."

"Dramatically?"

"Yes. Stop listening for ways to judge me, and hear what I'm trying to say."

"Okay," I said.

The elevator opened, and I stepped into the hall.

Val followed me toward the security door. "Joel insisted that I eat my PB and J in his office."

"Who's Joel?"

"Agent Marks. Pay attention. He texted me last night. He said Maddox has been weird. His baby brother is getting married next month—well, not married but remarried. No, that's not right either."

My face compressed. "Renewing their vows maybe?"

Val pointed at me. "Yes."

"Why are you sharing this with me?"

"He's going to see, you know...her."

"The one who burned him?"

"Affirmative. The last time he went home and saw her, he came back a new man." Her nose wrinkled. "Not in a good way. He was broken. It was scary."

"Okay."

"He's sweating the trip. He told Marks...this is fucking classified, do you hear me?"

I shrugged. "Go."

"He told Marks that he was kind of glad you transferred here."

I walked into my office and welcomed Val with a small smile, and she breezed past me. As the door fit snugly into the frame, I made a show of making sure it was closed, and then I flipped around, the wood of the door feeling cold and rough, even through my blouse.

"Oh my God, Val! What do I do?" I hissed, feigning panic. "He is *kind of glad?*" I made the most awful face that I was capable of and then began to pant.

She rolled her eyes and fell into my throne. "Fuck off."

"You can't tell me to fuck off while sitting in my chair."

"I can if you make fun of me." Her pants dragged against the dark leather as she leaned forward. "I'm telling you, this is a big deal. This is not like him. He doesn't get glad, not even kind of glad. He hates everything."

"Okay, but this is really non-intelligence here, Val. Even if it's atypical, you're pulling the fire alarm for a candle."

She arched one brow. "I'm telling you, you just knocked over his candle."

"You have better things to do, Val, and so do I."

"Drinks tonight?"

"I have to unpack."

"I'll help you, and I'll bring wine."

"Deal," I said as she left my office.

Sitting in my chair felt comforting. I was hiding in plain sight, my back protected, my body encompassed by the waist-high arms. My fingers clicked against the keyboard as small black dots filled in the white password box on the monitor. The first time I'd logged into the system, I remembered seeing the FBI emblem on the screen and feeling my pulse race. Some things never changed.

My inbox was full of messages from every agent on progress, questions, and leads. Constance's name practically leaped off the page, so I clicked it.

AGENT LINDY,

ASAC MADDOX REQUESTS A MEETING AT 1500 TO DISCUSS A DEVELOPMENT. PLEASE CLEAR YOUR SCHEDULE.

CONSTANCE

Shit.

Each minute that passed after that was more agonizing than my earlier walk to the fitness room. Five minutes till three, I wrapped up my current task and walked down the hall.

Constance's long black lashes fluttered when she noticed me, and she touched her ear. Words slipped through her bright red lips, low and inaudible. She turned a fraction of an inch toward Maddox's door. Her white-blonde hair fell behind her shoulder and then bounced back into its soft wave. She seemed to snap back to the present and smiled at me. "Please proceed, Agent Lindy."

I nodded, noting that she never took her eyes off me as I passed her small desk. She wasn't just Maddox's assistant. She was his guard dog in a tiny blonde package.

I took a breath and twisted the brushed nickel knob.

Maddox's office was made up of mahogany and lush carpets, but his shelves were bare and pathetic like mine, missing family photos and personal trinkets that could lead anyone to believe he had a life outside of the Bureau. The walls displayed his favorite memories, including plaques and awards along with a photo of him shaking hands with the director.

Three frames sat on his desk, staggered and facing away from me. It bothered me that I couldn't see what was inside of them. I wondered if they held pictures of her.

Maddox was standing in his navy suit, one hand in his pocket, staring out his beautiful corner office view. "Have a seat, Lindy."

I sat.

He turned. "I have a dilemma that you might be able to help me with."

A hundred different statements could have come from his mouth. That wasn't one I'd considered. "I'm sorry, sir. What was that?"

"I had a meeting with the S.A.C. earlier, and he feels you could be a solution to a recent issue," he said, finally sitting in his chair.

The blinds let in the full light of the afternoon sun, creating a glare on the desk's already glossy surface. It was large enough to seat six people, and I guessed it would be too heavy for two men to lift. I raised my toes to fit snuggly beneath the space between the wood and the rug. I let out a breath, feeling anchored enough to keep whatever unexpected thing Maddox was about to drop on me from blowing me away.

He tossed a file on the desk, and it slid toward me, stopping just short of the edge. As I picked it up and held the thick stack of papers in my hand, I was still too sidetracked by Maddox's previous statement to open it.

"Special Agent Polanski, the S.A.C., thinks I'm a solution," I said, suspicious.

Either I had seriously underestimated my value, or Maddox was full of shit.

"Just read it," he said, standing up again and walking toward the window. Gauging by his stern expression and stiff posture, he was nervous.

I opened the thick card stock to the first page, and then I continued to look over the numerous FD-302s, surveillance photos, and a list of the dead. One report contained charges and court transcriptions of a college kid named Adam Stockton. He was an organizer of some sort, and he had been sentenced to ten years in prison. I skimmed over most of it, knowing that wasn't what Maddox wanted me to see.

Several of the photos were shots of a man who looked a bit like Maddox—same height but with a buzz cut and arms covered in tattoos. There were more with a pretty young girl, early twenties, far more years of wisdom in her eyes than there should be. Some photos were individual shots, but most were of them together. I recognized her as the girl in some of the photos I'd posted on my office wall—Abernathy's daughter. The kid with the buzz cut and Abby were obviously a couple, but the way they held on to one another led me to believe their relationship was new and passionate. If not, they were very much in love. He held a protective stance in almost all the photos, but she stayed at his side, not at all intimidated. I wondered if he even noticed he stood that way when he was with her.

They were all students from Eastern State University. Further reading told of a fire that had burned down one of the buildings on campus, killing one hundred thirty-two college kids—at night. Before asking why that many kids would be in the basement of a school building that late, I turned the page to find my answer—a floating fight ring, and the Maddox look-alike was a suspect.

"Jesus Christ. What is this?" I asked.

"Keep reading," he said, his back still turned to me.

Almost immediately, two names jumped out at me—Maddox and Abernathy. After a few more pages, it all came together, and I looked up at my boss. "Your brother is married to Abernathy's kid?"

Maddox didn't turn around.

"You're messing with me."

Maddox sighed, finally facing me. "I wish I were. They're renewing their vows at the end of next month in St. Thomas...so the family can attend. Their first wedding was in Vegas almost a year ago—"

I held up the paper. "Just a few hours after the fire. She's a clever one."

Maddox walked slowly over to his desk and sat down again. His inability to sit still was making me even more nervous than he appeared to be.

"What makes you think it was her idea?" he asked.

"He doesn't seem like the type to let his girlfriend save him," I said, recalling his posture in the photos.

Maddox chuckled and looked down. "He's not the type to let anyone save him, which is why this is going to be particularly hard. Special Agent Polanski insists I need backup, and I have to agree with him."

"Backup for what?"

"I'm going to have to break it to him after the ceremony."

"That she married him to give him an alibi?"

"No," he said, shaking his head. "Abby might have married my brother for a reason, but that reason is because she loves him." He frowned. "It will destroy him to find out the truth even if she *was* trying to save him."

"Do you always do what's best for your brothers?"

He looked down at the pictures I couldn't see. "You have no idea." He sighed. "I did what I could after the fire, but as you can see from the list of the dead, a ten-year sentence from Adam isn't going to cut it. Adam was charged with two hundred sixty-four counts of involuntary manslaughter—two for each of the victims."

"How did the District Attorney get away with that?" I asked.

"Adam was indicted under two different theories of the crime. Criminal negligence manslaughter, and misdemeanor manslaughter."

I nodded.

"My hands were tied," Maddox continued. "I couldn't help my brother—until I let Polanski in on what made me one of the youngest ASACs in Bureau history. I had an in. He almost didn't believe me. My little brother was dating and is now married to the daughter of a person of investigative interest in one of our bigger cases—Mick Abernathy. I got Polanski—with the director's approval, of course—to waive the charges if Travis agreed to work with us, but cracking this case is going to take longer than his jail sentence might have been."

"He'll be an asset?" I asked.

"No."

"The FBI is recruiting him?" I said, astonished.

"Yes. He just doesn't know it yet."

My face screwed into disgust. "Why tell him at his wedding?"

"I won't tell him on his wedding day. I'll do it the morning after, before I leave. It has to be in person, and I don't know when I'll see him again. I don't go home anymore."

"What if he doesn't agree to it?"

Maddox blew out a long breath, wounded at the thought. "He'll go to prison."

"Where do I come in?"

Maddox turned a bit in his chair, his shoulders still tense. "Just…hear me out. It was one hundred percent the S.A.C.'s idea. He just happens to be right."

"What?" My mind was racing, and my patience was wearing thin.

"I need a date for the wedding. I need someone else from the Bureau to attend and witness the conversation. I don't know how he'll react. A female agent will be a good buffer. Polanski thinks you're the perfect candidate."

"Why me?" I asked.

"He mentioned you by name."

"What about Val? What about Constance?"

Maddox cringed and then stared at his finger while he tapped it on his desk. "He suggested someone who would fit in."

"Fit in," I repeated, confused.

"Two of my brothers are in love with women who…lack finesse."

"I lack *finesse*?" I asked, pointing to the center of my chest. "Are you fucking serious?" I craned my neck. "Have you met Val?"

"See?" Maddox said, pointing at me with his whole hand. "That is exactly something Abby would say—or…Camille, Trent's girlfriend."

"Trent's girlfriend?"

"My brother."

"Your brother Trent. And Travis. And you're Thomas. Who am I missing? Tiger and Toadstool?"

Maddox wasn't amused. "Taylor and Tyler. They're twins. They're between Trent and me."

"Why the Ts?" I had to ask, but I was beyond annoyed with the entire conversation.

He sighed. "It's a Midwestern thing. I don't know. Lindy, I need you to go to my brother's wedding with me. I need you to help me talk him into not going to prison."

"It shouldn't be that hard for you to convince him. The Bureau is a great alternative to prison."

"He'll be undercover. He will have to keep it from his wife."

"So?"

"He really, really loves his wife."

"So do our other undercover agents," I snapped, not feeling the slightest bit of sympathy.

"Travis has a past. His relationship with Abby has always been volatile, and Travis sees honesty as his commitment to their marriage."

"Maddox, you're boring me. Our undercover agents simply tell their significant others they can't discuss their job, and that's the end of it. Why can't he just do that?"

"He can't tell her anything. He'll be undercover on an investigation that could implicate Abby's father. That could certainly become an issue in their marriage. He won't willingly risk anything that could mean losing her."

"He'll get used to it. We'll just give him a simple, tight alibi and stick with it."

Maddox shook his head. "No part of this is simple, Liis. We'll have to be exceptionally creative to keep Abby from figuring it out." He sighed and looked up at the ceiling. "She's sharp as a goddamn tack, that one."

I narrowed my eyes at him, wary of the fact that he'd used my first name. "The S.A.C. wants me to go. Do you?"

"It's not a bad idea."

"Our being friends is a bad idea, but us posing as a couple for an entire weekend isn't?"

"Travis is…hard to explain."

"You think he'll get violent?"

"I know he will."

"I'm assuming you don't want me to shoot him if he does."

Maddox shot me a look.

"Then, can I shoot you?" I asked. He rolled his eyes, and I held up my hands. "I'm just trying to understand my role in all of this."

"Travis doesn't do well when he doesn't have choices. If he thinks he could lose Abby over it, he'll fight. Losing her for lying or losing her because he's in prison aren't great choices. He might turn down the deal."

"He loves her that much?"

"I don't think that's an adequate word to describe the way he feels about her. Threatening him with losing her is like threatening his life."

"That's awfully...dramatic."

Maddox considered that. "Drama is the nature of their relationship."

"Noted."

"Trent has organized a surprise bachelor party the night before in my hometown—Eakins, Illinois."

"I've heard of it," I said. When Maddox shot me a confused look, I continued, "I've driven by the exit a few times on my way to and from Chicago."

Maddox nodded. "The next day, we'll drive to O'Hare International Airport and then fly from there to St. Thomas. I'll have Constance email you the dates and itinerary."

I had mixed feelings about returning home so quickly after leaving. "Okay."

"Like I've mentioned, we'll be posing as a couple. My family believes I'm in marketing, and I'd like to keep it that way."

"They don't know you're an FBI agent?"

"That's correct."

"May I ask why?"

"No."

I blinked. "Okay. I assume we'll be sharing a hotel room in Eakins and in St. Thomas."

"Correct."

"Anything else?"

"Not at this time."

I stood. "Have a good afternoon, sir."

He cleared his throat, obviously surprised at my reaction. "Thank you, Agent Lindy."

Turning on my heels to leave his office, I was aware of everything—how fast I walked, the way my arms swayed, even how straight my posture was. I didn't want to give him anything. I didn't know myself how I felt about the upcoming trip, and I certainly didn't want him to speculate.

When I returned to my office, I shut my door and nearly collapsed into my chair. I crossed my legs at the ankles and hoisted them onto my desk.

Agent Sawyer's knuckles tapped on the door, and he expectantly stared at me through the glass wall. I waved him away.

Maddox had been glad I had transferred to San Diego, and the S.A.C. had thought I lacked finesse—even less than Fuck Off Val or Agent Davies the Slut. I looked down at my crisp light-blue button-down blouse and knee-length skirt.

I have motherfucking finesse. Just because I speak my mind means I'm not tactful?

My whole face flushed red with anger. I thought the days of women in the Bureau being called breast-feds and split-tails were over. Most male agents making sexist remarks would be quickly shut down by other male agents, even when they weren't aware of my or any other female's presence.

Lack finesse? I'm going to lack his finesse all over the fucking squad room.

I covered my mouth even though I hadn't sworn out loud. *They might have a point.*

The landline's shrill ring bleated twice, and I held it to my ear. "Lindy."

"It's Maddox."

I sat up tall even though he couldn't see me.

"There's one more reason you're a good candidate, one I didn't mention to the S.A.C."

"I'm positively on the edge of my seat," I said, monotone.

"We're posing as a couple, and I…think you're the only female agent who would be comfortable enough with me to play the part."

"I can't imagine why."

The line was silent for a solid ten seconds.

"I'm kidding. Good to know it's not solely because the S.A.C. thinks I have no class."

"Let's get one thing straight. The S.A.C. didn't say that, and neither did I."

"You kind of did."

"That's not what I meant. I would throat-punch someone if he ever said anything like that about you."

Now, it was my side of the line that was quiet. "Th-thank you." I didn't know how else to respond.

"Be on the lookout for that email from Constance."

"Yes, sir."

"Good day, Lindy."

I put the phone on its base and returned my ankles to their previous position on my desk, pondering the trip we would take in seven weeks. I was going to be spending several nights alone with Maddox, posing as his girlfriend, and I wasn't at all upset about it even though I wished I were.

I tried not to smile. I didn't want to smile, so I frowned instead, and it was the biggest lie I'd told since telling Jackson—and myself—that I was happy with him in Chicago.

Val lightly knocked on the glass with one knuckle and then tapped her watch. I nodded, and she walked away.

I wasn't sure how much Maddox wanted me to share. Keeping the secrets about our first night and my purpose in Squad Five was hard enough. Unfortunately for me, Val was my only friend in San Diego, and postulation happened to be her superpower.

CHAPTER SIX

MY FINGERS KNOTTED IN MY HAIR in frustration as I struggled to focus on the words on the screen. I'd been staring at my computer for more than two hours, and my vision was beginning to blur.

The blinds on the exterior windows were closed, but the sunset had slipped through the slits and then burned out hours before. After studying Travis's case file, I'd spent the rest of the evening looking for ways to get him out of prison time for the fire, but using him as an asset was not just the best idea. It was the only idea. Unluckily for Travis, his brother was so good at his job that the Bureau felt adding another Maddox would only be beneficial. So, he wasn't only an asset. He would be recruited.

A knock sounded, and Agent Sawyer slipped a file into the metal holder screwed on the front of my door. The holder was there so that agents wouldn't have to bother me with every approval request, but Sawyer opened the door just enough to poke his head into my office, a bright white Cheshire smile on his face.

"It's late," he said.

"I know," I said, resting my chin on the heel of my hand. I didn't take my eyes from the screen.

"It's Friday."

"I'm aware," I said. "Have a good weekend."

"I thought maybe you'd like to get dinner somewhere. You've got to be starving."

Maddox stepped into my office, cool and pleasant to me, and then he glowered at Sawyer. "Agent Lindy and I have a meeting in two minutes."

"A meeting?" Sawyer said, chuckling. Under Maddox's intense stare, his smile faded. He smoothed down his tie and then cleared his throat. "Really?"

"Good night, Agent Sawyer," Maddox said.

"Good night, sir," he said before disappearing down the hall.

Maddox ambled to my desk and sat in one of the club chairs, casually leaning back with both of his elbows perched on the arms.

"We don't have a meeting," I said, my eyes on the monitor.

"No, we don't," Maddox said, sounding tired.

"You made me his boss. You've got to let him speak to me at some point."

"I don't see it that way."

I leaned to the side to see his face, my face still squashed by my hand, and frowned at him, dubious.

"You look like hell," Maddox said.

"You look worse," I lied.

He looked like an Abercrombie model, including the stern yet impervious stare, and I happened to know that he looked like one under his suit and tie, too. I hid behind my computer again before he could catch my eyes lingering on those damn unforgettable lips.

"Hungry?" he asked.

"Starving."

"Let's go pick up something. I'll drive."

I shook my head. "I still have a lot to do."

"You have to eat."

"No."

"Goddamn, you're stubborn."

I looked around my monitor again for effect. "Agent Davies is saying I fucked my way to the top. Do you have any idea how hard it is to get the agents to take me seriously when I walk in here and get a promotion on day one?"

"It was day two actually. And Agent Davies *did* fuck her way to the top—well, to her top. She won't likely be promoted any further."

I raised an eyebrow. "Have you ever given her a raise?"

"Absolutely not."

"Well, Davies might have, but technically, she's right about me. It's gnawing at me. I'm putting in extra hours, so I can make myself believe that I earned the spot."

"Grow up, Liis."

"You first, Thomas."

I thought I heard him breathe out the tiniest hint of a laugh, but I didn't acknowledge it. I simply allowed myself a smug smile from behind the safety of the lit screen between us.

Car horns and sirens could be heard coming from the street below. Out there, the world continued, unaware that we worked late and lived lonely lives to make sure they could go to bed with one less mob boss, one less sex ring, and one less serial killer on the loose. The hunt-and-capture was what I worked for every day—or that was what my function used to be. Now, I was tasked with keeping Thomas's brother out of prison. At least, that was what it felt like.

My smug smile vanished.

"Tell me the truth," I said against my hand.

"Yes, I'm hungry," Thomas droned.

"That's not it. What is your objective? Taking Benny down or keeping Travis out of prison?"

"One is entangled with the other."

"Pick one."

"I practically raised him."

"That's not an answer."

Thomas took a deep breath and exhaled, his shoulders sagging as if the answer were weighing down on him. "I'd trade my life to save his. I would definitely walk away from this assignment. I've walked away before."

"From the job?"

"No, and no, I don't want to talk about it."

"Understood," I said. I didn't want to talk about her either.

"You *don't* want me to talk about it? Everyone else in this office is dying to know."

I glared at him. "You just said you didn't. There is something I want to know though."

"What?" he asked, wary.

"Who is in the pictures on your desk?"

"What makes you think it's a *who*? Maybe they're pictures of cats."

All emotion left my face. "You don't have cats."

"But I like cats."

I leaned back, and I hit my desk, frustrated. "You don't like cats."

"You don't know me that well."

I hid behind my monitor again. "I know that you either have a miracle lint brush, or you don't have cats."

"I could still *like* cats."

I leaned over. "You're killing me."

The faintest hint of a smile touched his lips. "Let's go to dinner."

"Not unless you tell me who is in those frames."

Thomas frowned. "Why don't you just look for yourself the next time you're in there?"

"Maybe I will."

"Good."

We were quiet for several seconds, and then I finally spoke, "I'll help you."

"To dinner?"

"I'll help you help Travis."

He shifted in the chair. "I didn't know you weren't planning to."

"Maybe you shouldn't consider me a sure thing."

"Maybe you shouldn't say yes," he snapped back.

I slammed my laptop closed. "I didn't say yes. I said I would watch for the email from Constance."

He narrowed his eyes at me. "I'm going to have to watch you."

A smug smile broke out across my face. "Yes, you are."

My cell phone chirped, and Val's name appeared on the screen. I picked up the phone and held it to my ear. "Hey, Val. Yes, just finishing up. Okay. See you in twenty." I pressed the End button and laid my phone on the desk.

"That hurts," Thomas said, checking his own phone.

"Deal with it," I said, opening the lower drawer to retrieve my purse and keys.

His brow furrowed. "Is Marks going?"

"I don't know," I said, standing before pulling my purse strap over my shoulder.

Vacuums were being pushed back and forth somewhere down the hall. Only half the lights were on. Thomas and I were the only employees left in the wing besides the cleaning staff.

Thomas's expression made me feel guilty. I tilted my head. "Do you want to go?"

"If Val will be there, it would be less awkward if Marks were going," he said, standing.

"Agreed." I thought about it for a moment. "Invite him."

Thomas's eyes sparked, and he lifted his cell phone, tapping out a quick message. Within seconds, it beeped back. He looked up at me. "Where?"

"A place downtown called Kansas City Barbeque."

Thomas laughed once. "Is she giving you the official tourist tour?"

I smiled. "It's the same bar from *Top Gun*. She said she didn't do those things when she moved here, and she's never gotten to it. Now, she has an excuse."

Thomas tapped on his phone, a grin spreading quickly across his face. "KC Barbeque it is."

I sat on the end stool, glancing around the room. The walls were covered in *Top Gun* memorabilia—posters, pictures, and signed headshots of the cast. To me, it didn't look anything like the bar in the movie, except for the jukebox and the antique piano.

Val and Marks were deep in conversation about the pros and cons for the solicitation notice of the 9mm pistols versus our standard issue Smith & Wesson. Thomas was on the other side of the L-shaped bar, standing in the middle of a small herd of California girls any Beach Boy would be proud of. The women were all giggling as they drank and took turns at the dartboard, clapping and cheering every time Thomas hit a bull's-eye.

Thomas didn't seem to be overly flattered by the attention, but he was having a good time, glancing over at me every now and again with a relaxed smile.

He had taken off his jacket and rolled up the sleeves of his oxford, revealing several inches of his thick tanned forearms. His tie was loose, and his top button had been left undone. I willed away the jealousy threatening to bubble to the surface every time I looked over at his new fangirls, but I could still feel those arms around me, pulling me into different positions and watching as they flexed while he—

"Liis!" Val said, snapping her fingers. "You didn't hear a flippin' word I said, did you?"

"No," I said before finishing my drink. "I'm going to head out."

"What? No!" Val said, pouting. Her protruding bottom lip pulled back in as she smiled. "You don't have a ride. You can't leave."

"I called a taxi."

Val's eyes reflected her feelings of betrayal. "How dare you."

"See you Monday," I said, situating my purse strap.

"Monday? What about tomorrow? You're going to waste a perfectly good Saturday night?"

"I have to unpack, and I would actually like to spend time in the condo I'm paying for."

Val was back to pouting. "Fine."

"Good night, Lindy," Marks said before turning his attention back to Val.

I pushed the door open, smiling politely to the patrons sitting outside on the patio. The multicolored string lights hanging overhead made me feel like I was on vacation. I still wasn't used to the fact that the balmy temperature and camisoles were now my normal. Instead of trudging through the frozen tundra of Chicago in a down coat, I could step outside in a summer dress and sandals if I wanted, even in the wee hours of the morning.

"Leaving?" Thomas said, seeming rushed.

"Yes. I'd like to get completely unpacked this weekend."

"Let me drive you."

"You look"—I leaned over to peek at his groupies through the window—"busy."

"I'm not." He shook his head as if I should have known better.

When he looked at me that way, I felt like the only person in the city.

My heart fluttered in my chest, and I begged any hatred I still had for him to make itself known.

"You're not driving me home. You've been drinking."

He sat his half-empty bottle of Corona on a table. "I'm good. I swear."

I glanced at my wrist.

"That's nice," Thomas said.

"Thanks. It was a birthday present from my parents. Jackson never understood why I'd wear something so tiny that didn't have any numbers on it."

Thomas covered my watch with his hand, his fingers wrapping around my small wrist one and a half times. "Please let me drive you."

"I've already called a cab."

"They'll get over it."

"I—"

"Liis"—Thomas slid his hand from my wrist to my hand, leading me toward the parking lot—"I'm going that way anyway."

The warmth in his smile made him seem more like the stranger I had taken home and less like the ogre at the office. He didn't let go of my hand until we were at his black Land Rover Defender. It looked almost as old as I was, but Thomas had clearly made some upgrades and modifications, and he kept it meticulously clean.

"What?" he said, noticing the look on my face after he sat in the driver's seat.

"This is just such an odd vehicle to own in the city."

"I agree, but I can't give her up. We've been through too much. I bought her on eBay when I first moved here."

I had left behind my four-year-old silver Toyota Camry in Chicago. I hadn't had the money saved up to ship it, and that long of a road trip hadn't sounded appealing in the least, so it was sitting in my parents' drive with the words *For Sale* and my cell phone number written in white shoe polish on the front windshield. I hadn't thought of eBay. I was so determined not to think about Jackson or home that I hadn't thought about anyone or anything inside of Chicago's city limits. I hadn't called my old friends or even my parents.

Thomas left me to my thoughts, lost in his own, as he navigated his SUV through traffic to our building. My hand had felt lonely ever since he let it go to open my door. Once he parked and jogged around to my side to be a gentleman again, I tried not to hope that he would take my hand, but I failed. However, Thomas didn't fail to disappoint me.

I walked with my arms crossed against my chest, pretending like I wouldn't have taken his hand anyway. Once inside, Thomas pressed the button, and we waited in silence for the elevator. Once the doors opened, he motioned for me to step inside, but he didn't follow.

"You're not coming?"

"I'm not tired."

"Are you going all the way back?"

He thought about that and then shook his head. "Nah, I'll probably go across the street."

"To Cutter's Pub?"

"If I go upstairs with you right now—" he said as the doors slid closed. He didn't get to finish.

The elevator climbed five floors and then set me free. Feeling ridiculous, I hurried to the window at the end of the hall and watched Thomas walk across the street with his hands in his pockets. A weird sadness came over me until he paused and looked up. When his eyes met mine, a gentle smile stretched across his face. I waved at him, and he waved back and then continued on.

Feeling half embarrassed and half exhilarated, I walked to my condo and dug around in my purse for my keys. The metal grated against each other as I jiggled the lock and turned the knob. Immediately, I closed the door behind me, and one after another, I slid the chain and flipped the dead bolt.

The boxes stacked in my condo were beginning to look like furniture. I let my purse slide from my shoulder onto the small table next to me, and I kicked off my shoes. It was going to be a long solitary night.

Three loud knocks on the door made me jump, and without checking the peephole, I scrambled to open the locks before yanking the door open so quickly that the wind swept my hair.

"Hi," I said, blinking.

"Don't look so letdown," Sawyer said, brushing past me into my living room.

He sat on my couch, leaning back into the cushions and stretching his arms out over the top. He looked more comfortable in my condo than I did.

I didn't bother asking an FBI agent how he knew where I lived. "What the hell are you doing here, unannounced?"

"It's Friday. I've been trying to speak with you all week. I live in the next building over. I was outside, smoking my e-cig, and saw Maddox walk in here with you, but then he walked toward Cutter's without you."

"I'm not understanding where any of that translates into an invitation."

"Sorry," he said, not an ounce of apology in his voice. "Can I come over?"

"No."

"It's about Maddox's kid brother."

That gave me pause. "What about him?"

Sawyer enjoyed having my full attention. "Did you read the file?"

"Yes."

"All of it?"

"Yes, Sawyer. Stop wasting my time."

"Did you read the part about Benny trying to employ Travis? The S.A.C. ordered Maddox to make his brother an asset. He has an in no one else does."

"I know this already." I didn't want to let him in on the fact that Travis had already been slated for recruitment. My gut told me to keep that to myself.

"Did you also know that it's a shit idea? Abby Abernathy is the way to go."

"She doesn't get along with her father. Travis is the more viable choice."

"She whisked Travis off to Vegas and lied about the alibi. Trenton was at the fight. He knew his brother was there. The whole family was in on it."

"Except Thomas."

He sighed in frustration and sat forward, resting his elbows on his knees. "It's Thomas now?"

I glared at him.

"I've been telling Thomas for a year that we should use Abby. She would be a better asset."

"I disagree," I said simply.

He scooted to the edge of the couch and held out his hands. "Just…hear me out."

"What is the point? If Travis finds out we've coerced his wife, the operation will implode."

"So, the better option is to bring him, the unstable one, on as an asset?" he said, deadpan.

"I think Maddox knows his brother, and he is the lead on this. We should trust him."

"You've known him for a week. You trust him?"

"No, not even a week. And yes. You should, too."

"He's too close to this case. This is his brother. Hell, even the director is too close. For some unknown reason, he's practically adopted Maddox. They should all know better. This is not me being a jackass. This is reason, and it's making me crazy that no one is listening. Then, you come in—someone unattached and put into a place of authority. I thought I finally got my chance, and I'll be damned if Maddox isn't actively keeping me away from you."

"I'll give you that," I said.

"What's worse is the louder I am, the less they hear."

"Maybe you should try speaking more softly."

Sawyer shook his head. His smoldering blue eyes snuffed out when he looked away from me. "Good God, Lindy. You need some help unpacking?"

I wanted to send him on his way, but an extra set of hands would make it go so much faster. "Actually—"

He held up his hands again. "I know my reputation at the office. I admit to half of it—okay, most of it. But I'm not a dick all the time. I'll help you and go home. I swear."

I glared at him. "I'm a lesbian."

"No, you're not."

"Right, but the chances are better for me to become a lesbian than for me to have sex with you."

"Understood. Although I find you extremely attractive—I won't deny that in the real world, I'd try my damnedest to take you home from the bar—you should know that, even though I am a jerk and a man-whore at times, I'm not stupid. I wouldn't sleep with my boss."

Sawyer's comment made my cheeks flush, and I turned my back to him. His Southern charm wasn't lost on me even though reason told me he was a waste of time for any woman wanting respect or a relationship.

Sawyer might be a womanizer, and he might even be an asshole most of the time, but he had no problem with transparency. Kept at arm's length, Sawyer could actually be an asset and maybe even a friend.

I pointed to the kitchen. "Let's start there."

CHAPTER SEVEN

I WOKE UP TO A NEARLY CLEAN BEDROOM. All my clothes were either hanging in the closet or folded and put away in the dresser drawers. Sawyer and I had managed to unpack every box and even clean up most of our mess—aside from some packing nuts and empty boxes that we'd torn down and stacked by the front door.

Wearing a gray sweatshirt and navy lounge pants, I wrapped my fuzzy white robe around me and then opened my bedroom door, looking out into the kitchen and living room. They were one in the same, separated only by the kitchen counter that doubled as an island and possibly a breakfast bar.

My condo was small, but I didn't need much room. The thought of having a whole space to myself made me want to take in a deep breath and spin around like Maria in *The Sound of Music*—until I remembered that I wasn't alone.

Sawyer was lying on my couch, still asleep. We'd blazed through two and a half bottles of wine before he passed out. One of his arms was draped over his face, covering his eyes. One socked foot was on the floor, likely to keep the room from spinning. I smiled. Even drunk, he'd kept his promise not to make a pass at me, and he'd earned an infinite amount of respect by the time I left him on the couch for my room.

Poking through my pathetically stocked cabinets, I was trying to find something to eat that wouldn't offend my hangover. Just as I reached up for the box of saltine crackers, someone knocked on the door.

I padded over in my pink-and-white gingham slippers—a Christmas present from my mother the year before. *Damn*, I thought. *Need to call her today.*

Releasing the chain lock and dead bolt, I turned the knob and peeked through the crack in the door.

"Thomas," I said, surprised.

"Hey. I'm sorry for ditching you last night."

"You didn't ditch me."

"You're just waking up?" he said, his eyes pouring over my robe.

I pulled the belt tighter. "Yeah. I kept the party going while I unpacked."

"Need some help?" he asked.

"No, I'm finished."

His eyes danced around a bit, his investigator senses kicking in. I'd seen that expression so many times before.

"You finished all that unpacking by yourself?"

My hesitation to answer prompted him to touch his hand to the door and slowly push it open.

His anger was instant. "What the fuck is he doing here?"

I returned the door to its former position. "He's sleeping on the couch, Thomas. Jesus, do the math."

He leaned in and whispered, "I've been on that couch before, too."

"Oh, fuck you," I said.

I pushed the door to shut it, but Thomas held it open.

"I told you if he bothered you to let me know."

I crossed my arms. "He wasn't bothering me. We had a nice night."

His eyes flickered, and his brows pulled inward. He took a step toward me and kept his voice low as he said, "If you're worried about how you're perceived, you shouldn't have let Sawyer spend the night."

"Is there something you need?" I asked.

"What did he say to you? Did he discuss the case?"

"Why?"

"Just answer the questions, Lindy," he said through his teeth.

"Yes, but I don't think it's anything he hasn't said to you."

"He wants to make Abby an asset."

I nodded.

"And?" he asked.

I was surprised that he was asking me.

"Your brother won't allow it. Besides, I don't think she can be trusted. According to the file, she has helped her father numerous times despite their volatile relationship. She won't turn him in, except maybe for Travis. We'd have to arrest him first though. Then, maybe she'd play."

Thomas sighed, and I inwardly cursed myself for thinking aloud.

"*You* would have to arrest him," Thomas said.

"What do you mean?"

Thomas nearly whispered, "It would blow my cover."

"You're not undercover. What the hell are you talking about?"

Thomas shifted his weight. "It's hard to explain, and I won't while I'm in the hall and while Sawyer is pretending to be asleep on your couch."

I turned, and one of Sawyer's eyes popped open.

He sat up, grinning. "To be fair, I was asleep until you knocked on the door. This couch is comfy, Lindy! Where did you get it?" he asked, pushing down on the cushions.

Thomas opened the door wider and pointed to the hall. "Out."

"You can't kick him out of my condo," I said.

"Get the fuck out!" Thomas yelled, the veins in his throat bulging.

Sawyer stood up, stretched, and then grabbed his things off my long rectangular coffee table, his keys scraping against the glass as he did so. He stood between me and the doorjamb, just inches from my face. "See you Monday morning."

"Thanks for the help," I said, trying to sound apologetic while still remaining professional. It was an impossible balance.

Sawyer nodded to Thomas and then left us for the hallway. Once the elevator opened and then closed again, Thomas looked at me with a stern glare.

I rolled my eyes. "Oh, stop. You are trying too hard."

I walked off, and Thomas followed me inside.

I retrieved the saltines from the cabinet and held them out. "Breakfast?"

Thomas seemed confused. "What?"

"I'm hungover. Crackers are for breakfast."

"What do you mean, I'm trying too hard?"

I looked up at him. "You like me."

"I...you're okay, I guess," he said, stumbling over his words.

"But you're my boss, you don't think we should date, so now you're scaring away any interested parties."

"That's quite a theory," he said.

I pulled apart the plastic package, put a stack of saltines on a plate, poured a glass of tepid water, and used the counter for a table. "Are you saying I'm wrong?"

"You're not wrong. But you're emotionally unavailable, remember? Maybe I'm just doing Sawyer a favor."

The crackers crunched between my teeth, and the cotton mouth I was experiencing from too much alcohol became worse. I pushed the plate away and took a drink of water.

"You shouldn't be so hard on Sawyer. He's just being a team player. You're trying to save your brother. This is important to you. For whatever reason, your family doesn't know you're a fed, and now, you're forcing your brother to join the ranks. We all get it, but no need to piss on every idea your team brings you."

"You know, Liis, your observations aren't always correct. Sometimes, things go deeper than what you see on the surface."

"The reasons leading to the origin of the problem aren't always simple, but the solution always is."

Thomas sat on the couch, looking distraught. "They don't get it, Liis, and you definitely don't get it."

My tough shell melted at the sight of his tough shell melting. "I might if you explain it to me."

He shook his head, rubbing his face with his hand. "She knew this would happen. That's why she made him promise."

"Who's *she*? Camille?"

Thomas looked up at me, completely pulled out of his line of thought. "What the hell made you think of her?"

I walked the ten feet to the couch and sat next to him. "Are we going to work together on this or not?"

"We are."

"Then, we have to trust each other. If something is between me and getting the job done, I remove whatever it is."

"Like me?" he asked with a half smile.

I recalled our argument in the fitness room and wondered how I'd found the courage to tell the ASAC to get out of my way. "Thomas, you have to fix this."

"What?"

"Whatever is messing with your head. Sawyer seems to think you're too close to this case. Is he right?"

Thomas frowned. "Sawyer has wanted this case since I brought it to the supervisor. He wanted it when I was promoted to supervisor, and he wanted it when I was promoted to ASAC."

"Is it true? Were you promoted because of the break you got in the case?"

"Travis dating Abernathy's daughter?"

I waited for his answer.

He looked across the room, his expression somber. "For the most part. But I've also worked my ass off."

"Then, quit screwing around, and let's bring these guys in."

Thomas stood and began to pace. "Bringing them in means nailing them, and the easiest way to do that is to use my little brother."

"So, do it."

"You know it's not that easy. You can't be that naive," Thomas snapped.

"You know what has to be done. I'm not sure why you're making it so hard."

Thomas thought about that for a moment and then sat next to me again. He covered his mouth and nose with his hands, and then he closed his eyes.

"Do you want to talk about it?" I asked.

"No," he said, his voice muffled.

I sighed. "Do you really not want to talk about it? Or is this where I demand that you do?"

He let his hands fall to his lap, and he sat back. "She had cancer."

"Camille?"

"My mother."

The air in the room became heavy, so much so that I couldn't move. I couldn't take a breath. All I could do was listen.

Thomas's eyes were fixed on the floor, his mind trapped in a bad memory. "Before she died, she spoke to each of us. I was eleven. I've thought about it a lot. I just can't"—he took a deep breath—"imagine what it was like for her—trying to tell her sons everything she wanted to teach us over a lifetime, but having to do so in just a few weeks."

"I can't imagine what that was like for *you*."

Thomas shook his head. "Every word she said, even every word she tried to say, is branded into my memory."

I leaned back against the cushion, my head propped by my hand, listening as Thomas described how his mother had reached out for him, how beautiful her voice had been even though she could barely speak, and how much he knew she'd loved him, even in her last moments. I thought about what kind of woman must have raised a man like Thomas along with four other boys. What kind of person could say good-bye with enough strength and love to last her children the rest of their childhoods? His descriptions of her left a knot in my throat.

Thomas's eyebrows pulled together. "She said, 'Your dad is going to take this hard. You're the oldest. I'm sorry, and it's not fair, but it's up to you, Thomas. Don't just take care of them. Be a good brother.'"

I rested my chin on my hands, watching the various emotions scroll across his face. I couldn't relate, but I definitely empathized, so much so that I had to resist wrapping my arms around him.

"The last thing I said to my mother was that I'd try. What I'm about to do to Travis doesn't feel like trying, not one fucking bit."

"Really?" I asked, dubious. "All the work you've done on this case? All the strings you had to pull to get Travis recruited instead of sent to prison?"

"My dad is a retired police detective. Did you know that?" Thomas looked at me with his dark hazel eyes. He was neck-deep in his past, family baggage, guilt, and disappointment.

I wasn't sure how much worse his story could get. Part of me was afraid he was going to admit to being abused.

Hesitant, I shook my head. "Did he...hit you?"

Thomas's face screwed into disgust. "No. No, nothing like that." His eyes lost focus. "Dad checked out for a few years, but he's a good man."

"What do you mean?" I said.

"It was right after she spoke to me for the last time. I was crying in the hallway, just outside the bedroom door. I wanted to get it all out, so the boys wouldn't see me. I heard Mom ask Dad to quit his job at the station, and she made him promise that he'd never let us follow in his footsteps. She had always been proud of him, of his job, but she knew her death would be hard on us, and she didn't want Dad in a line of work that could make us orphans.

Dad loved the job, but he promised. He knew Mom was right. Our family couldn't take another loss."

He rubbed his thumb on his lips. "We came too close with Trenton and Travis. Along with Abby, they almost died in that fire."

"Does your dad know?"

"No. But if something had happened to them, he wouldn't have survived it."

I touched his knee. "You're good at being a federal agent, Thomas."

He sighed. "They won't see it that way. I spent the rest of my childhood trying to be a grown-up. I lost a lot of sleep trying to think of something else to be. I couldn't let my dad break his promise to her. He loved her too much. I couldn't do that to him."

I reached for his hand and held it in mine. His story was so much worse than I'd thought. I couldn't imagine how much guilt he carried around with him every day, loving the job he wasn't supposed to have.

"When I decided to apply for the Bureau, it was the hardest, most exciting thing I'd ever done. I've tried to tell them so many times, but I just can't."

"You don't have to tell him. If you truly believe he won't understand, then don't. It's your secret to keep."

"Now, it's going to be Travis's secret to keep."

"I wish"—I put my other hand on top of his—"you could see this the way I do. You're protecting him the only way you can."

"I potty-trained Travis. I bathed him every night. My dad loved us, but he was lost in his grief. For a while after he got his new job, he used to drink until he passed out. He's made up for it. He apologizes all the time for taking the easy way out. But I raised Trav. I bandaged his scrapes. I got in so many fights over him and fought next to him. I can't let him go to prison." His voice broke.

I shook my head. "You're not. The director agreed to recruit him. He's home free."

"Do you understand what I'm dealing with here? Trav will have to lie to our family and his wife, like I've done. But I chose this, and I know how hard it is, Liis. Travis doesn't get a choice. Not only will Dad be disappointed, but Travis will also be undercover. Only the director and our team will know. He is going to have to lie to everyone he knows because I knew his connection to Benny could get me this promotion. I'm his fucking brother. What kind of person does that to his own brother?"

Thomas's self-loathing was difficult to watch, especially knowing there was no reprieve.

"You didn't do this just for a promotion. You might tell yourself that, but I don't buy it." I squeezed his hand. His misery was so heavy that even I could feel it. "And you didn't force him to engage in illegal activity. You're just trying to spare him the consequences of his actions."

"He's a kid," Thomas said, his voice faltering. "He's just getting ready to turn twenty-one, for Christ's sake. He's a fucking kid, and I bailed on him. I left for California and didn't look back, and now, he's in some serious shit."

"Thomas, listen to me. You've got to get this straight in your head. If you don't believe in the reasons for Travis's recruitment, he sure as hell isn't going to."

He cupped my hands in both of his. Then, he brought my fingers to his mouth and kissed them. My entire body leaned toward him a fraction of an inch as if by a gravitational pull I couldn't control. As I watched his lips warm my skin, I felt jealous of my own hands.

Never had I wanted to defy my own rules so ardently that my conscience was at war in my own head. Not even half of these conflicting emotions had existed the night I decided to leave Jackson. The effect Thomas had on me was wonderful and maddening and terrifying.

"I remember the guy I met my first night here, the one without the pressure of running a field office or making the tough decision to protect his brother. No matter what you tell yourself, you're a good person, Thomas."

He looked over at me and pulled his hand away from mine, indignant. "I'm no fucking saint. If I told you the story about Camille, you wouldn't be looking at me like that."

"You mentioned that she's Trent's girlfriend. I can guess."

He shook his head. "It's worse than you think."

"I'd say helping Travis avoid a prison sentence is atonement."

"Not even close." He stood.

I reached for him but missed. I didn't want him to leave. I had an entire day and nothing to unpack. Now that Thomas was in my living room, he seemed to fill up the empty space. I was afraid it would feel lonely when he left.

"We can do this, you know," I said. "Travis will be free. He can stay home with his new wife, and he'll have a good job. It'll all work out."

"It'd better. God owes me one, more than one."

He wasn't in my living room. He was miles away from me.

"We just have to stay focused," I said. "This has to be the best damn thing either of us has ever pulled off."

He nodded, considering my words.

"And what about Camille?" I asked. "Do you have that handled?"

Thomas walked toward the door, putting his hand on the knob. "Another time. I think we've had enough truth for one day."

When the door slammed, my shoulders flew up to my ears, and I closed my eyes. After the few decorations Sawyer had nailed to the walls the night before stopped rattling, I sat back against the couch cushions in a huff. Thomas was supposed to make it easier to hate him, and after what he'd shared with me, it was impossible.

I wondered who at the Bureau knew about his personal conflicts—with his brother and the Vegas case, and keeping his career from his family—maybe Marks, likely the S.A.C., and definitely the director.

Thomas had made me his partner on this. For whatever reason, he trusted me, and just as inexplicably, that made me want to work that much harder to wrap up this case.

Val had said before that Thomas had a loyal circle and to be careful what I said. Now, I was part of that circle, and I was curious if it was because he needed to use my talents like he did Sawyer's or if it was just that he needed *me*.

I covered my face, thinking about his lips on my skin, and I knew that I was hoping for both.

CHAPTER EIGHT

"ABSOLUTELY NOT," I said to Agent Davies.

She gritted her teeth, sitting stiffly in my office.

"You're not getting three million dollars of taxpayer money for some half-cocked scheme."

"It's not a half-cocked scheme, Lindy. It's right there in the file. If we wire three million to that account, we'll have Vick's trust."

"You know how much a middleman's trust is worth to me?"

"Three million?" Davies said, her big eyes only half hopeful.

"No. Stop wasting my time." I continued typing on my laptop, checking my schedule.

Val and I had a lunch meeting at Fuzzy's, and then I had to ask Thomas if I could speak with the other language expert, Agent Grove, about some discrepancies I had found in his FD-302.

Davies slapped my desk and stood up. "Just another goddamn bossy..." Her grumbling trailed off as she got closer to my door.

"Agent Davies," I called.

She turned around, her long brown ponytail flipping as she did so. The annoyed expression on her face hardened when her eyes met mine.

"You need to get one thing straight. I am not bossy. I'm the fucking boss."

Davies's stern look softened, and she blinked. "Have a nice day, Agent Lindy."

"Likewise, Agent Davies." I motioned for her to shut the door, and as it closed, I put on my headphones and listened to the digital file Thomas had sent me this morning.

The file Agent Grove had translated a few days before was accurate, except for a few key elements. I'd meant to ask Thomas about it earlier, but something felt off. It was mostly a number here and there, but then Grove had listed a suspect by the wrong name and begun leaving things out altogether.

I pulled off the headset and walked out into the squad room, noticing Grove wasn't at his desk. "Val," I called, "have you seen Maddox?"

She walked over to me, holding a small bag of potato chips in one hand and licking the salt off the other. "He's interviewing someone over at the Taliban Welcome Center."

I frowned. "Really? We're really going to call it that?"

"It's what everyone calls it," she said, shrugging.

Val was referring to the million-dollar building that sat in front of our multimillion-dollar building. It served as a security checkpoint for visitors, and it was where we would question persons of interest. That way, if they or their friends attempted to bring explosives in, the main building wouldn't be at risk.

Someone had dubbed this checkpoint as the Taliban Welcome Center, and for some bizarre reason, the nickname had stuck.

I flicked my ID badge—habit to make sure I had it on before I left—and I headed out. It was normally a nice jaunt across the parking lot to the checkpoint building, but low gray clouds were rumbling across the sky, and huge raindrops began to fall a few moments after I'd stepped onto the concrete.

The air smelled metallic, and I breathed in deep. The last week had been spent mostly indoors. That was something I hadn't prepared for. It was easy to work behind a desk in freezing Chicago temperatures. Working so much when it was downright balmy was proving to be more difficult as the gorgeous days came, one after another.

I looked up at the sky, seeing flashes of lightning at the edge of the city. It would be easier to be at work in stormy weather.

I pushed through the glass double doors, flicking my hands and spraying the carpet with rainwater. Despite being soaked, I was in a good mood.

I looked to the agent at the desk with a broad smile. She wasn't impressed with my positivity, my manners, or the fact that I'd walked that far in the rain.

My smile fell away, and I cleared my throat. "Special Agent Maddox?"

She took a long look at my badge and then nodded behind her. "He's in interrogation room two."

"Thank you," I said. I walked over to the security door and bent over a bit while holding my badge to the black box on the wall near the door. I felt ridiculous, and someday soon, I would have to find a retractable badge holder.

The bolt lock clicked, and I pushed through. I walked down the hall and then through a door before seeing Thomas standing alone, watching Agent Grove question an unknown subject—also known as an unsub—a sullen, lanky Asian man in a bright track suit.

"Agent Lindy," Thomas said.

I crossed my arms, aware that my white blouse was wet and I was cold. "How long has he been at it?"

"Not long. The subject has been cooperating."

I listened to them conversing in Japanese. Immediately, I frowned.

"What made you come this way?" Thomas asked.

"I had some questions about a few of Grove's transcriptions. I need your permission to speak with him."

"For the Yakuza case?"

"Yes."

He hummed, unaffected. "Your function here is confidential."

"Someone left a stack of his reports on my door. I assumed Grove knew I was also a specialist and wanted me to look them over."

"Assumptions are dangerous, Liis. I put them there."

"Oh."

"Did you find anything?"

"A lot of things."

I looked through the glass at the three people inside. Another agent was sitting in the corner, taking notes but otherwise looking extremely bored.

"Who's that?" I asked.

"Pittman. He wrecked his third vehicle. He's on desk duty for a while."

I looked to Thomas. He was unreadable.

"You don't seem surprised that I found some discrepancies," I said, watching Grove through the one-way mirror. I pointed. "There. He just translated that eleven former members of Yakuza are living in a building that also houses other subjects of Bureau investigations."

"So?"

"The unsub relayed that the members are in fact current members of Yakuza, and their number is eighteen, not eleven. Grove's omitting. He's either shit at Japanese, or he's unreliable."

Agent Grove stood and then left the unsub in the room alone with the transcribing agent. He slowly walked out before closing the door behind him. When he saw the two of us, he startled but quickly recovered.

"Agent Maddox," he said in a nasal tone.

Anyone else might have missed the slight trembling in his fingers when he pushed up his glasses. He was a pudgy man with copper skin. His eyes were so dark that they were nearly black, and his wiry mustache twitched when he spoke.

Thomas gestured to me with the same hand that held his coffee. "This is Agent Lindy, the new supervisor for Squad Five."

"I've heard the name," Grove said, eyeing me. "From Chicago?"

"Born and raised."

Grove had the look I'd seen often right before a person asked me if I was Korean, Japanese, or Chinese. He was trying to decide if I could speak the language he had been incorrectly translating.

"Maybe you should come in here and help. He's got a weird accent. Keeps tripping me up," Grove said.

I shrugged. "Me? I don't speak Japanese. I've been thinking of taking lessons though."

Thomas spoke up, "Maybe you could work with her, Grove?"

"Like I have time for that," he grumbled, mindlessly rubbing his sweaty palms against each other.

"Just a thought," Thomas said.

"I'm grabbing coffee. I'll see you around."

Thomas lifted his chin once, waiting until Agent Grove left the room.

"Good call," Thomas said, watching Pittman doodle.

"How long have you known?" I asked.

"I've had my suspicions for at least three months. I was sure when I missed an arrest after walking in on an empty room that I knew had been crawling with Yakuza two days prior."

I raised an eyebrow.

Thomas shrugged. "I was going to bring him in to translate the Title Threes we'd gotten on Benny's guys in Vegas, but after that missed arrest, I thought better of it. Instead, I wanted to bring in someone new, someone better."

"Someone who wasn't a double agent?"

Thomas turned to me with the smallest hint of a smile. "Why do you think I brought you here?"

"Will you arrest him?" I asked. "What will you do?"

He shrugged. "I doubt we'll keep using him as a translator."

I made a face. "I'm serious."

"Me, too."

Thomas walked with me down the hall and out to the parking lot, tossing his coffee and opening an umbrella. "You should invest in one of these, Liis. It's spring, you know."

He hadn't said my name as acerbically as before. He'd spoken it softly, his tongue caressing each letter, and I found myself glad that we had the excuse of the rain to keep close.

I dodged puddles, inwardly enjoying it when Thomas struggled to keep the umbrella over my head. Finally, he resorted to putting his free hand around my waist and squeezing me to his side. If we came upon a puddle, he could simply and effortlessly lift me over it.

"I have never liked the rain," Thomas said as we stopped in front of the lobby doors while he shook off his umbrella. "But I might have changed my mind."

I grinned up at him, trying my best not to make obvious the ridiculous giddiness I felt over his innocent flirtation.

Once inside the lobby of the main building, Thomas was back to his typical ASAC demeanor. "I'll need a FD-three-oh-two on your findings by the end of the day. I'm going to need to report this to the S.A.C."

"On it," I said, turning for the elevator.

"Liis?"

"Yes?"

"Will you be working out today?"

"Not today. I'm having lunch with Val."

"Oh."

I relished the flicker of disappointment in his eyes. "I'll be there tomorrow."

"Yeah, okay," he said, trying to play off the small blow to his ego.

If he looked any unhappier, I wouldn't be able to thwart the smile threatening to break out across my face.

Once inside the elevator, when the thrill wore off, I was thoroughly annoyed with myself. I'd essentially kicked him out of my bedroom the night we met because I was sure I would be too busy enjoying my freedom. Being with Jackson had been suffocating, and a transfer had seemed like the perfect solution.

Why in the hell do I feel this way about Thomas? Despite my feelings about starting a new relationship and considering his temper and emotional baggage, what is it about him that makes me lose my ability to reason?

Whatever it was, I needed to get a handle on it. We had to focus on getting through our assignment in St. Thomas, and something messy like feelings wouldn't help anyone.

The elevator opened to reveal Val smiling brightly in the hallway. After taking in the sight of me, her good mood vanished. "Haven't you heard of an umbrella, Liis? Jesus."

I rolled my eyes. "You act as if I'm covered in dog shit. It's rain."

She followed me to my office and sat in one of the twin chairs in front of my desk. She crossed her legs and arms and glared at me. "Spill it."

"What are you talking about?" I said, kicking off my heels and placing them next to each other by the floor vent.

"Really?" She tucked her chin. "Don't be that girl. Chicks before dicks."

I sat down and laced my fingers together on top of my desk. "Just tell me what you want to know, Val. I have things to do. I think I just got Agent Grove fired—or arrested."

"What?" Her eyebrows shot up for half a second, and then she was frowning again. "You might be an ace at diversion, but I know when someone's not telling me something, and you, Liis, have a secret."

I covered my eyes with my hand. "How can you tell? I've got to get better at this."

"What do you mean, how can I tell? Do you know how many interrogations I've sat in on? I just know. I'd say I'm psychic, but that's stupid, so I'll just say, 'Thank you, Dad, for being a cheating bastard and heightening my bullshit-o-meter.'"

I pulled my hand away and gave her a look.

"What? I tell the truth—unlike you, you...fake, foul friend."

I wrinkled my nose. "That was harsh."

"So is knowing that your friend doesn't trust you."

"It's not that I don't trust you, Val. It's just none of your business."

Val stood and walked around the club chair, placing her hands on the back. "Quite frankly, I'd rather you not trust me. And...you're no longer invited to Fuzzy's."

"What?" I shrieked. "C'mon!"

"No. No Fuzzy's for you. And they love me, Liis. Do you know what that means? No Fuzzy's for lunch. No Fuzzy's *forever.*" She emphasized every syllable of the last word. Then, she widened her eyes and turned on her heels before shutting the door behind her.

I crossed my arms and pouted.

Five seconds later, my landline rang, and I picked up the phone. "Lindy," I snapped.

"Hurry up. I'm hungry."

I smiled, grabbed my purse and shoes, and hurried to the hall.

CHAPTER NINE

"So," VAL SAID AS SHE CHEWED, wiping the mixture of mayo and mustard from the corner of her mouth, "you have a date with Maddox in three weeks. Is that what you're telling me?"

I frowned. "No. It was what you pulled out of me."

She smiled, pursing her lips to keep the large bite of BLT from tumbling out.

I rested my chin on my fist, pouting. "Why can't you just leave things alone, Val? I need him to trust me."

She swallowed. "How many times have I told you? There are no secrets in the Bureau. Maddox should have assumed that I'd find out eventually. He's acutely aware of my talents."

"What is that supposed to mean?"

"Curb the jealousy, O.J. I mean that Maddox knows we're friends, and he knows I can sniff out any secret better than a coon dog."

"A *coon dog*? Who are you right now?"

"My grandparents live in Oklahoma. I used to visit every summer," she said dismissively. "Listen, you're doing a crackerjack job as supervisor. The S.A.C. clearly has an eye on you. You're going to be at Quantico before you can say *office affair*."

I nearly choked on my fry. "Val, you're killing me."

"He can't keep his eyes off of you."

I shook my head. "Stop."

She teased me with a knowing look. "He smiles sometimes when you walk by. I don't know. It's kind of cute. I've never seen him like this."

"Shut up."

"So, what about Travis's wedding?"

I shrugged. "We're going to spend the night in Illinois, and then we'll go to St. Thomas."

Val's grin was contagious.

I chuckled. "What? Knock it off, Val! It's work."

She threw a fry at me, and then she allowed me to finish my lunch in peace.

We left Fuzzy's to head back to the office.

As we passed Marks's office, he waved at Val. "Hey! Meet me at Cutter's tonight," he said.

"Tonight?" She shook her head. "No, I have to buy groceries."

"Groceries?" he said, making a face. "You don't cook."

"Bread. Salt. Mustard. I have nothing," she said.

"Meet me afterward. Maddox is coming." His eyes floated to me for just a fraction of a second, long enough to make my cheeks flush pink.

I retreated to my office, not wanting to seem eager to hear of Thomas's plans. Just as I sat in my throne and woke up my laptop, Sawyer knocked on the partially open door.

"Bad time?" he asked.

"Yes," I said, rolling the mouse. I clicked on the icon for my email and frowned as I read the numerous subject lines. "How in the hell does this happen? I'm gone for an hour, and I have thirty-two new messages."

Sawyer shoved his hands into his pockets and leaned against the doorjamb. "We're needy. There's an email from me."

"Great."

"Do you want to go to Cutter's tonight?"

"Is that the only bar in the neighborhood?"

He shrugged, walking toward my desk and falling into a chair. He leaned back, his knees spread and his fingers intertwined at his chest.

"This isn't my living room, Agent."

"Sorry, ma'am," he said, sitting up. "Cutter's is just where we go. It's close for a lot of us who live in the area."

"Why do so many of us live in that area?" I asked.

He shrugged. "Housing has a good relationship with the property owners. It's fairly close to the office. It's a nice neighborhood, and for Midtown, it's pretty affordable." He smiled. "There's a little eatery in Mission Hills called Brooklyn Girl. It's pretty fantastic. Want to go there?"

"Where is Mission Hills?"

"About ten minutes from your condo."

I thought about it for a second. "Just food, right? It's not a date."

"God, no—not unless you want to buy me dinner."

I chuckled. "No. Okay. Brooklyn Girl at eight thirty."

"Boom," he said, standing.

"What was that?"

"I don't have to eat alone. Pardon me while I celebrate."

"Get out of here," I said, waving him away.

Sawyer cleared his throat, and then I noticed the door hadn't closed when it should have. I glanced up to see Thomas standing in the doorway. His short hair was still damp from his post-workout shower.

"How long have you been standing there?" I asked.

"Long enough."

I barely acknowledged his taunt. "You really should stop hovering in my doorway. It's creepy."

He sighed, shutting the door behind him before approaching my desk. He sat, waiting patiently, while I looked over my emails.

"Liis."

"What?" I said from behind the monitor.

"What are you doing?"

"Checking my email, also known as work. You should try it."

"You used to call me sir."

"You used to make me." An awkward long silence prompted me to lean over and meet his eyes. "Don't make me explain."

"Explain what?" he asked, genuinely intrigued.

I looked away, annoyed, and then gave in. "It's just dinner."

"At Brooklyn Girl."

"So?"

"It's my favorite restaurant. He knows that."

"Jesus, Thomas. This is not a pissing match."

He considered that for a moment. "Maybe not to you."

I shook my head in frustration. "What does that even mean?"

"Do you remember the night we met?"

Every bit of my sass and nerve melted away, and I instantly felt the same way I had the first few seconds after he climaxed inside me. The awkwardness put me in my place faster than intimidation ever could.

"What about it?" I asked, chewing on my thumbnail.

He hesitated. "Did you mean what you said?"

"Which part?"

He stared into my eyes for what seemed like an eternity, planning what he would say next. "That you're emotionally unavailable."

He hadn't just taken me off guard. All my guards were taken off faster than any other offed guards in the history of offed guards.

"I don't know how to answer that," I said. *Well done, Liis!*

"Does that go for everyone or just me?" he asked.

"Nor that."

"I've just been…" His expression changed from casually flirty to curious and flirty. "Who's the SWAT guy you left behind in Chicago?"

I glanced behind me as if someone who might be hanging on the seventh-floor window could hear. "I'm at work, Thomas. Why the hell are we talking about this now?"

"We can talk about it over dinner if you'd like."

"I have plans," I said.

The skin around his eyes tightened. "A date?"

"No."

"If it's not a date, then Sawyer won't care."

"I'm not canceling on him because you want to win whatever game you're playing. This is already old. You make me tired."

"Then, it's settled. We'll discuss your ex-ninja at my favorite restaurant at eight thirty." He stood.

"No, we won't. None of that sounds appealing—at all."

He looked around and playfully pointed at his chest.

"No, you're not appealing either," I snapped.

"You're a terrible liar for a fed," Thomas said with a smirk. He walked to my door and opened it.

"What is with everyone today? Val is acting crazy, and you're insane…and arrogant, by the way. I just want to come to work, go home, and maybe not eat alone once in a while with whomever the hell I want, without drama or whining or contests."

The whole of Squad Five was staring into my office.

I gritted my teeth. "Unless you have an update for me, Agent Maddox, please allow me to continue my current task."

"Have a good day, Agent Lindy."

"Thank you," I said in a huff.

Before he closed the door, he poked his head back in. "I was just getting used to you calling me Thomas."

"Get out of my office, Thomas."

He shut the door, and my cheeks burned bright as an uncontrollable smile spread across my face.

Miniature rivers rushed down each side of the street, a city's worth of dirt and debris escaping down the large square drains at each intersection. Tires sloshed in high-pitched tones as they careened down the wet asphalt, and I stood in front of the striped awning and large glass windows that featured *Brooklyn Girl* in vintage font.

I couldn't stop smiling about the fact that I wasn't saddled with a heavy coat. The low clouds overhead were backlit by the moon, and the sky had spit and poured on San Diego off and on all day, yet there I stood in a sleeveless white blouse, a coral linen blazer, and skinny jeans with sandals. I'd wanted to wear my suede slingback heels, but I hadn't wanted to chance getting them wet.

"Hey," Sawyer said into my ear.

I turned and smiled, elbowing him.

"I got us a table," Thomas said, breezing past us and opening the door. "Three, right?"

Sawyer looked like he'd swallowed his tongue.

Thomas's eyebrows lifted. "Well? Let's eat. I'm starved."

Sawyer and I traded glances, and I walked in first, followed by Sawyer.

Thomas shoved his hands into his pockets as he stood at the hostess's podium.

"Thomas Maddox," the young woman said, a sparkle in her eye. "It's been a long time."

"Hi, Kasie. Table for three, please."

"Right this way." Kasie smiled, taking three menus and leading us to a corner booth.

Sawyer sat first near the wall, and I sat in the chair next to him, leaving Thomas to sit across from us. Both men looked happy with the arrangement at first, but Thomas's eyebrows pulled together when Sawyer scooted his chair a bit closer to mine.

I suspiciously eyed him. "I thought this was your favorite restaurant?"

"It is," Thomas said.

"She said you haven't been in here in a long time."

"Nope."

"Why?" I asked.

"Didn't you used to bring your girl here?" Sawyer asked.

Thomas lowered his chin and glowered at Sawyer, but when Thomas's eyes met mine, his features softened. He looked down, situating his silverware and napkin. "The last time I came here was with her."

"Oh," I said, my mouth suddenly dry.

A young waitress approached our table with a smile. "Hi, guys."

Sawyer looked up at her with a familiar gleam in his eye. "Someone's got a date after work. I'm jealous."

Tessa blushed. "New lipstick."

"I knew it was something." Sawyer's eyes lingered on her a big longer before he looked down at the menu.

Thomas rolled his eyes, ordered a bottle of wine without looking at the list, and then she was gone again.

"So," Sawyer said, turning his entire body toward me, "did you figure out the painting?"

"No," I said with a quiet laugh, shaking my head. "I don't know why it's so heavy. It's still propped against the wall where I want to hang it."

"So weird there's not a stud anywhere along that wall," Sawyer said, desperately trying not to seem nervous.

Thomas shifted in his seat. "I have anchors. How heavy is it?"

"Too heavy for the drywall, but I think an anchor would work," I said.

Thomas shrugged, looking far more comfortable with the situation than Sawyer or me. "I'll bring one down later."

From my peripheral, I saw the smallest movement in Sawyer's jaw. Thomas had just secured time alone with me later. I wasn't sure if other women enjoyed being in this position, but I was borderline miserable.

Tessa returned with a bottle and three glasses.

As she poured, Sawyer winked at her. "Thanks, sweetheart."

"You're welcome, Sawyer." She could barely contain her glee as she teetered on the heels of her feet. "Uh, have you decided on an appetizer?"

"The roasted stuffed marrow," Thomas said, making a point not to take his eyes off of me.

The intensity of his stare made me squirm, but I didn't look away. On the outside at least, I wanted to seem impervious.

"I'll just have the hummus," Sawyer said, looking disgusted at Thomas's choice.

Tessa turned on her heels, and Sawyer watched her walk all the way back to the kitchen.

"Excuse me," Sawyer said, motioning that he needed out of the booth.

"Oh." I scooted over and stood, letting him get out.

He walked by me with a smile and then toward what I assumed was the restroom, past the gray walls and modern rustic wall art.

Thomas smiled as I returned to my seat. The air conditioner kicked on, and I pulled my blazer tighter around me.

"Would you like my jacket?" Thomas said, offering his blazer. It perfectly matched the walls. He also wore jeans and laced brown leather Timberland boots.

I shook my head. "I'm not that cold."

"You just don't want to be wearing my jacket when Sawyer comes out of the restroom. But he won't notice because he'll be chatting it up with Tessa."

"What Sawyer thinks or feels doesn't concern me."

"Then, why are you here with him?" His tone wasn't accusatory. In fact, it was so unlike his usual demanding loud voice that his words nearly blended into the hum of the AC.

"I'm not sitting across from him. At the moment, I'm here with you."

The corners of his mouth turned up. He seemed to like that, and I inwardly cursed myself for the way that made me feel.

"I like this place," I said, glancing around. "It sort of reminds me of you."

"I used to love this place," Thomas said.

"But not anymore. Because of her?"

"My last memory of this place is also my last memory of her. I don't count the airport."

"So, she left you."

"Yes. I thought we were going to talk about your ex, not mine."

"Did she leave you for your brother?" I asked, ignoring him.

His Adam's apple bobbed as he swallowed, and he glanced toward the restrooms, looking for Sawyer. As predicted, Sawyer was standing at the end of the counter near the drink station, making Tessa giggle.

"Yeah," Thomas said. He puffed, like something had knocked the breath out of him. "But she wasn't mine to begin with. Camille has always belonged to Trent."

I shook my head and furrowed my brow. "Why do that to yourself?"

"It's hard to explain. Trent has loved her since we were kids. I knew it."

His confession surprised me. From what I knew of his childhood and his feelings toward his brothers, it was hard to imagine Thomas pulling something so heartless.

"But you pursued her anyway. I just don't understand why."

His shoulders moved up just a tiny bit. "I love her, too."

Present tense. A tinge of jealousy twinged in my chest.

"I didn't mean to," Thomas said. "I used to go home quite a bit, mostly to see her. She works at the local bar. One night, I went straight to The Red and sat down in front of her station, and then it just hit me. She wasn't a little girl in pigtails anymore. She was all grown-up and smiling at me.

"Trent talked about Camille all the time, but in a way—to me, at least—I never thought he'd go for it. For the longest time, I thought he'd never settle down. Then, he started seeing this other girl...Mackenzie. That's when I decided he was past his crush on Camille. But pretty quickly after that, there was an accident, and Mackenzie died."

I sucked in a tiny sharp breath.

Thomas acknowledged my shock with a nod and continued, "Trent wasn't the same after that. He drank a lot, slept with whomever, and left school. One weekend, I came home to check on him and Dad, and then I went to the bar. She was there." He winced. "I tried not to."

"But you did."

"I reasoned that he didn't deserve her. It's the second most selfish thing I've ever done, and both of them were to my brothers."

"But Trent and Camille ended up together?"

"I work a lot. She's there. He's there. It was bound to happen once Trent decided to chase her. I couldn't really protest. He loved her first."

The sad look in his eyes made my chest ache. "Does she know what you do?"

"Yes."

I arched an eyebrow. "You told her who you work for but not your family?"

Thomas thought about my words and shifted in his seat. "She won't tell them. She promised she wouldn't."

"So, she's lying to all of them?"

"She's omitting."

"To Trent as well?"

"He knows we were seeing each other. He thinks we were keeping it a secret from him because of the way he felt about Camille. He still doesn't know about the Bureau."

"Do you trust her not to tell him?"

"Yes," he said without hesitation. "I asked her to keep quiet about the fact that we were dating. For months, no one knew but her roommate and a few of her coworkers."

"It's true, isn't it? You didn't want your brother to know you had stolen her," I said, smug.

His face twisted, disgusted at my lack of finesse. "In part. I also didn't want Dad poking her for information. She would have had to lie. It would have just made things more difficult than they already were."

"She had to lie anyway."

"I know. It was stupid. I acted on a temporary feeling, and it turned into something more. I put everyone in a bad position. I was a selfish dick. But I did…I do…love her. Trust me, I'm getting payback."

"She's going to be at the wedding, isn't she?"

"Yeah," he said, twisting his napkin.

"With Trent."

"They're still together. They live together."

"Oh," I said, surprised. "And that has nothing to do with why you want me to go?"

"Polanski wants you to go."

"You don't?"

"Not because I'm trying to make Camille jealous, if that's what you're getting at. They love each other. She's in my past."

"Is she?" I asked before I could stop myself. I braced for his reply.

He looked at me for a long time. "Why?"

I swallowed. *That is the real question, isn't it? Why do I want to know?* I cleared my throat, chuckling nervously. "I don't know why. I just want to know."

He breathed a laugh and looked down. "You can love someone without wanting to be with them. Just like you can want to be with someone before you love them."

He looked up at me, a spark in his eye.

From my peripheral, I saw that Sawyer was standing next to our table, waiting with Tessa, who had a tray in her hand.

Thomas didn't look away from me, and I couldn't look away from him.

"Can I, uh...excuse me," Sawyer said.

I blinked a few times and looked up. "Oh. Yes, sorry." I stood to let him by, and then I returned to my seat, trying not to shrink under Thomas's unfaltering stare.

Tessa placed the appetizers on the table along with three small plates. She filled Thomas's half-empty glass, the dark merlot splashing inside, but I put my hand over mine before she could pour.

Sawyer lifted his glass to his lips, and an awkward silence hung over the table while the rest of the restaurant hummed with a steady chatter, broken up only by intermittent laughter.

"Did you tell her about Camille?" Sawyer asked.

The hairs on the back of my neck stood on end, and my mouth suddenly felt parched. I gulped the last of the red liquid in my glass.

Thomas bared his teeth and squinted his eyes, looking regretful. "Did you tell Tessa about that rash?"

Sawyer nearly choked on his wine. Tessa tried to think of something to say but failed, and after a few bounces, she retreated to the kitchen.

"Why? Why are you such an asshole?" Sawyer said.

Thomas chuckled, and I fought a smile but lost, giggling into my water glass.

Sawyer began to laugh, too, and he shook his head before slathering his slice of pita with hummus. "Well played, Maddox. Well played."

Thomas looked up at me from under his brow. "How are you getting home, Liis?"

"You're driving me."

He nodded once. "I didn't want to assume, but I'm glad you agree."

CHAPTER TEN

"THANK YOU," I said quietly.

I tried not to look at the sliver of beautifully tanned skin between Thomas's belt and the bottom hem of his white T-shirt. He was hanging the painting, one of the first things I'd purchased after training. It was a canvas print, wrapped around wood, and it was too heavy to be wall decor.

"It's creepy as hell," Thomas said, stepping off my dining room chair onto the carpet.

"It's a Yamamoto Takato. He's my favorite Japanese modern artist."

"Who are they?" Thomas asked, referring to the two sisters on the painting.

They were resting outside at night. One sister was looking on, quietly enjoying whatever mischief was happening before them. The other was looking back at Thomas and me, sullen and bored.

"Spectators. Listeners. Like us."

He looked unimpressed. "They're weird."

I crossed my arms and smiled, happy that they were finally in their place. "He's brilliant. You should see the rest of his work. They're tame in comparison."

His expression told me he didn't approve of this new piece of information.

I lifted my chin. "I like them."

Thomas took in a breath, shook his head, and sighed. "Whatever frosts your cookies. I guess I'll, uh...head out."

"Thanks for taking me home. Thanks for the anchor. Thanks for hanging the girls."

"The girls?"

I shrugged. "They don't have names."

"Because they're not real."

"They're real to me."

Thomas picked up the chair and returned it to the table, but he gripped the top, leaning over a bit. "Speaking of things that aren't real...I've been trying to think of a way to talk to you about certain aspects of the trip."

"Which ones?"

He stood up and walked toward me, leaning down just inches from my face, slightly turning his head.

I pulled away. "What are you doing?"

He backed off, satisfied. "Seeing what you would do. I was right to bring this up now. If I don't show affection, they'll know something is up. You can't pull away from me like that."

"I won't."

"Really? That wasn't a knee-jerk reaction just then?"

"Yes...but I've let you kiss me before."

"When you were drunk," Thomas said with a smirk. He walked to the middle of the room and sat on my couch like he owned the place. "That doesn't count."

I followed him, watched him for a moment, and then sat on his right, leaving not even air between us. I nuzzled my cheek against his chest and slid my hand across his rigid abdomen before digging my fingers into his left side, just enough so that my arm stayed in place.

My entire body relaxed, and I crossed my right leg over my left, letting my calf overlap his knee so that every part of me was at least a little bit draped over him. I cuddled up against him with a smile because Thomas Maddox—the astute, always-in-control Special Agent—was as still as a statue, his heart thundering in his chest.

"I'm not the one who needs practice," I said with a grin. I closed my eyes.

I felt his muscles ease, and he wrapped his arms around my shoulders, letting his chin rest on top of my head. He let all the air escape from his lungs, and it seemed like a long time before he took another breath.

We stayed that way, without anywhere to be, listening to the quietness of my condo and the noise from the street. Tires still sloshed against the wet asphalt, horns honked, doors from cars slammed. Once in a while, a person would shout, car brakes would whine, and a dog would bark.

Inside, sitting with Thomas—on the very couch we'd christened the night we met—felt like an alternate universe.

"This is nice," he said finally.

"*Nice?*" I was mildly offended. I thought it felt amazing. No one had held me that way since Jackson in Chicago, and even then, it hadn't felt like this.

I didn't think that I would miss someone touching me, especially when I hadn't appreciated Jackson's affection before. But being without it for less than a month had made me feel lonely, and maybe even a little depressed. That was typical for anyone, I imagined, but I was sure that the sadness wouldn't have come so strong and so soon had I not experienced Thomas's hands on me during my first night in San Diego. I'd had to miss them every day after that.

"You know what I mean," he said.

"No. Why don't you tell me?"

His lips pressed against my hair, and he inhaled, deep and peaceful. "I don't want to. I just want to enjoy it."

Fair enough.

I opened my eyes, alone and lying on my couch. I was still fully dressed, covered with the wool throw that had been folded on the chair.

I sat up, rubbed my eyes, and then paused. "Thomas?" I called. I felt ridiculous. It was worse than the morning after our one-night stand.

My watch read three a.m., and then I heard a bump upstairs. I looked up with a smile. It was nice knowing that he was so close. But then I heard something else, something that made my stomach turn.

A groan.

A moan.

A yelp.

Oh God.

A rhythm of bumping against a wall along with moans began to filter down to my condo, and I looked around, not knowing what to think. *Did he leave here and go to Cutter's? Meet a girl? Take her home?*

But Thomas wouldn't do that. I had been the only one since…maybe I'd gotten him out of his slump.

Oh God.

"Oh God!" a woman's muffled cry repeated my thought aloud, filling my condo.

No. This has to stop.

I stood up and began to search for something long to bang against the ceiling. His embarrassment didn't matter in the least. I didn't even care if I was *that* neighbor—the spinster downstairs who didn't like hearing music, loud laughter, or sex. I just needed that woman's abnormally loud orgasm to stop.

I climbed onto the dining room chair, the same one Thomas had used earlier, with a broom in hand. Just before I started banging the handle against the ceiling, someone knocked on the door.

What in the hell?

I opened it, fully aware that either I looked absolutely insane or the person on the other side of the door would be the crazy one, and I would have to use the broom on some psycho.

Thomas was standing in the doorway with dark circles under his eyes, looking exhausted. "Can I stay here?"

"What?"

"Why are you holding a broom?" he asked. "It's after three in the morning. Are you cleaning?"

I narrowed my eyes. "Don't you have company?"

He looked around, seeming confused by my question, and then shifted his weight from one leg to the other. "Yes."

"Shouldn't you be at your place then?"

"Uh…I'm not getting much sleep up there."

"Clearly!"

I tried to slam the door, but he caught it and followed me inside.

"What is wrong with you?" he asked. Then, he pointed to the stray dining room chair. "What's up with the chair?"

"I was going to climb up on it and use this!" I said, holding out the broom.

"For what?" His nose wrinkled.

"On the ceiling! To make it stop! To make her stop!"

Recognition lit his eyes, and he was instantly embarrassed. "You can hear that?"

I rolled my eyes. "Yes. The whole building can hear it."

He rubbed the back of his neck. "I'm sorry, Liis."

"Don't apologize," I seethed. "It's not like we…it's not real."

"Huh?"

"Please don't apologize! It just makes me feel more pathetic!"

"Okay! I'm sorry! I mean…"

I sighed. "Just…go."

"I…was going to ask if I could stay here tonight. But I guess if you can hear her—"

I tossed the broom at him, but he hopped over it.

"What the hell, Liis?"

"No, you can't stay here! Go back upstairs to your one-night stand! Seems like you've become a pro."

His eyes grew wide, and he held up his hands. "Oh! Whoa. No. That wasn't…that's not me. Up there. With her."

"What?" I closed my eyes, completely confused.

"I'm not with her."

I glared at him. "Obviously. You just met her."

His hands were moving back and forth in a horizontal motion. "No. I'm not up there, fucking her."

"I know," I emphasized each word. I might as well have been talking to a wall.

"No!" he yelled in frustration.

The banging began again, and we both looked up. The woman began to yelp, and a low moan filtered through the ceiling—a man's voice.

Thomas covered his face. "Jesus Christ."

"Someone has a woman in your condo?"

"My brother," he groaned.

"Which one?"

"Taylor. He's staying here for a few days. He texted me, wondering why I wasn't at home. I left here to meet him upstairs, but when I got there, he was pissed about something and didn't want to sit at the condo. So, I took him over to Cutter's. Agent Davies was there, and—"

I pointed to the ceiling. "That's Agent Davies?"

Thomas nodded his head.

"Oh, thank God," I said, covering my eyes with my hand.

He frowned. "Huh?"

"Nothing."

Davies cried out.

I shook my head and pointed to the door. "You've got to tell them to quit that shit. I have to get some sleep."

Thomas nodded again. "Yeah. I'll go." He turned for the door, but then he stopped, flipped around, and pointed at me. "You thought that was me. You were pissed."

I made a face. "No, I wasn't."

"Yeah, you were. Admit it."

"So what if I was?"

"Why were you mad?" he asked, his eyes begging me for something.

"Because it's three a.m., and I should be sleeping."

"Bullshit."

"I have no idea what you're talking about!"

I knew exactly what he meant, and he knew that I was trying to play dumb.

He smiled. "You thought that was me banging some chick from the bar, and you were mad at me. You were jealous."

After several seconds of being unable to come back with a believable response, I blurted out, "So?"

Thomas raised his chin and then reached behind him to grip the doorknob. "Good night, Liis."

I maintained the dirtiest look I could until he shut the door, and then I walked over to the broom, scooped it up, and pushed the chair back to the table.

After a minute or so, the yelping and banging stopped.

I trudged to my room, stripped off my clothes, and slipped on a T-shirt before falling into the bed.

Not only did I not hate Thomas, I liked him. Worse than that, he knew it.

CHAPTER ELEVEN

I FLIPPED MY WRIST OVER TO CHECK MY WATCH, cursing myself for sleeping in. After poking a pair of fake diamond studs into the holes in my ears, I slipped on my heels, grabbed my purse, and opened the door.

Thomas stood there with a Styrofoam cup in each hand. "Coffee?"

I pulled the door closed and twisted the key in the lock. "Is there milk in that coffee?" I asked.

"Nope. Six sugars and a two creamers."

"How do you know how I take my coffee?" I asked, taking the cup he'd pushed toward me.

We walked together to the elevator, and Thomas pressed the button.

"Constance."

"Constance knows you bought me coffee?"

"Constance told me to buy you coffee."

The doors opened, and we stepped inside.

I turned to him, confused. "She's up early," I grumbled. "Why would Constance tell you to do this?"

He shrugged. "She thought you might like it if I did."

I turned to face forward. He was answering me without answering me, my very least favorite thing. I was going to have to ask Val to teach me her human-lie-detector trick.

"No more questions?" Thomas asked.

"No."

"*No?*"

"You won't give me a real answer anyway."

"Constance knows I like you. She says I've been different since you've been here, and she's right."

"Thomas," I said, turning to him, "I...appreciate that, but I'm—"

"Emotionally unavailable. I know. But you're also just coming out of a relationship. I'm not asking you to move in with me."

"What are you asking?"

"Let me take you to work."

"That's not a question."

"Okay. Can we have dinner alone?"

I turned to him as the elevator opened. "Are you asking me on a date, Maddox?"

I walked into the lobby, my heels clicking against the floor.

After a few seconds of hesitation, he nodded once. "Yes."

"I don't have time for anything messy. I'm committed to the job."

"As am I."

"I like to work late hours."

"As do I."

"I don't like to report to anyone."

"Nor do I."

"Then, yes."

"Yes, I can take you to work? Or yes, we can have dinner?"

"Yes to both."

He smiled, triumphant, and then he used his back to push open the lobby doors, keeping me in view. "My vehicle's this way."

During the drive to work, Thomas explained his evening with Taylor, what time Agent Davies had left his condo, and how inconvenient it was to have a drop-in guest even if it was his brother.

The freeway was still damp from the rain the day before. He weaved his Land Rover in and out of traffic, and although I was used to driving in Chicago, San Diego was totally different, and I wasn't sure if I would be prepared once I found a vehicle.

"You look nervous," Thomas said.

"I hate the freeway," I grumbled.

"You'll hate it more when you drive it. When does your car get here? You're going on three weeks without it."

"It's not coming. My parents are selling it for me. I'm going to look for a new one when I have some time, but for now, public transportation works."

Thomas made a face. "That's ridiculous. You can just ride with me."

"It's really fine," I said.

"Just meet me out front in the mornings. We leave at the same time anyway, and we're going to the same place. Plus, you're doing me a favor. I can drive in the carpool lane."

"Okay," I said, looking out the window. "If you don't mind."

"I don't mind."

I glanced over at him. His transformation from angry, volatile boss to gentle, content neighbor—possibly more—had been gradual, so I hadn't noticed until we were side by side, the morning sun highlighting the calm in his eyes. We rode the rest of the way to the Bureau in comfortable silence.

The next time Thomas spoke was to the guard at the security gate.

"Agent Maddox," Agent Trevino said, taking our badges. He leaned down to identify me and smirked.

"Hi, Mig," Thomas said. "How's the family?"

"All fine. Nice of you to drive Agent Lindy to work this morning."

Thomas took back his badge. "We live in the same building."

"Mmhmm," Trevino said, sitting back before pressing the button to open the gate.

Thomas drove through and chuckled.

"What's so funny?"

"Trevino," Thomas said, resting his elbow on the bottom of the window and touching his lips with his fingers.

I frowned. Anytime anything came into contact with his lips, a mixture of depression and jealousy swirled inside me. It was an awful feeling, and I wondered when it would stop. "Am I a running joke?"

Thomas looked over at me and switched his driving hand. Then, my hand was in his, and he squeezed.

"No. Why would you think that?"

"What is so amusing?"

Thomas pulled into the parking garage and put the gear into park. He turned back the key, and the engine silenced. "Me. He's laughing at me. I don't bring people to work. I don't smile when I check in, and I damn sure don't ask him about his family. He knows it's...he knows. Things have been different since you came here."

"Why is that?" I stared at him, my eyes begging him to say the words.

Admittedly, I was too proud and stubborn to break my vow to the Bureau without insurance. Coffee, odd jobs around my condo, even his hand in mine weren't enough. I was okay with being second to his job. When we were both committed to the Bureau, it somehow canceled the other out. But I wouldn't come in third.

His cell phone rang, and when he noticed the name on the display, his entire demeanor changed. His eyebrows pulled in, and he sighed.

"Hey," Thomas said, his face tight. He let go of my hand and looked away. "I told you I would. I, uh..." He rubbed his eyes with his thumb and index finger. "I can't. My flight doesn't land until an hour prior to Trav's arrival at the hotel. Okay...tell me what?"

Thomas looked down, and his shoulders sagged. "You are? That's great," he said, failing to cover the devastation in his voice. "Uh, no, I understand. No, Trent, I get it. It's okay. Yeah, I'm happy for you. I am. Okay. All right. See you then."

Thomas pressed End and then let the phone fall to his lap. He held the steering wheel with both hands, his grip twisting so hard that his knuckles turned white.

"Want to talk about it?"

He shook his head.

"Okay. Well...I'll be in my office if you change your mind."

Just as I reached for the lever, Thomas grabbed me by the arm and pulled me to him, his amazingly soft lips melting against mine. Everything around us blurred, and I was transported back to the night we'd met—the desperate hands, his tongue deep in my mouth, his blazing hot sweaty skin against mine.

When he finally let me go, I grieved. Even though it had been my lips against his, when we'd parted, I was still left with that awful feeling.

"Damn it, Liis. I'm sorry," he said, looking just as shocked as I was.

I was breathing slow but deep, still leaned in a bit.

"I know you don't want a relationship," he said, angry with himself. "But I'll be goddamned if I can't stay away from you."

"I can relate," I said, smoothing my hair away from my face. "Trent?" I asked, nodding to his cell phone.

He looked down and then back at me. "Yeah."

"What did he say that upset you?"

Thomas hesitated, clearly not wanting to answer. "He was talking to me about Travis's bachelor party."

"And?"

"He's the entertainment."

"So?"

Thomas shifted nervously. "He, uh…has a deal with Camille." He shook his head. "A while back, she agreed to marry him if he did something crazy and embarrassing. He's going to do it at Trav's party, and then he's…" His eyes fell. He looked heartbroken. "He's going to ask Camille to marry him."

"Your ex."

He nodded slowly.

"The one you're still in love with. And then you kiss me to stop thinking about it?"

"Yes," he admitted. "I'm sorry. It was a shit thing to do."

My first reaction was to be angry. But how could I be angry when kissing him was all I'd thought about since we met? And how could I be jealous? The woman he loved would very soon be engaged, and he'd practically just given his blessing. All of that logic did me no good. I was envious of a woman I'd never met and who would never be with Thomas. I couldn't be mad at him, but I was furious with myself.

I pulled at the lever. "Squad Five is meeting at three."

"Liis," he called after me.

I walked away as fast as my heels would allow, all the way to the elevator.

The doors closed behind me, and I stood in silence as the numbers climbed. People got on and off—agents, assistants, city leaders—all speaking in hushed tones, if they spoke at all.

When the doors opened on the seventh floor, I stepped out and tried to hurry past Marks's office. He was always early, and Val was usually in his office, chatting. I snuck by his open door, hearing Val's voice, and quickly slipped through the security doors. I walked around the corner of the first cubicle, passed another two, and then ducked into my office, closing the door.

I sat in my throne and turned my back to the wall of windows, and I stared at my bookshelf and the view of the city below. I heard a knock but ignored it, and then someone put a file in the holder on my door, leaving me alone. I let the high back of the chair conceal me from the squad room, and I twisted the long black strands of my hair around my finger, thinking about the kiss, the night before, and every time I'd been alone with Thomas since I met him.

He was still in love with Camille. I didn't understand, and worse, I wasn't sure of my feelings either. I knew that I cared for him. If I were being honest, that was a gross understatement. The way my body responded to his presence was addictive and impossible to ignore. I wanted Thomas in a way that I'd never felt for Jackson.

Is it worth the mess it might make at work? Is it worth the mess he could make of me?

I pulled my hair out of my mouth after realizing I had been chewing on it. I hadn't done that since I was a girl. Thomas was my neighbor and my boss. It was illogical and unreasonable to attempt to be anything more, and if I wanted to stay in control of the situation, I had to surrender to that fact.

My door swung open.

"Liis?"

It was Thomas.

I slowly turned around and sat up straight. The anguish in his eyes was unbearable. He was being pulled in two directions just like I was.

"It's okay," I said. "You're not the one I'm mad at."

He shut the door and walked over to one of the club chairs before sitting down. He leaned down, putting his elbows on the edge of my desk. "That was totally out of line. You didn't deserve that."

"You had a moment. I get it."

He stared at me, rattled by my answer. "You're not a moment, Liis."

"I have a set goal that I am determined to achieve. Any feelings I might have for you won't get in the way of those goals.

Sometimes, you make me forget, but I always come back to the original plan—a plan that doesn't include a significant other."

He let my words simmer for a bit. "Is that what happened with you and Jackson? He didn't fit into your guidelines for the future?"

"This isn't about Jackson."

"You don't talk about him much." He sat back.

Shit. I didn't want to get into this conversation with him.

"That's because I don't need to."

"Weren't you engaged?"

"Not that it's any of your business, but yes."

Thomas raised an eyebrow. "Nothing, huh? Didn't shed a single tear?"

"I don't really...do that. I drink."

"Like that night at Cutter's?"

"Exactly like that night at Cutter's. So, I guess we're even."

Thomas's mouth fell open, not even attempting to hide his wounded ego. "Wow. I guess so."

"Thomas, you of all people should understand. You were faced with the same decision when you were with Camille. You chose the Bureau, didn't you?"

"No," he said, slighted. "I tried to hang on to both."

I sat back and clasped my hands together. "And how did that work out for you?"

"I don't like this side of you."

"That's unfortunate. From now on, this is the only side you're going to get." I stared him straight in the eyes, unwavering.

Thomas began to speak, but someone knocked on the door and pushed it open.

"Agent Lindy?" a smooth but high-toned voice came from the hall.

"Yes?" I said, recognizing Constance standing in the doorway.

"You had a visitor downstairs. I brought him up."

Before I had the chance to wonder who on earth would be visiting, Jackson Schultz walked around Constance and stood in my doorway.

"Oh. My. God," I whispered.

Jackson was in a French-blue button-down shirt and patterned tie. The only times I'd seen him look so well dressed was the night he proposed and at Agent Gregory's funeral. The hue of his shirt set off his azure eyes. They used to be my favorite thing about him, but in that moment, I could only notice that they were as round as his face. Jackson had always been fit, but his smoothly shaved head made him appear more portly than he was.

The longer we had been together, the more his less appealing features and habits had grown noticeable—the way he'd suck food through his teeth after a meal; lean to the side when he passed gas, even in public; or not always wash his hands after he had been in the restroom for half an hour. Even the three deep wrinkles where his skull met his neck made me cringe.

"Who the hell are you?" Thomas asked.

"Jackson Schultz, Chicago SWAT. Who the hell are you?"

I stood up. "Special Agent Maddox is San Diego's ASAC."

"Maddox?" Jackson laughed once, unimpressed.

"Yes, as in the asshole who runs this place." Thomas looked to Constance. "We're in a meeting."

"Sorry, sir," Constance said, not looking sorry at all.

She didn't fool me. She'd told Thomas what kind of coffee to buy, and once she'd learned Jackson was in the building, she'd swiftly escorted him to my office to remind her boss that he had competition. I wasn't sure whether to strangle her or laugh, but it was clear that she cared about Thomas, and it was nice to know she thought well enough of me to push him in my direction.

"Agent Maddox, we were just wrapping up, weren't we?" I asked.

Thomas looked at me and then back to Jackson. "No. Agent Schultz can wait the fuck outside. Constance?"

One corner of her mouth turned up. "Yes, sir. Agent Schultz, if you'll just follow me."

Jackson kept his eyes on me while he followed Constance until they were both out of sight.

I narrowed my eyes at Thomas. "That was unnecessary."

"Why didn't you tell me he was visiting?" Thomas barked.

"Do you really think I knew?"

His shoulders relaxed. "No."

"The quicker you allow him in here, the quicker he'll leave."

"I don't want him here."

"Stop."

"What?" Thomas snapped, pretending to stare at the various photographs and Post-its on my wall or the bookshelf or neither.

"You're being childish," I said.

He lowered his chin to glower at me. "Get rid of him." He kept his voice low.

In the recent past, I might have been intimidated, but Thomas Maddox didn't scare me anymore. I wasn't sure that he ever had.

"You made such a big deal of me being jealous last night. You know I left him and have zero interest, and look at you."

He pointed at the door. "You think I'm jealous of Mr. Clean? You're fucking joking, right?"

"We both know you're too fucked up in there"—I pointed to my own head—"to worry about my ex-fiancé or about me in general."

"That's not true."

"You're still in love with her!" I said too loud.

Every member of Squad Five present in the squad room leaned forward or back in their chairs to watch through the glass wall of my office. Thomas walked over and lowered the blinds for one section and then the other, and then he shut the door.

He frowned. "What does that have to do with anything? I can't like you and still love her?"

"Do you? Like me?"

"No, I just asked you on a date because I enjoy being shot down."

"You asked me to dinner right before you had a meltdown. You're not over her, Maddox."

"There you go with the Maddox again."

"You're not over her," I said, hating the sadness in my voice. "And I have goals."

"You've mentioned that."

"Then, we agree that it's pointless."

"Fine."

"*Fine?*" I asked, embarrassed about the tinge of panic in my voice.

"I'm not going to push it. If I get over Camille and you get over your…thing…we'll reconvene."

I stared at him in disbelief. "You weren't just saying that to Constance. We were really having a meeting."

"So?"

"This isn't something you can outline, Thomas. You can't tell me how it's going to go down, and we're not going to *reconvene* about progress. That's not how it works."

"It's how we work."

"That's ridiculous. You're ridiculous."

"Maybe, but we're the same, Liis. That's why it didn't work out with other people. I'm not going to let you run away, and you're not going to put up with my shit. We can think about whether or not it's efficient to be together until we retire, or we can just accept it now. The fact is, we plan things, we organize, we control."

I swallowed.

Thomas pointed to the wall. "Before you, I was a lonely workaholic, and even though you had someone, so were you. But you and I can make this work. It makes complete sense for us to be together. When you tell Mr. Ninja out there to kick rocks, let me know, and I'll take you to dinner. Then, I'm going to kiss you again and not because I'm distraught."

I swallowed. I tried to keep my voice from wavering as I said, "Good. It's a little disconcerting to be kissed when you're distraught over another woman."

"It won't happen again."

"Make sure that it doesn't."

"Yes, ma'am." He opened the door, walked through, and closed it.

I fell into my chair, taking deep breaths to calm myself. *What the hell just happened?*

CHAPTER TWELVE

"HI," JACKSON SAID FROM THE LOVE SEAT in the small waiting area down the hall. He stood, towering over me. "You look beautiful. California looks good on you."

I tilted my head to the side, offering an appreciative grin. "It's only been a few weeks."

He looked down. "I know."

"How are your parents?"

"Dad just got over a cold. Mom swore that if I brought you flowers, you'd change your mind."

I pulled my mouth to the side. "Let's take a walk."

Jackson followed me to the elevator. I pushed the button for the first floor, and we rode in silence.

When the doors slid open again, the lobby was bustling with activity. First thing in the morning, agents were either coming in or leaving to conduct interviews, to go to the courthouse, or to do the hundreds of other tasks that fell in the spectrum of our duties. Visitors were getting checked in, and a small group of junior high children were beginning a tour.

We walked together toward the backside of the building, and I pushed open the double doors that led to the courtyard. Nestled between the two buildings was a beautiful sitting area with patio furniture, river rocks, patches of green fescue, and a monument for fallen agents. I'd always wanted to spend a few minutes there to gather my thoughts or just sit in the quiet, but between lunch dates with Val and fitness-room time with Thomas, I hadn't really found a spare moment.

Jackson sat in one of the cushioned wicker love seats. I stood in front of him, fidgeting. We didn't speak for nearly a minute, and then I finally took a breath.

"Why didn't you call first?" I asked.

"You would have told me not to come." His voice was pitifully sad.

"But you came anyway," I said, squinting from the bright morning sun.

When Jackson bent over and held his forehead in his hands, I was glad we were alone.

I took a step back, afraid for a second that he might cry.

"I haven't been handling this well, Liisee. I haven't been able to sleep or eat. I had a meltdown at work."

His nickname for me made me cringe. It wasn't his fault. I'd never told him that I hated it. Seeing him so vulnerable when he was usually in command of his emotions made me uncomfortable, and my guilt compiled it tenfold.

Jackson wasn't a bad guy. But falling out of love with him had made everything he did grotesque to me, and the harder I'd tried to feel different, the more I couldn't stand him.

"Jackson, I'm at work. You can't do this here."

He looked up at me. "I'm sorry. I just meant to ask you to lunch."

I sighed and sat next to him. "I hate that you're hurting. I wish I felt different, but I...just don't. I gave it a year, like I promised."

"But maybe if I—"

"It's nothing you did. It's not even something you didn't do. We just don't work."

"You work for me."

I put my hand on his back. "I'm sorry. I really, truly am. But what we had is over."

"You don't miss me at all?" he asked.

His body was so much larger than mine that he shaded me from the sun.

I remembered seeing him at training. The other female trainees had thought he was so attractive and sweet. And he was. After all their efforts to catch Jackson Schultz, I'd managed to catch him with no effort at all. He was attracted to confidence and brilliance, he'd said. And I had both.

Here he was, begging me to want him, when he could walk out of here and make a number of women swoon, women who would love him and appreciate his bad habits along with the traits that I'd fallen in love with.

After some hesitation, I decided the truth wasn't pleasant, but it was necessary. I simply shook my head.

"Holy shit." He laughed once without humor. "Did you move out here for someone? It's not my business, I understand that, but I still gotta know."

"Absolutely not."

He nodded, satisfied. "Well, my plane doesn't leave until Wednesday. I guess there are worse places to be stuck."

"Can you change your flight?" I'd known before I asked that he wouldn't.

Not only was Jackson terrible at letting go, he was also completely helpless at things like changing a plane ticket, making reservations, or scheduling appointments. I was sure his mother had taken care of his travel arrangements for him to even come here.

"The *Top Gun* bar is here. You'd really like it," I said.

"Yeah." He chuckled. "That sounds pretty great."

"I'll walk you out. I'm really…I'm just sorry, Jackson."

"Yeah. Me, too."

I guided him across the lawn and back into the main building. He didn't say a single word as we walked across the lobby and to the entrance.

"I just…I have to say it once…before I leave. I love you."

I kissed his cheek. "Thank you. I don't deserve that, but thank you."

He smirked. "I know you can handle that jerk-off upstairs, but if it gets old, you can always come home."

I snickered. "He's not a problem."

"Good-bye, Liis." Jackson kissed my forehead and turned, pushing through the door.

I took a deep breath and suddenly felt exhausted.

Trudging back into the elevator, I leaned against the back wall until the chime signaled that I was at my floor, and then I stepped out into the hallway, forcing one foot in front of the other.

"Liis?" Marks called as I passed his office. "Get in here."

I stopped and turned around, surprised at the gratefulness I felt for the invitation. I slumped in his chair. "What?"

He raised an eyebrow, momentarily halting the continuous clicking on his keyboard. "I told you. You're trouble."

"What makes you say that?" I asked.

"Everybody can tell that he's different. He's practically happy when you're around."

"I'm missing why that makes me trouble."

"Is your ex staying with you for a few days?"

"Of course not."

"Why not?"

I sat up. "Do you make a habit of asking questions that are none of your damn business?"

"Let me guess. You transferred here to get away from him? You told Tommy you were emotionally unavailable, and now, he's chasing you because you turned him down. Only this isn't a game to you. You really aren't available."

I rolled my eyes and sat back. "Let's not pretend he doesn't have issues of his own."

"Exactly. So, why don't you both make it easier on this department and knock it the hell off?"

"You have your own problems. Concentrate on those instead of mine." I stood.

"I saw what it did to him...when Camille left the last time. It was even worse when he came back after Trent and Cami's car accident. Cami chose Trent, but Tommy has never stopped loving her. I'm not trying to be a dick here, Liis, but he's my friend. I might be in your business, but Tommy was different after he'd lost Cami—and not for the better. He's just now showing signs of the man he used to be before she broke his heart."

"Tommy?" I said, unimpressed.

Marks craned his neck at me. "Is that all you got out of everything I just told you? This isn't a pissing match, Liis. I'm not trying to take him from you. I'm trying to save him from you."

As bitter as it tasted, I tried to swallow the shame. My struggle was clear because the anger in Marks's eyes vanished.

"I can appreciate that you're committed to the job and that you're focused," he said. "But if you can't find a way to love the job and him, too...just don't fuck him over while you're trying to figure out if you've got a heart."

The shame was quickly replaced by anger. "Eat shit, Marks," I said before leaving his office.

I buzzed myself through the security door and marched to my office.

"Lindy," Agent Sawyer began.

"Not now," I said before slamming the door to my office to make a point.

Once again, I was in my chair with the back facing the glass wall. The blinds were closed from when Thomas had been in here before, but I still needed to feel the tall back between me and the squad room.

After a small knock on the door, it opened. By the lack of greeting and the sound of someone sitting in the club chair, I knew it could only be Val.

"Fuzzy's today?"

"Not today. I definitely need to spend my lunch hour in the fitness room."

"Okay."

I spun around. "That's it? No interrogation?"

"I don't have to. I've been watching you all morning. First, you hide in here, and Maddox runs in after you. Then, your ex shows up, and Maddox is up here, yelling at everyone like he used to." She waggled her eyebrows. "He's got it bad."

I looked away. "I just broke Jackson's heart—again. What the hell was I thinking? I knew something had happened to Thomas. Hell, you told me on day one he'd been burned. Marks is right."

Val stiffened. "What did Marks say?"

"That I should stay away from Thomas. That I couldn't commit to Jackson, and it's likely that I can't commit to anyone else."

Val made a face. "You're lying. He isn't that much of a brazen dick."

"He is when it comes to me. And to clarify, yes, I was paraphrasing."

"Then, those are your fears talking. But if you like Maddox, Liis, don't let a failed relationship govern your next one. Just because you didn't love Jackson doesn't mean you can't love Maddox."

"He still loves her," I said, not trying to hide the wounded tone in my voice.

"Camille? She was the one who got away, Liis. He'll probably always love her."

A sick feeling came over me, and I curled my shoulders inward, feeling actual physical pain seeping all the way into my bones.

We haven't known each other for that long. Why do I have such strong feelings for him?

I couldn't ask that though. It made me too vulnerable, made me feel too weak.

I spoke aloud the only question I could, "Do you think he can love two people?"

"Can you love one?" she snapped back.

I shook my head, touching my fingers to my lips.

Val had no sympathy in her eyes. "You're really kind of bringing this on yourself. Be with him or not. But Marks is right. Don't fuck with Maddox's emotions. I realize you told him once that you're emotionally unavailable, but you're behaving differently."

"Because I like him. I think I more than like him. But I don't want to."

"Then, be straight with him, and don't give him mixed signals."

"It's hard not to when that's all I've got going on here," I said, motioning to the space between my head and heart.

She shook her head. "I understand that, but you're going to have to make a decision and stick with it, or you'll just look like a bitch."

I sighed. "I don't have time for this. I have a job to do."

"Then, get your shit straight, and do it." Val stood up and left my office without another word.

I sat at my desk, my hands folded, as I glared down at them. She was right. Marks was right. Jackson was right. Not only was I in no position to experiment with my commitment phobia, but also, Thomas was definitely not the guy to try it with.

I stood and made my way to Constance's desk. Unsure if I was breathless or just nervous, I asked to see Special Agent Maddox.

"He's in his office," Constance said without checking her earpiece. "Go right in."

"Thank you," I said, breezing past her.

"Hey," Thomas said, standing and smiling the moment he recognized who was barging in.

"I can't...do this. The date. I'm sorry."

Thomas's guard instantly flew up, and I hated myself for it.

"Did you change your mind about Jackson?" he asked.

"No! No...I'm...not sure I feel any different about relationships than I did when I left Chicago, and I don't think it's fair to you to try."

Thomas's shoulders relaxed. "That's it? That's your spiel?"

"Huh?"

"Unless you can look me in the eye right now and tell me you didn't like it when I kissed you this morning, I'm not buying it."

"I...you..." That wasn't the response I'd expected. "You've had your heart broken. I just broke someone's heart."

Thomas shrugged. "He wasn't right for you."

He walked around his desk and toward me. I took several slow small steps backward until my backside was touching the massive conference table.

Thomas leaned in, just inches from my face.

I recoiled. "We have an assignment next week, sir. We should probably focus on a game plan."

He closed his eyes and inhaled through his nose. "Please stop calling me sir."

"Why does it bother you so much now?"

"It doesn't bother me." He shook his head, scanning over my face with such longing I couldn't move. "Our assignment is to pose as a couple."

His minty breath was warm on my cheek. The need to turn and feel his mouth on mine was so urgent that my chest ached.

"Since when did you start calling me sir again?"

I looked up at him. "Since now. The attraction is obvious, but—"

"That's an understatement. Do you have any idea how hard it is for me to see you walking around the office in a skirt, knowing you never wear panties?"

I puffed out a breath. "There is something between us. I'm aware. We slept together less than twenty minutes after we'd met, for Christ's sake. But I'm trying to do you a favor. Do you hear me? I want this to be very clear. I like you...a lot. I admit it. But I suck at relationships. More importantly, I don't want you to get hurt again. And...neither do your friends."

Thomas smirked. "You've been talking to Marks, haven't you?"

"I'm also trying to spare us the squad-room theatrics that we both know will come if this doesn't work out."

"Are you saying I'm dramatic?"

"Temperamental," I clarified. "And I can't follow through. We were doomed from the start."

"You stayed with Jackson for how many years after you had known you didn't want to marry him?"

"Too many," I said, ashamed.

Thomas watched me for a moment, analyzing me. I hated that feeling. The power and control that came with being on the other side was much more preferable.

"You're scared," he said. His words were gentle, understanding.

"Aren't you?" I asked, looking up, straight into his beautiful hazel eyes.

He bent down and kissed the corner of my mouth, lingering there for a while, savoring it. "What are you scared of?" he whispered, cupping my elbows.

"The truth?"

He nodded, his eyes closed, his nose tracing my jaw.

"In a few days, you're going to see Camille, and you'll be heartbroken. I won't like it, and neither will the office."

"You think I'm going to get hurt and start being an angry asshole again?"

"Yes."

"You're wrong. I'm not going to lie. It won't be fun. I'm not going to enjoy it. But...I don't know. Things don't seem as hopeless as they did before." He intertwined his fingers with mine and squeezed. He looked so relieved, so happy to be saying these things out loud. He didn't seem to be nervous or afraid at all. "And you're right. We need to focus and finish this assignment to ensure that Trav gets out of trouble. By then, maybe you can let go of this ridiculous notion that you can't be successful at both your career and a relationship, and once we've both got a clear conscience, you can decide if we're going on that date or not."

I frowned.

He chuckled, touching his thumb to my chin. "What now?"

"I'm not sure. Something's not right. You're too okay about this."

"Talk to Val. Ask her if I'm lying."

"She doesn't work like that."

"Yes, she does. Ask her." I opened my mouth to speak, but he pressed my lips closed with his thumb. "Ask her."

I leaned away. "Fine. Have a good day, sir."

"Don't call me sir. I want you out of the habit before we go to the ceremony."

"Agent Maddox," I said before walking quickly from his office.

"I don't like that either," he called after me.

A wide grin spread across my face. I looked over at Constance as I passed, and she was smiling, too.

CHAPTER THIRTEEN

Val HELD THE WINE GLASS TO HER LIPS. Her legs were stretched out across my couch in her charcoal-gray lounge pants, and she had on a light-blue T-shirt that read, WELL, THE PATRIARCH ISN'T GOING TO FUCK ITSELF.

"It's been over three weeks," she said, her thoughts as deep as they could be while floating in wine. She held the corkscrew like a weapon between her fingers, but then she crossed her legs like a lady.

"What's your point?" I asked.

"He's just so…I don't want to say he's in love. It's a little premature for that. But he's so…in love."

"You're absurd."

"What about you?" she asked.

"I like him," I said after a little thought. "A lot." There was no point in lying to Val.

"What is that like? To actually like Thomas Maddox? I've hated him for so long that it's so foreign. To me, he's not really human."

"Maybe that's what I like."

"Lie."

"I meant that he does have a human side, and I like that I'm the only one he allows to see it. It's sort of our secret—something he keeps just for me."

She swirled the wine around in her glass and then tipped it back against her mouth, swallowing the last bit. "Oh, be careful. That sounds dangerously like you're in it to win it, sunshine."

"You're right. I take it back."

"Well, on that depressing note, the wine is gone, so I am gone."

"I feel used."

"But you enjoyed it." She winked. "See you in the morning."

"You want me to walk you?"

"I'm on the next block," she said, her drunken look of disapproval not at all intimidating.

"What is that like?" I asked. "Living in the same building as Sawyer?"

"I used to like it." She picked up the empty bottle and carried it to the kitchen counter. "But that didn't last long. Now, I just ignore him."

"Why does everyone detest him so much?"

"You'll learn," she said.

I frowned. "Why does it have to be such a secret? Why can't you just tell me?"

"Trust me when I say that being told he's a bastard doesn't help. You have to experience it for yourself."

I shrugged. "And Marks? Doesn't he live there, too?"

"He lives downtown."

"I don't know what to think about him," I said, standing. "I think he hates me."

"Marks and Maddox have a bromance. It's gross." She walked with an astonishing amount of balance for being a bottle and a half in.

I laughed. "I'm going to bed."

"All right. Good night, geese with an L." She showed herself out, and I heard the elevator ding.

Already in drinking-wine-at-home clothes, I fell onto my mattress, facedown on top of my yellow-and-gray comforter.

My ears perked up when a knocking noise broke the silence. At first, I thought it was someone down the hall, but then it was louder.

"Val," I called, annoyed that I had to stand again. I walked across the kitchen and living room to open the door. "You should have just stayed—" My voice pinched off when I recognized Jackson standing in the doorway, looking desperate and drunk.

"Liis."

"Jesus Christ, Jackson. What are you doing here?"

"I went to the *Top Gun* bar like you said. Got drunk. There are some hot, *hot*"—he squinted his eyes—"women in this town." His face fell. "It made me miss you even more," he whined, trudging past me into the living room.

My entire body tensed. He wasn't part of my new life, and it made me nearly frantic to have Jackson standing in my new Jackson-free condo. "You can't be here," I began.

"I don't want to do those things without you," he slurred. "I want to experience San Diego with you. Maybe if…if I transferred here, too—"

"Jackson, you're drunk. You barely listen to me when you're sober. Let's call you a cab."

I walked toward my phone, but Jackson got to it before I could, and he tossed it across the room. It skidded across the floor and slammed against the baseboard.

"What the hell is wrong with you?" I yelled before quickly covering my mouth.

I scurried over to retrieve my phone from the floor. It was lying on its face next to the baseboard it had collided with. I inspected it to make sure it wasn't damaged. Miraculously, it wasn't cracked or even dinged.

"I'm sorry!" Jackson yelled back, leaning forward and holding up his hands. "Don't call a cab, Liisee."

He intermittently swayed from side to side to keep his balance. I couldn't remember ever seeing him so intoxicated.

"I'll just sleep here with you."

"No," I said, my tone firm. "You're not staying here."

"Liis," he said, walking toward me, his round eyes half closed and glossed over. He wasn't even looking at me but past me, weaving back and forth. He took my shoulders in his hands and leaned in, his lips puckered and his eyes closed.

I dodged, and we both tumbled to the floor.

"Damn it, Jackson!" I scrambled up, and I watched him struggle to get his bearings.

Reaching up and rocking to sit up, he looked like a turtle on its shell. I groaned.

He climbed to his knees and began to blubber.

"Oh no. Oh, please. Please stop," I said, holding out my hands.

I helped him up and then began to dial the number for a cab. Jackson swatted my phone from my hands, and again, it crashed to the floor.

I let go of his arm, letting him fall—hard. "That's it! I've tried to be nice. Get out!"

"You can't just kick me out of your life, Liis! I love you!" He slowly climbed to stand.

I covered my eyes. "You are going to be so embarrassed tomorrow."

"No, I'm not!" He grabbed my shoulders and shook me. "What's it going to take for you to hear me? I can't just let you go! You're the love of my life!"

"You're not giving me a choice," I said, grabbing hold of his fingers and bending them backward.

He cried out, more from shock than pain. That move might have worked on any other drunken idiot but not FBI SWAT. Even drunk, Jackson quickly maneuvered from my grasp and was grabbing at me again.

The door blew open, the knob banging into the wall. One minute, I was in Jackson's grasp, and the next, Jackson was in someone else's.

"What the fuck are you doing?" Thomas said, holding Jackson's back against the wall with a murderous glare. He had two fistfuls of Jackson's shirt.

Jackson heaved Thomas away and swung, but Thomas ducked and then pushed Jackson right back against the wall, holding him there by using his forearm like a bar across his throat.

"Don't. Fucking. Move," Thomas said, his voice low and menacing.

"Jackson, do as he says," I warned.

"What are you doing here?" Jackson asked. He looked to me. "Does he live here? Are you living together?"

I rolled my eyes. "Jesus."

Thomas glanced over his shoulder at me. "I'm going to take him down and put him in a cab. What hotel is he at?"

"I have no idea. Jackson?"

Jackson's eyes were closed, and he was breathing deep, his knees sagging beneath him.

"Jackson?" I said loudly, poking at his shoulder. "Where are you staying?" When he didn't answer, my shoulders fell. "We can't put him in a cab while he's passed out."

"He's not staying here," Thomas said, a tinge of anger still in his voice.

"I don't see another option."

Thomas leaned over, letting Jackson fall forward over his shoulder, and then carried him to the couch. More careful than I'd thought he would be, Thomas helped Jackson lie back and then tossed a throw over him.

"C'mon," he said, taking my hand.

"What?" I asked with just a bit of resistance as he pulled me toward the door.

"You're staying with me tonight. I have an important meeting in the morning, and I won't be able to sleep, worrying that he's going to wake up and wander into your bed."

I pulled my hand back. "I would hate for you not to be at your best during your meeting."

Thomas sighed. "Cut me some slack. It's late."

I raised an eyebrow.

He looked away, annoyed, and then back at me. "I admit it. I don't want him fucking touching you." He was enraged at the thought, and then it seemed to melt away. He took a step toward me, tenderly gripping my hips. "Can't you see through my bullshit by now?"

"Can't we just...I don't know...say what we think or feel?"

"I thought I was," Thomas said. "Your turn."

I picked at my nails. "You were right. I'm scared. I'm afraid I can't do this even if I want to. And I'm not sure you can either."

He pressed his lips together in a hard line, amused. "Get your keys."

I took the few steps to my phone and bent down to retrieve it, and then walked to the counter and swiped the keys up with one hand, my purse with the other. As I slid on my slippers, I couldn't help but glance back once more to Jackson. His limbs were splayed out in every direction, his mouth was open, and he was snoring.

"He'll be fine," Thomas said, holding out his hand for me.

I joined him in the hall, locking the door behind us. We passed the elevator and climbed the stairs in silence. Once we arrived at his door, Thomas swung the door open and gestured for me to walk inside.

Thomas flipped on the light, revealing a space so immaculate it didn't look lived in. Three magazines were fanned out on the coffee table, and a like-new couch sat against the wall.

Everything was in its place—plants, magazines, and even pictures. It included everything that made up a home, but beneath the homey embellishments, it was too perfect, sterile even. It was as if Thomas were trying to convince himself that he had a life outside of the Bureau.

I walked over to a console table next to the flat screen on the opposite side of the room. Three silver frames held black-and-white photos. One, I assumed were his parents. Another showed Thomas with his brothers, and I was amazed at how much the younger four looked alike. Then, there was one of Thomas and a woman.

Her beauty was distinctive, seeming to be wild and effortless. Her razor-cut short hair and cleavage-baring tight shirt surprised me. She wasn't who I'd thought would be Thomas's type at all. Her thick eyeliner and smoky eyes were that much more prominent in grayscale. Thomas held her like she was precious to him, and I felt a lump form in my throat.

"Is she Camille?" I asked.

"Yes," he said, his voice tinged with disgrace. "I'm sorry. I'm rarely home. I forget it's there."

My chest ached. The picture in that frame was the only answer I needed. Despite my efforts, I was falling for Thomas, but he was still in love with Camille. Even in a perfect world where two people who were obsessed with their jobs could make a relationship work, we had the added obstacle of unrequited love. At the moment, it was Thomas's problem, but if I allowed myself to have deeper feelings, it would be mine.

I was always a firm believer that a person couldn't love two people at the same time. *If Thomas still loves Camille, what does that mean for me?*

An obnoxious siren went off in my head, so loud I could barely think. These feelings for Thomas, Agent Maddox, my boss needed to stop now. I glanced at his couch as I worried that I would one day be begging him to love me in return, showing up drunk and emotional at his door before passing out on his couch like Jackson was on mine.

"If you don't mind, I'll just make a pallet on the floor. The couch doesn't look that comfortable."

He chuckled. "Taylor said the same thing. You're welcome to the bed."

"I think, given our history, that is a particularly bad idea," I said, quoting him from before.

"What do you plan to do when we go to St. Thomas?" he asked.

"It will be your turn to take the floor." I tried to keep the hurt out of my voice.

Thomas left me for his bedroom and then came out with a pillow and a tightly rolled sleeping bag.

I eyed his haul. "Do you keep that in case of sleepovers?"

"Camping," he said. "You've never been?"

"Not since running water became a thing."

"The bed is all yours," he said, ignoring my jab. "I just put on fresh sheets this evening."

"Thank you," I said, passing him. "I'm sorry we woke you."

"I wasn't asleep. I have to admit that it was startling to hear a man yelling in your living room."

"I apologize."

Thomas dismissively waved his hand and then walked over to turn out the light. "Stop apologizing for him. I was out the door before I had time to think."

"Thank you." I put my hand on the doorjamb. "Get some sleep. I don't want you to be mad at me if you can't concentrate during your meeting."

"There is only one reason I wouldn't be able to concentrate during my meeting, and sleep isn't it."

"Enlighten me."

"We're going to be spending the better part of the weekend together, and I have to talk my brother into something he won't want to do. Sunday is important, Liis, and you're the biggest distraction in my life at the moment."

My cheeks flushed, and I was thankful the lights were dim. "I'll try not to be."

"I don't think you can help being a distraction any more than I can help thinking about you."

"I understand now why you said being friends would be a bad idea."

Thomas nodded. "I said that three weeks ago, Liis. The situation has changed."

"Not really."

"We're more than friends now, and you know it."

I looked over at the picture of Thomas and Camille and pointed to it. "She is what scares me, and she is what won't go away."

Thomas walked over to the picture and set it down on its face. "It's just a picture."

The words I wanted to say caught in my throat.

He took a step toward me.

I pushed away from the doorjamb, holding a hand out. "We have a job to do. Let's focus on that."

He couldn't hide his disappointment. "Good night."

CHAPTER FOURTEEN

THOMAS TOSSED A THICK STACK OF PAPERS onto my desk, his jaw dancing under his skin. He paced back and forth, breathing through his nose.

"What is this?"

"Read it," he growled.

Just as I opened the file folder, Val rushed in, stopping abruptly between the door and Thomas. "I just heard the news."

I frowned and skimmed over the words. "The Office of the Inspector General?" I said, looking up.

"Shit," Val said. "*Shit.*"

The report was titled *A Review of the FBI's Handling and Oversight of Agent Aristotle Grove.*

I looked up at Thomas. "What did you do?"

Val closed the door and approached my desk. "Grove is downstairs. Will they arrest him today?"

"It's likely," Thomas said, still fuming.

"I thought you took care of this," I said, closing the file and pushing it forward.

"Took care of it?" Thomas said, his eyebrows shooting toward his hairline.

I leaned forward, keeping my voice low. "I told you Grove was feeding you bad intel. You sat on it too long."

"I was compiling evidence against him. That was part of the reason I brought you here. Val was in on it, too."

I looked to my friend, who stared at the file as if it were on fire.

She was biting her lip. "I didn't have to speak Japanese to know he was full of shit," she said. "Wait—are you the language specialist he brought in on this?"

I nodded.

Thomas pointed at her. "That's confidential, Taber."

Val nodded, but she seemed uncomfortable that she hadn't sniffed that one out.

Sawyer blew in, straightening his tie just as the door closed behind him. "I came as soon as I heard. What can I do?" he asked.

Val shrugged. "What you do best."

Sawyer seemed disappointed. "Seriously? Again? He is my least favorite target. You know if we took a black light Grove's bedroom room, every inch would be glowing."

Val covered her mouth, disgusted.

I stood, pressing my fists down on my desk. "Would someone mind explaining what the hell everyone is talking about?"

"We have to be extremely careful with how we proceed," Thomas said. "Travis could be in real trouble if this isn't seamless."

Val sat in the club chair, defeated. "When Maddox transferred to HQ in Washington before he was promoted to ASAC, he caught a lead on one of Benny's goons from an agent working in HQ's Asian Criminal Enterprise Unit."

I looked to Thomas, dubious. "You caught a lead on one of your Italian mob bosses in Vegas from the Asian Crime Unit in Washington?"

Thomas shrugged. "I'd call it luck, but I've worked on this case day and night since it landed on my desk. There isn't a fingerprint I haven't checked or a backlog I haven't accessed."

Val sighed, impatient. "You can call it bad luck. The goon was a kid. His name was David Kenji. Travis beat him unconscious one night in Vegas to protect Abby."

"That's not in Travis's file," I said, looking to Thomas.

He looked away, allowing Val to continue.

Val nodded. "That was intentionally kept out, so it wouldn't throw up any red flags for Grove. He can't know anything about Travis. If he passes on the plan to any Yakuza, Travis is no longer an asset to the Bureau."

"Why would Grove pass on info about Travis's recruitment to any Yakuza?" I asked.

Val sat forward. "David is the son of Yoshio Tarou's sister."

"Tarou, as in the second-in-command of Goto-gumi in Japan?" I said, in disbelief.

Goto-gumi was one of the oldest syndicates of the original Yakuza Japanese gang. Tarou was a prominent boss, leading Goto-gumi since the 1970s. Tarou didn't just intimidate his enemies. He was creative with his executions, leaving their mutilated bodies for all to see.

Val nodded. "Tarou's sister lived with him until she died when David was fourteen."

I nodded. "Okay, so you're telling me Travis is also a target of Yakuza?"

Thomas shook his head.

I frowned. "I'm not hearing why there's a goddamn Inspector General's report on my desk."

"Tarou is bad news, Liis," Thomas said. "Grove has been passing him information via the Yakuza he's interviewed here, and more recently, he's been speaking to Tarou directly. That's why we've had no traction on their criminal activity despite all the interviews. They've been one step ahead."

"So, we let the IG arrest Grove. Who cares?" I asked.

Thomas's face fell. "It gets worse. David died a couple of months ago. He was beaten unconscious during a fight, and no one has seen him since."

"Does Tarou think it was Travis?" I asked.

"Keep in mind," Sawyer chimed in, "David's run-in with Travis was over a year ago, and to their knowledge, Travis hasn't been to Vegas since."

"The fights were run by the mob," Val said. "Benny pitted David against someone out for blood. Uncle Tarou blamed Benny and sent several of his guys over to the States to get an explanation from Benny. The fighter who killed David was found all over the desert—well, not all of him. We have reason to believe the men Tarou sent over are part of this Yakuza nest we've been interviewing."

I frowned, still confused. "Why was the nephew of Tarou doing low-level goon work for Benny?"

"The mother," Val said simply as if I should have known. "When his mother died, David blamed Tarou. There was a fight. David left and came to the States. He gravitated toward what he knew and ended up with Benny."

"This is a train wreck," I said.

Val looked up to Thomas and then back at me. "We were waiting to pull the trigger on Grove because we knew he was playing both sides, but now that we've cracked the connection with Benny, we don't know what intel from our case he's turned over to them."

"Shit," I said. "How much does he know?"

Thomas took a step toward me. "Like I said, I've been suspicious of him for a while. Sawyer has been keeping track of his activities."

"What kind of activities?" I asked.

Sawyer crossed his arms. "Daily activities—what he eats, where he sleeps. I know what gives him indigestion, what soap he uses, and what porn sites he jacks off to."

"Thanks for that," I said.

Sawyer chuckled, "Surveillance, boss. I'm damn good at surveillance."

"Like the master," Val said.

Sawyer smiled at her. "Thanks."

Val rolled her eyes. "Fuck off."

Sawyer continued, "Maddox kept Grove in the dark about the Vegas case for the most part, but when the cases began to intertwine, Grove became interested…and so did Tarou. Benny is smoothing things over with Tarou, and with these guys, money can turn enemies into friends. The fights are big money. Benny wants a champion, and Travis is a sure thing."

Val sat back in the chair. "We can control what Grove learns at the Bureau, but if Benny or Tarou mention Travis Maddox to Grove, it's all over. He'll make the connection."

I sighed. "Travis's deal, even Abby's access…"

Thomas nodded. "The case. All of it. We'll have to turn in what we've got and wrap it up without Travis or Abby."

"And Travis will no longer be an asset to the Bureau. He'll go to prison."

The weight of my words seemed to bear down on Thomas, and he used the bookshelf for support.

I looked at the file lying askew halfway between Val and me. "The Inspector General just blew us out of the water."

Sawyer shook his head. "Grove doesn't know yet. We need to get on the phone, delay his arrest, and drag this out just a little longer."

"You should have told us your contact was Liis," Val scolded. "We could have avoided this."

Thomas glared at her, but she didn't yield.

"How?" he asked. "Telling you that Liis was keeping tabs on Grove was going to keep the IG's office from writing that report? Are you fucking joking?"

"Knowing we could use Liis to check Grove's transcriptions would have been helpful," Sawyer said.

"I *was* having Liis check them, Sawyer," Thomas said, annoyed. "You think she's been listening to Taylor Swift on her headphones in here?"

I shook my head. "Why the secrecy?"

Thomas held out his hands and let them fall to his sides. "It's Spy one-oh-one, kids. The fewer people you tell, the less risk you take. I didn't want Grove to know I had another Japanese translator in the unit. He needed to keep tabs on all the interviews for Tarou, and another Japanese-speaking agent could have gotten in the way. She might have ended up a target just to keep Grove in charge of the Yakuza interrogations."

"Oh," Val said. "You needed to protect her."

Sawyer rolled his eyes. "That's absurd. He didn't even know her to want to protect her." It took him a moment, but when Sawyer recognized the shame in my eyes, his mouth fell open. His index finger waggled between Thomas and me. "You two were…"

I shook my head. "It was before. He didn't know I was here to work at the Bureau."

"Discussing line of work comes right after name-swapping." Sawyer cackled. "You one-nighted the new hire, Maddox? No wonder you jumped on her ass at her first meeting. You don't like surprises. This is all beginning to make sense."

"We don't have time for this," Thomas sneered.

Sawyer stopped laughing. "Is that why you gave her the promotion?"

The small smile on Val's lips vanished. "Oh, shit."

Thomas lunged for Sawyer, and Val and I stood between them, bouncing like pinballs as we pushed them apart.

"All right! I'm sorry!" Sawyer said.

"A little fucking decorum, please!" I yelled. "We're grown adults! At work!"

Thomas stepped back, and Sawyer smoothed his tie and then sat down.

"Grow up!" I snarled at Thomas.

Thomas touched his fingers to his mouth while he calmed down. "My apologies," he said through his teeth. "I'll call Polanski. We need to get that report buried and intercept the warrant for Grove's arrest—at least for now."

Val straightened her clothes. "You call the S.A.C. I'll call the IG's office."

"I'll tail Grove. See if he suspects anything," Sawyer said.

Thomas's expression turned severe. "We have to keep a tight lid on this."

"Understood," Sawyer and Val said.

They left Thomas and me alone in my office, and we stared at one another.

"You left out your key agents to protect me?" I asked.

"Marks knew."

I tilted my head. "Marks isn't even on this case."

Thomas shrugged. "I can trust him."

"You can trust Val, too."

"Val talks too much."

"We can still trust her."

Thomas gritted his teeth. "I shouldn't have to explain myself. It's dangerous, Liis. These people we're dealing with, if they get a hold of your name—"

"That is the stupidest thing I've ever heard," I snapped.

Thomas blinked, surprised at my reaction.

"I can shoot a target at eighty-five yards with a twenty-two pistol, I can take down an assailant twice my size, and I deal with your arrogant ass at least twice a day. I can handle Benny, the Yakuza, and Grove. I'm not Camille. I am an agent of the FBI, same as you, and you will respect me as such. Do you understand me?"

Thomas swallowed, carefully thinking about his next answer. "I don't think you're weak, Liis."

"Then, *why*?"

"Something happened to me when I met you."

"We had great sex. You're attracted to me. That doesn't mean you shut out your best agents. That's another reason it's a bad idea for us to explore whatever this is," I said, gesturing in the air between us.

"No, it's more than that. From the very beginning...I knew."

"You knew what?" I snapped.

"That I would have to be careful. I lost someone I loved before, and it changed me. I gave up someone I loved before, and it crushed me. I know that when you leave, Liis, however it goes down...it will end me."

I closed my open mouth and stuttered out the next words, "What makes you think I'm going anywhere?"

"Isn't that what you do? Run? Isn't that your whole goal in life? To move on?"

"That's not fair."

"I'm not just talking about promotions, Liis. We are poking not one but two deadly mafia rings. They don't know we're onto Grove. If Grove finds out that you speak the language and can out him, they will see you as a problem. You know how these people are. They're really good at erasing problems."

"But Grove doesn't know, and Val or Sawyer wouldn't have told him."

"I wasn't going to chance it," he said, sitting in the chair Val had previously occupied.

"So, now, we have two problems. He's going to notice when your brother starts working for the FBI. If you want this to work with Travis, we have to get rid of Grove."

"And we can't get rid of Grove without Tarou knowing we're onto him and Benny. The case will implode."

I stood there, at a complete loss. "What are we going to do?"

"We're going to stall. The timing has to be perfect."

"So, we don't just have to pull off one miracle but two."

"You have to be careful, Liis."

"Don't start. We have to focus."

"Goddamn it! I'm more focused than I've been in a long time. When I walked into that squad room and saw you sitting there...I admit it, okay? Knowing I brought you in to expose Grove scared the shit out of me, and it still does. It has nothing to do with you needing protection or you being a female agent and everything to do with the fact that, at any moment, you could have a target on your back, and it'd be my fucking fault!" he yelled the last part, the veins in his neck bulging.

"It's the job, Thomas. It's what we do."

Thomas picked up the file and tossed it across the room. Papers exploded in every direction before floating down to the floor. "You're not listening to what I'm saying! This is serious!" He leaned down, his palms flat on my desk. "These people will kill you, Liis. They won't think twice about it."

I forced my shoulders to relax. "We're leaving for Eakins on Saturday and attending a ceremony in the Virgin Islands on Sunday, and we have to persuade your brother to lie to his wife for the rest of his life before we leave Monday morning because our boss wants an answer. Let's concentrate on that first."

Thomas's face fell, defeated. "Just…stay away from Agent Grove. You're not the best liar."

"Yet you trust me to convince your family that we're a couple all weekend."

"I know what it feels like to have you wrapped up in my arms," he said. "I trust that."

He closed the door behind him, and after several moments, I finally let out the breath I hadn't known I was holding.

CHAPTER FIFTEEN

"LET ME CARRY THAT," Thomas said, sliding my leather tote off my shoulder and onto his.

"No, I've got it."

"Liis, girlfriends like this stuff. You need to get your head on straight. Stop being an agent, and start playing the part."

I nodded, unhappily conceding. We had just arrived at San Diego International Airport. I was glad we could breeze through the business-class line. On the final Saturday of spring break, the airport was particularly crowded. Dodging the human traffic on the way to our gate was making an already tense Thomas even more anxious.

"I'm not looking forward to doing this again in the morning or again on Monday morning," Thomas grumbled.

Noticing women taking second and third glances at Thomas made it hard not to stare at him myself. He was wearing a somewhat tight gray T-shirt with a navy sport coat and jeans, his brown leather belt matching his Timberlands. When I got close enough, I could smell his cologne and found myself breathing deeper.

He hid his eyes behind a pair of aviator sunglasses and kept a forced smile despite being loaded down with our luggage and the knowledge that he would see his family—and Camille—soon.

We sat in the terminal, and Thomas situated our bags around him. He'd only brought a carry-on. The rest was my medium-sized roller luggage, a roller carry-on, and a leather tote.

"What do you have in this thing?" he asked, slowly lowering the leather tote to the floor.

"My laptop, creds, keys, snacks, headset, wallet, a sweater, gum..."

"Did you pack a coat?"

"We'll be in Illinois for one night, and then we're off to the Virgin Islands. I can make it for that long with a sweater unless the bachelor party is outside."

"I'm not sure you're going to the bachelor party."

"Trent is proposing to Camille at the bachelor party, right?"

"Seems that way," he said, his voice suddenly quiet.

"If she can go, I can go."

"She's a bartender."

"I'm an FBI agent. I win."

Thomas stared at me. "I mean that she might be working the party."

"So will I."

"I doubt other females will be there."

"I'm okay with that," I said. "Look, I'm not leaving you to witness that alone. I'm not even in love with Jackson, and I can't imagine how awkward I would feel being present while he proposed."

"How did the next morning go? You never said."

"He was gone. I called his mom, and she said that he got home okay. We haven't spoken."

Thomas laughed once. "Showed up at your place, begging. What a vagina full of sand."

"Focus. We won't have time to drop me off. We'll have to go straight there, and I'm not waiting in the car. Just tell your brothers we go everywhere together. Tell them that I'm an overbearing, jealous girlfriend. Honestly, I don't care. But if you wanted background decoration, you should have brought Constance."

Thomas smiled. "I wouldn't have brought Constance. She's very nearly engaged to the S.A.C.'s son."

"Really?" I asked, surprised.

"Really."

"Another boat you missed while pouting over Camille."

Thomas made a face. "Constance isn't my type."

"Yes, because beautiful, smart, and blonde is so icky," I deadpanned.

"Not all men are into sweet and loyal."

"You're not?" I said, dubious.

He looked down at me, amused. "My type seems to be feisty women who are emotionally unavailable."

I glared at him. "I'm not the one who is in love with someone else."

"You're married to the Bureau, Liis. Everyone knows it."

"Exactly what I've been trying to tell you. Relationships are a waste of time for people like us."

"You think being in a relationship with me would be a waste of time?"

"I know it would. I wouldn't even come second. I would be third."

He shook his head, confused. "Third?"

"After the woman you're in love with."

At first, Thomas seemed too insulted to argue, but then he leaned into my ear. "Some days, you make me wish I'd never told you about Camille."

"You didn't tell me about her, remember? It was Val."

"You need to get over it."

I touched my chest. "*I* need to get over it?"

"She's an ex-girlfriend. Stop being a brat."

I gritted my teeth, afraid of what would come out of my mouth next. "You miss her. How am I supposed to feel about that? You still have a picture of her in your living room."

Thomas's face fell. "Liis, c'mon. We can't do this now."

"Can't do what? Fight over an ex-girlfriend? Because a real couple wouldn't do that." I crossed my arms and sat back against the seat.

Thomas looked down, laughing once. "I can't argue with that."

We waited at the gate until the desk agent called business class for boarding. Thomas loaded up with our carry-ons and my tote, refusing to let me help. We slowly stepped forward in line, listening to the machine beep each time the ticket agent scanned a boarding pass.

Once we were through, Thomas followed me down the jetway, and then we were stopped again near the door of the plane.

I noticed the females staring—this time, the flight attendants—looking past me to Thomas. He seemed unaware. Maybe he was just used to it at this point in his life. At the office, it was easy to pretend he wasn't beautiful, but out in the real world, the reactions of others reminded me of how I'd felt the first time I saw him.

We settled in our seats, buckling in. I finally felt relaxed, but Thomas was on edge.

I put my hand on his. "I'm sorry."

"It's not you," he said.

His words stung. Although unintentional, they had a deeper meaning. He was about to watch the woman he loved agree to marry someone else. And he was right. The woman he loved wasn't me.

"Try not to think about her," I said. "Maybe we can step out before it happens. Get some air."

He looked at me as if I should have known better. "You think I'm stressed about Trenton's proposal?"

"Well…" I began but didn't quite know how to finish.

"You should know the picture is gone," he said matter-of-factly.

"The picture of Camille? Gone where?"

"In a boxful of memories—where it belongs."

I looked at him for the longest time, a twinge forming in my chest.

"Are you happy?" he asked.

"I'm happy," I said, half-ashamed, half-bewildered.

Holding back now would make me gratuitously stubborn. He had put her away. I had no excuse.

I reached over and laced my fingers in his, and he brought my hand up to his mouth. He closed his eyes and then kissed my palm. Such a simple gesture was so intimate, like tugging at someone's clothes during a hug or the tiniest touch on the back of the neck. When he did things like that, it was easy to forget he'd ever thought of someone else.

After the passengers settled into their seats and the flight attendants informed us how to survive a possible plane crash, the plane taxied to the end of the runway and then surged forward, the speed climbing and the fuselage rattling, until we took off in a quiet smooth motion.

Thomas began to fidget. He turned around and then faced forward.

"What's wrong?" I asked.

"I can't do this," Thomas whispered. He looked over at me. "I can't do this to him."

I kept my voice low. "You're not doing anything to him. You're the messenger."

He looked up at the vent above his head and reached up, turning the knob until air was blowing full blast in his face. He settled back into his seat, looking miserable.

"Thomas, think about it. What other option does he have?"

He clenched his teeth as he always did when he was annoyed. "You keep saying I'm protecting him, but if I hadn't told my director about Travis and Abby, he wouldn't have to choose."

"That's true. Prison would be his only choice."

Thomas looked away from me and out the window. The sun reflected off the sea of white clouds, making him squint. He closed the shutter, and it took my eyes a moment to adjust.

"This is impossible," I said. "We have a job to do, and if we have all this personal junk swimming around in our heads, we're going to make a mistake, and this entire operation will go south. But its very nature is personal. This assignment involves your family. And we're here, together, with our own...issues. If we don't figure out a way, Thomas, we're fucked. Even if—*when* Travis says yes, if you're not on your A game, Grove is going to sniff this out."

"You're right."

"I'm sorry. What did you say?" I teased, touching my fingers to my ear.

The flight attendant leaned in. "Can I get you a beverage?"

"White wine, please," I said.

"Jack and Coke," Thomas said.

She nodded and stepped toward the row behind us, asking the same.

"I said you're right," Thomas said begrudgingly.

"Are you nervous about seeing Camille tonight?"

"Yes," he said without hesitation. "The last time I saw her, she was in the hospital, pretty banged up." He noticed my surprised expression and continued, "She and Trenton were driving just outside of Eakins when they were hit by a drunk driver."

"I can't decide if your family is really lucky or really accident-prone."

"Both."

The flight attendant brought our drinks, setting down napkins first and then our glasses. I took a sip of wine as Thomas watched. He paid special attention to my lips, and I wondered if he had the same jealous thoughts as I did when his lips would touch things other than my mouth.

Thomas broke his stare and looked down. "I'm happy for Trent. He deserves it."

"And you don't?"

He laughed nervously and then looked up at me. "I don't want to talk about Camille."

"Okay. It's a long flight. Talk, nap, or read?"

The flight attendant returned with a notepad and pen. "Miss...Lindy?"

"Yes?"

She smiled, dozens of gray strands shooting out like lightning bolts from her French braid. "Would you like the grilled chicken with sweet chili sauce or our grilled salmon with lemon caper butter?"

"Uh...the chicken, please."

"Mr. Maddox?"

"The chicken as well."

She scribbled on her notebook. "Everyone okay with beverages?"

We both looked at our nearly full glasses and nodded.

The attendant smiled. "Fantastic."

"Talk," Thomas said, leaning toward me.

"What?"

He stifled a laugh. "You asked, talk, nap, or read. I choose talk."

"Oh." I smiled.

"But I don't want to talk about Camille. I want to talk about you."

I wrinkled my nose. "Why? I'm boring."

"Have you ever broken a bone?" he asked.

"No."

"Ever cried over a guy?"

"Nope."

"How old were you when you lost your virginity?"

"You...were my first."

Thomas's eyes nearly popped out of his head. "What? But you were engaged..."

I giggled. "I'm just kidding. I was twenty. College. Not anything or anyone to speak of."

"Illegal drugs?"

"No."

"Ever drank enough that you passed out?"

"No."

Thomas thought for approximately thirty seconds.

"I told you," I said, a tad embarrassed, "I'm boring."

Then, he asked his next question, "Have you ever slept with your boss?" He smirked.

I shrank into my seat. "Not on purpose."

He threw his head back and laughed.

"It's not funny. I was mortified."

"Me, too, but not for the reason you think."

"Because you were afraid of what Tarou or Benny would do to me if Grove found out why I was there?"

Thomas frowned. "Yes." He swallowed hard and then looked down at my lips. "That night with you…it changed everything. I was going to give it a few days, so I wouldn't look completely pathetic when I knocked on your door. I came to work that morning and immediately told Marks that he was coming with me to Cutter's. I was hoping to run into you again."

I smiled. "Yeah?"

"Yeah," he said, looking away again. "I'm still concerned. I'm going to have to keep a close eye on you."

"Darn," I teased.

Thomas didn't seem happy about my response. "I'm not the one who keeps tabs on people, remember?"

"Sawyer?" I asked.

When Thomas affirmed my suspicion with a nod, I chuckled.

"It's not funny," he said, unamused.

"It's a little funny. No one will tell me why they dislike him, except to say he's a bastard or an asshole. Neither you nor Val will give me anything specific. He helped me unpack. He was at my condo all night and didn't try to sleep with me. He's got the sleazy barfly thing going on, but he's harmless."

"He's not harmless. He's married."

My mouth fell open. "Excuse me?"

"You heard me."

"No, it sounded like you said Agent Sawyer is married."

"He is."

"*What?*"

Thomas was beyond annoyed, but I couldn't wrap my head around what he was telling me.

He leaned closer. "To Val."

"What?" My voice lowered an octave. Now, I knew he was messing with me.

"It's true. They were like Romeo and Juliet at first, and then it turned out that Sawyer has a small issue with commitment. Val has sent him divorce papers several times. He keeps dragging it out. They've been separated for almost two years."

My mouth was still hanging open. "But…they live in the same building."

"No," he said, chuckling. "They live in the same condo."

"Shut the front door!"

"Different bedrooms. They're roommates."

"Val makes me tell her *everything*. This is just…I feel betrayed. Is that rational? I do."

"Yeah," Thomas said, shifting in his seat. "She's definitely going to kill me."

I shook my head. "I did not see that coming."

"I'd ask you not to tell her that I told you, but when we get back, she'll take one look at you and know."

I turned to face him. "How does she do that?"

He shrugged. "She's always had a bullshit detector, and then the FBI helped her hone her skill. With pupil dilation, delay of response, looking up and to the left, and whatever inner radar she has that goes off, she can detect more than just lies now. She detects omission even if you've got news on your mind that you're keeping to yourself. Val knows all."

"It's unsettling."

"That's why you're her only friend."

My mouth pulled to one side, and I cocked my head to the other. "That's sad."

"Not many people can handle Val's gift or her brazen use of it. *That's* why Sawyer's such a dick."

"He cheated?"

"Yes."

"Knowing she would find out?"

"I believe so."

"So, why won't he divorce her?" I asked.

"Because he can't find anyone better."

"Oh, I hate him," I snarled.

Thomas pushed a button, and his seat began to recline. A satisfied smile stretched across his face.

"No wonder she's never let me come over," I mused.

His grin became wider, and he wedged the pillow under his head. "Have you ever—"

"No. No more questions about me."

"Why not?"

"There is literally nothing to speak of."

"Tell me about what happened with you and Jackson. Why didn't it work out?"

"Because our relationship was nothing to speak of," I said, forming my lips over the words like he had to read my lips to understand.

"Are you telling me your entire life was boring until you came to San Diego?" he asked, in disbelief.

I didn't answer.

"Well?" he said, shifting until he was comfortable.

"Well what?"

"Knowing you now, I'd almost believe you didn't have it in you to be so spontaneous. It makes sense. You left Cutter's with me that night to have something to talk about." Arrogance flickered in his eyes.

"Don't forget, Thomas. You don't know me that well."

"I know you bite your thumbnail when you're nervous. I know you twist your hair around your finger when you're in deep thought. You drink Manhattans. You like Fuzzy's Burgers. You hate milk. You're not particularly fussy about the cleanliness of your home. You can run farther than I can during our lunch hour, and you like weird Japanese art. You're patient, you give second chances, and you don't make hasty judgments about strangers. You're professional and highly intelligent, and you snore."

"I do not!" I sat straight up.

Thomas laughed. "Okay, it's not snoring. You just…breathe."

"*Everyone* breathes," I said, defensive.

"My apologies. I think it's cute."

I tried not to smile but failed. "I lived with Jackson for years, and he never said anything."

"It's the tiniest wheeze, barely noticeable," he said.

I shot him a dirty look.

"To be fair, Jackson was in love with you. He probably didn't tell you a lot of things."

"Good thing you're not, so I can hear all the humiliating things about myself."

"As far as everyone is concerned, I'm in love with you today and tomorrow."

His words made me pause. "Then, play the part and pretend that you think I'm perfect."

"I can't recall thinking otherwise." Thomas didn't crack a smile.

"Oh, please," I said, rolling my eyes. "Does my first FD-three-oh-two ring a bell?"

"You know why I did that."

"I'm not perfect," I grumbled, biting the corner of my thumbnail.

"I don't want you to be."

He scanned over my face with such affection that I felt like the only other person in the fuselage. He leaned toward me, his eyes fixated on my lips. I had just begun to close the gap when the flight attendant approached.

"Would you open your tray table?" she asked.

Thomas and I both blinked and then fiddled with the mechanics of getting the trays out of the arm of the seat. His popped out first, and then he helped me with mine. The attendant gave us that what-a-cute-couple look and then spread napkins on both of our trays before setting our meals before us.

"More wine?" she asked.

I looked at my half-empty glass. I hadn't even realized I'd been drinking it. "Yes, please."

She filled my glass and then returned to the other passengers.

Thomas and I ate our meals in silence, but it was clear what we thought of our microwaved grilled chicken with a teaspoon of sweet chili sauce and limp mixed vegetables. The pretzel roll was the best part of the meal.

The man sitting in the aisle seat in front of us kept his feet propped on the wall in front of him and talked to his neighbor about his burgeoning evangelical career. The silver-haired man behind us talked to the woman next to him about his first novel, and after asking some basic questions, she revealed that she was thinking of writing one, too.

Before I was finished with my warm chocolate chip cookie, the pilot came over the PA system to announce that he would begin the descent soon, and our flight would land in Chicago ten minutes earlier than expected. Once he finished his announcement, a symphony of seat belts unclicking and bodies shifting could be heard, and the pilgrimages to the restrooms began.

Thomas closed his eyes again. I tried not to stare. Since we'd met, I had done nothing but deny my feelings for him while I fought ferociously for my independence. But I was free only when he touched me. Outside of our intimate moments, I would be held captive by thoughts of his hands.

Even if it was just for appearances, I hoped that pretending would satisfy my curiosity. If Thomas seeing Camille changed anything, at least remembering the best memories of the weekend would be a better alternative to mourning our fake relationship when we got home.

"Liis," Thomas said, his eyes still shut.

"Yes?"

"The moment we land, we're undercover." He looked at me. "It's important that any connections with Mick or Benny have no clue that we're federal agents."

"I understand."

"You're free to talk about anything from your life, except for your time at the Bureau. That will be interchanged by your undercover career as a replacement professor in cultural studies at the University of California, San Diego. We have all the records in place there."

"I've packed my university credentials."

"Good." He closed his eyes again, settling into his seat. "You've researched the school, I assume?"

"Yes, and your family and a few others who you might have mentioned if we were in an actual relationship—Shepley, America, Camille, the twins; your dad, Jim; his brother, Jack; Jack's wife, Deana; and your mom."

His lips curved up. "Diane. You can say her name."

"Yes, sir."

It was a natural thing to say, practically ingrained, and I didn't mean anything by it, but Thomas's eyes popped open, and his disappointment was hard to miss.

"It's Thomas. Just Thomas." He turned his shoulders to face me head-on. "I have to admit, I thought this would be easier for you. I know it will be distracting to be in Chicago again, but are you sure you can do this? It's important."

I bit my lip. For the first time, I truly worried that I would slip and not only put the whole operation at risk, but also put Thomas in danger of being at odds with his family for lying. But if I voiced my concerns, the Bureau would send another female agent to play the part, likely one out of the Chicago office.

I took his hand in mine, tenderly rubbing my thumb against his skin. He looked down at our hands and then back at me.

"Do you trust me?" I asked.

Thomas nodded, but I could tell he was uncertain.

"When we set down, not even you will be able to tell the difference."

CHAPTER SIXTEEN

"HEY, DICKHEAD!" ONE OF THE TWINS SAID, walking across baggage claim toward Thomas with open arms. He had just a dusting of hair on his head, and the skin around his honey-brown eyes wrinkled when he smiled.

"Taylor!" Thomas set down our luggage and tightly wrapped his arms around his brother.

They were the same height, and both towered over me.

At first glance, a passerby might mistake them for friends, but even under his peacoat, Taylor was just as ripped. The only difference was that Thomas had thicker muscles, making it obvious that he was the older brother. Other things tipped off that they were related. Taylor's skin tone was just a shade lighter, geography being the likely culprit.

When Taylor hugged Thomas, I noticed that they also had identical strong large hands. Being around all five of them at the same time would be incredibly daunting.

Thomas patted his brother's back, almost too hard. I was glad he didn't greet me that way, but his brother wasn't fazed. They let go, and Taylor hit Thomas's arm, again hard enough that it was audible.

"Damn, Tommy! You're a fuckin' diesel!" Taylor made a show of squeezing Thomas's bicep.

Thomas shook his head, and then they both turned to stare at me with matching grins.

"This," Thomas said, beaming, "is Liis Lindy."

There was a reverence in his voice when he spoke, and he regarded me in the same way he'd held Camille on the pier in the picture. I felt precious to him, and I had to push on my toes to keep from leaning forward.

Just a few weeks before, Thomas had said my name as if it were a swear word. Now, when he formed his mouth around it, I melted.

Taylor gave me a bear hug, lifting me off the ground. When he set me down, he smirked. "Sorry about keeping you up the other night. I had a rough week."

"At work?" I asked.

His face turned red, and I inwardly celebrated at being able to make a Maddox brother blush.

Thomas smirked. "He got dumped."

The feeling of victory vanished, and guilt jarred me into silence. That didn't last long when I remembered the yelping and wall-banging. "So, you slept with—" I almost slipped and said Agent Davies. "I'm sorry. It's none of my business."

Thomas couldn't hide his relief.

Taylor took a long deep breath and blew it out. "I wasn't going to bring this up until later, but I was really messed up over it and really drunk. Falyn and I worked it out, and she'll be in St. Thomas, so I'd appreciate it if...you know..."

"Falyn is your girlfriend?" I asked.

Taylor looked so deeply ashamed. It was hard to judge him.

I shrugged. "I never saw you. Anything I reported would be speculation anyway." *Damn it, Liis. Stop sounding like an agent.*

Taylor lifted my tote and slipped it over his shoulder. "Thanks."

"Could I just..." I reached for the tote.

Taylor leaned down to give me better access. I pulled out my sweater, and Thomas helped me slip it on.

Taylor began walking, and Thomas reached back for my hand. I took his hand, and we followed his brother to the exit.

"I drove around for half an hour before I found a parking spot in the main lot," Taylor said. "It's spring break, so everyone is traveling, I guess."

"When did you get into town? What are you driving?" Thomas asked.

Suddenly, I didn't feel so bad. Thomas sounded more like FBI than I did.

"I've been here since yesterday."

The moment Taylor stepped foot in the street, he pulled a box of cigarettes from his pocket and flipped one in his mouth. He dug into the pack again and pulled out a lighter. He lit the end and puffed until the paper and tobacco glowed orange.

He blew out a puff of smoke. "Have you been to Chicago before, Liis?"

"I'm from here actually."

Taylor stopped abruptly. "Really?"

"Yes," I said, my voice rising an octave as if it were a question.

"Huh. Millions of people in San Diego, and Thomas bags a girl from Illinois."

"Taylor, Jesus," Thomas scolded.

"Sorry," Taylor said, turning to look at me.

He had Thomas's same charming expression, one that would make the average girl swoon, and I was beginning to realize it was just a Maddox trait.

"Is Falyn at Dad's?" Thomas asked.

Taylor shook his head. "She had to work. She's meeting me in St. Thomas, and then we'll fly back together."

"Did Trav pick you up from the airport? Or did Trent?" Thomas asked.

"Honey," I said, squeezing Thomas's hand.

Taylor laughed. "I'm used to it. He's always been like this."

He walked ahead, but Thomas's eyes softened, and he brought my hand up to his mouth for a tender tiny kiss.

Taylor nodded. "Shepley did. Travis is with Shepley all day, so I drove Trav's car to come get you. He doesn't know we're in town. He thinks he'll see us all in St. Thomas tomorrow, like the girls."

"Are all the girls in St. Thomas?" I asked.

Thomas gave me a look. He knew exactly what I was asking.

"Not all the girls. Just Abby and her bridesmaids." We walked into the main lot, and Taylor pointed straight ahead. "I'm all the way down by the fence."

After hiking a hundred yards or so in the cold wind, Taylor pulled a set of keys from his pocket and pressed a button. A silver Toyota Camry chirped a few cars ahead.

"Am I the only one who thinks it's strange that Travis has a car now?" Thomas said, staring at the vehicle.

A gold chain was looped around the rearview mirror and then separated into several strands. The ends were looped through small holes in white poker chips. They looked personalized with black-and-white striped borders and red writing in the middle.

Taylor shook his head, pushing another button to open the trunk. "You should see him driving it. He looks like a pussy."

"Glad I'm selling mine then," I said.

Thomas laughed and then helped Taylor load our luggage. Thomas came around and opened the passenger door for me, but I shook my head.

"It's okay. Sit in the front with your brother." I opened the back door. "I'll sit back here."

Thomas leaned down to kiss my cheek, but then he noticed I was gawking into the backseat. He stared as well.

"What the fuck is that?" Thomas asked.

"Oh! It's Toto! I'm babysittin'," he said with a proud smile that showed off a deep dimple in one cheek. "Abby would probably kill me if she knew I left him in the car alone, but I was only gone for ten minutes. It's still warm in the car."

The dog wiggled its entire back end, wearing a navy-and-gold striped sweater and standing on a plush wool pet bed.

"I..." I began, looking to Thomas. "I've never had a dog."

Taylor laughed. "You don't have to take care of him. You just have to share a seat with him. I have to strap him in though. Abby is kind of a fruitcake about this dog."

Taylor opened the other side and secured Toto into the nylon harness. Toto must have been used to it because he sat still while Taylor snapped each clip into place.

Thomas rolled the seat cover under until it revealed a hair-free section of the seat.

"There you go, honey." The corners of his mouth were trembling as he tried not to smile.

I stuck out my tongue, and he shut the door.

The seat belt clicked when I pushed it into the buckle, and I heard Taylor laughing.

"You pussy-whipped douche waffle."

Thomas gripped the handle. "She can hear you, fuckstick. My door is open."

Taylor opened his door and bent down, looking sheepish. "Sorry, Liis."

I shook my head, half-amused and half in disbelief at their
banter. It was as if we had fallen down a rabbit hole and landed in a
frat house full of drunken toddlers. Suddenly, *Eat Me* had a whole
new meaning.

Thomas and Taylor buckled in, and then Taylor backed out of
his spot. The drive to the bachelor party was full of colorful insults
and updates on who was doing whom and who was working
where.

I noted that Trenton and Camille weren't mentioned at all. I
wondered how that went over with the family, knowing she'd dated
both Thomas and then Trenton, and how they felt about her, if
they disliked her at all because Thomas didn't come home anymore
to avoid causing awkwardness for them or further pain for himself.
Shame washed over me when, for less than a second, I hoped they
didn't like her at all.

Taylor pulled into the driveway of the Rest Inn and then drove
to the backside of the building. Twice as many cars were parked
back there than in the front.

Taylor turned off the ignition. "Everyone is parking here, so
we don't tip him off."

"Cap's? The bachelor party we've waited a year to throw Travis
is going to be at Cap's?" Thomas said, unimpressed.

"Trent planned it. He's taking classes again and working full-
time. Plus, he's on a budget. Don't bitch if you didn't offer to
help," Taylor said.

I expected Thomas to lash out, but he accepted the scolding.
"Touché."

"What about the, um…" I pointed to the dog looking up at me
like he was going to lunge for my throat at any moment—or maybe
he just wanted a pat on the head. I couldn't be sure.

A car pulled up next to us, and a woman hopped out, leaving
the engine running and the headlights on.

She opened the back door and smiled at me. "Hey, there." She
looked at Thomas and stopped smiling. "Hey, T.J."

"Raegan," Thomas said.

I already loathed the nickname. Taylor didn't refer to him that
way. The woman was exotically beautiful with her layers of
chestnut hair, the wavy ends stopping at just above her waistline.

Raegan unclipped Toto's harness and then gathered his things.

"Thanks, Ray," Taylor said. "Abby said everyone else was going to the wedding."

"No problem," she said, trying not to look at Thomas. "Kody can't wait. He's been wanting a dog so bad, but I don't know how people keep a puppy from being lonely while they go to work and school." She looked down at Toto and touched her nose to his, and he licked her cheek. She giggled. "Dad offered doggy daycare, so we'll see. Maybe babysitting for a few days will help us decide. Should I walk him? I don't want a mess in my car."

Taylor shook his head. "I just took him right before I picked them up. He should be good until you get home. Did Abby tell you about the harness?"

"She told me—in detail." Raegan scratched the dog's head and then turned around, opening her back door. She let the dog walk around on the backseat while she buckled in the harness, and then he sat, astonishingly well-behaved, while she buckled him in again.

"Okay," Raegan said. "That's it. Good to see you, Taylor." Her expression instantly lost all emotion when she looked at Thomas. "T.J."

She had to be an ex-girlfriend. Between the nickname and overly cool demeanor, he must have really burned her.

She smiled at me again. "I'm Raegan."

"Liis…nice to meet you," I said, completely unsettled by her one-eighty.

She hurried around the front of her car and then disappeared inside. The car pulled away, and Taylor, Thomas, and I sat in silence.

"Okay then!" Taylor said. "Let's party."

"I don't understand this," Thomas said. "He's not a bachelor."

Taylor patted his brother's shoulder, again so hard that it made me wince in reaction. "The whole point of this weekend is to celebrate what we missed out on because that little bastard eloped. And, Tommy…" Taylor's grin faded.

"I know. Trenton called me," Thomas said.

Taylor nodded, a touch of sadness in his eyes, and then he pulled on the door lever before setting off across the parking lot.

When I opened my door, the cold air was shocking. Thomas rubbed my arms, breathing out a small cloud that was a stark contrast to the night surrounding us.

"You can do this," I said, already shivering.

Beautiful
REDEMPTION
159

"You've forgotten how cold it gets here? Already?"

"Shut up," I said, walking toward the building where Taylor had gone.

Thomas jogged to catch up and took my hand. "What did you think of Taylor?"

"Your parents should be proud. You have exceptional genes."

"I'm going to take that as a compliment and not a pass at my brother. You're mine for the weekend, remember?"

I smirked, and he playfully jerked me against him, but then I realized how much truth was behind his lighthearted remark. We stopped at the door, and I watched Thomas psych himself up for whatever was on the other side.

Without knowing what else to do, I rose up on the balls of my feet and kissed his cheek. He turned, catching me square on the lips. That one gesture began a chain reaction. Thomas's hands went straight up to my cheeks, gingerly cupping my face. When my mouth parted and his tongue slipped inside, I gripped his sport coat in my fists.

The music inside suddenly became louder, and Thomas released me.

"Tommy!"

Another brother—obvious because he looked so much like Taylor—was holding open the door. He was wearing only a yellow nylon Speedo, barely big enough to conceal his man parts, and a matching wig. The hideous bright yellow acrylic on his head was a mess of curls and frizz, and he flirtatiously bounced it with one hand.

"Like it?" the brother said. In small steps, he pirouetted, revealing that bit of fabric he wore wasn't a Speedo at all but a thong.

After getting an unexpected eyeful of his snow-white hindquarters, I looked away, embarrassed.

Thomas looked him up and down and then breathed out a laugh. "What the hell are you wearing, Trenton?"

A half smile dimpled one of Trenton's cheeks, and he gripped Thomas's shoulder. "It's all part of the plan. Come in!" he said, moving his hand in small circles toward himself. "Come in!"

Trenton held open the door as we walked inside.

Cardboard renditions of breasts hung from the ceiling, and golden confetti in the shape of penises were sprinkled all over the floor and tables. A table sat in the corner, crowded with liquor bottles and buckets of ice filled with various brands of beer. Wine bottles were absent, but there was a cake in the shape of very large pink breasts.

Thomas leaned down to speak into my ear, "I told you it wasn't a good idea for you to come here."

"You think I'm offended? I work in a field that is predominantly male. I hear the word *titties* at least once a day."

Thomas conceded, but he paused to look at his hand just after patting his little brother's shoulder. The body glitter covering Trenton's skin had rubbed off on Thomas's palm, and it shimmered under the disco ball above. Thomas was immediately horrified.

I grabbed a napkin off a table and handed it to Thomas. "Here."

"Thanks," he said, half-amused and half-repulsed.

Thomas took my hand. The glittery-wadded napkin was mashed between our palms as he pulled me through the crowd. Loud music assaulted my ears, the bass humming in my bones. Dozens of men were standing around, and there were just a handful of women. I instantly felt sick, wondering when I would run into Camille.

Thomas's hand felt warm in mine, even with the buffer of the napkin. If he was nervous though, it didn't show. He greeted several college-aged men as we crossed the room. When we reached the other side, Thomas held out his arms and hugged a portly man before kissing his cheek.

"Hi, Dad."

"Well, hello there, son," Jim Maddox said in a gruff voice. "It's about damn time you came home."

"Liis," Thomas said, "this is my dad, Jim Maddox."

He was quite a bit shorter than Thomas, but he had the same sweetness in his eyes. Jim looked upon me with kindness and almost thirty years' worth of practiced patience from raising five Maddox boys. His short and sparse silver hair was now multiple colors from the party lights.

Jim's hooded eyes brightened with realization. "This is your girl, Thomas?"

Thomas kissed my cheek. "I keep telling her that, but she doesn't believe me."

Jim opened his arms wide. "Well, c'mere, cupcake! Nice to meet you!"

Jim didn't shake my hand. He pulled me into a full-on hug and squeezed me tight. When he released me, Thomas hooked his arm around my shoulders, much more cheerful to be amid his family than I'd expected.

Thomas pulled me into his side. "Liis is a professor at the University of California, Dad. She's brilliant."

"Does she put up with your shit?" Jim asked, trying to speak over the music.

Thomas shook his head. "Not at all."

Jim laughed out loud. "Then, she's a keeper!"

"That's what I keep telling him, but he doesn't believe me," I said, nudging Thomas with my elbow.

Jim laughed again. "Professor of what, sis?"

"Cultural studies," I said, feeling a bit guilty for yelling at him.

Jim chuckled. "She must be brilliant. I haven't a clue what in the Sam Hill that means!" He put his fist to his mouth and coughed.

"You want a water, Dad?"

Jim nodded. "Thank you, son."

Thomas kissed my cheek and then left us alone to track down the water. I wasn't sure if I'd ever get used to his lips on my skin. I hoped I never would.

"How long have you worked for the college?" Jim asked.

"This is my first semester," I said.

He nodded. "Is that a nice campus out there?"

"Yes." I smiled.

"You like San Diego?" he asked.

"Love it. I lived in Chicago before. San Diego's weather is preferable."

"You're from Illinois originally?" Jim asked, surprised.

"I am," I said, trying to mouth the words precisely so that I wouldn't have to yell so loud.

"Huh," he said with a chuckle. "I sure wish Tommy lived closer. But he never really belonged here. I think he's happier out there," he said, nodding as if in agreement with himself. "How did you two meet?"

"I moved into his building," I said, noticing a woman speaking to Thomas by the beverage table.

His hands were in his pockets, and he was staring at the floor. I could tell that he was being purposefully stoic.

Thomas nodded, and she nodded. Then, she threw her arms around him. I couldn't see her face, but I could see his, and as he held her, his pain could be felt from where I stood.

The same deep ache from before burned in my chest, and my shoulders pulled in. I crossed my arms over my midsection to camouflage the involuntary motion.

"So, you and Thomas...this is new?" Jim asked.

"Relatively new," I said, still staring at Thomas and the woman clinging to him.

Trenton was no longer dancing. He was watching them, too, almost exactly parallel from me.

"Is the woman with Thomas...is that Camille?"

Jim hesitated, but then he nodded. "Yes, she is."

After a full minute, Thomas and Camille were still wrapped in each other's arms.

Jim cleared his throat and spoke again, "Well, I've never seen my boy so happy as when he introduced me to you. Even if it is new, it's in the present...unlike other things...that are in the past."

I shot a small smile in Jim's direction, and he pulled me to his side with a squeeze.

"If Tommy hasn't told you that yet, he should."

I nodded, trying to process the dozens of emotions swirling within me at the same time. Feeling such hurt was quite surprising for a girl who was happily married to her job. If I didn't need Thomas, my heart didn't know it.

CHAPTER SEVENTEEN

Thomas's eyes popped open, and he looked directly at me. He released Camille, and without telling her good-bye or even giving her a second look, he walked past her, sweeping up a bottle of water on his way to where Jim and I stood.

"Did you interrogate her sufficiently while I was gone, Dad?" Thomas asked.

"Not as well as you would have, I'm sure." Jim turned to me. "Thomas should have been a detective."

Despite the uncomfortable proximity to the truth, I held a smile.

Thomas had a strange expression as well, but his features smoothed. "Are you having a good time, honey?"

"Please tell me that was good-bye," I said. I didn't try to keep Jim from hearing. It was an honest request, one that I could ask and still keep our cover intact.

Thomas gently took me by the arm and brought me to an unoccupied corner of the room. "I didn't know she was going to do that. I'm sorry."

I felt my expression crumble. "I wish you could have seen that through my eyes and then hear you say she's in the past with my ears."

"She was apologizing, Liis. What was I supposed to do?"

"I don't know...not look heartbroken?"

He stared at me, speechless.

I rolled my eyes and pulled on his hand. "C'mon, let's get back to the party."

He pulled away from me. "I am, Liis. I *am* heartbroken. What happened is fucking sad."

"Great! Let's go!" I said, my words dripping with false excitement and sarcasm.

I shouldered past him, but he grabbed my wrist and pulled me against him. He held my hand near his cheek and then turned to kiss my palm, closing his eyes.

"It's sad because it's over," he said against my hand, his breath warm on my skin. He turned and looked down into my eyes. "It's sad because I made a choice that has changed my relationship with my brother forever. I hurt her and Trenton and myself. The worst part is that I thought it was justified, but now, I'm afraid it was all for nothing."

"What do you mean?" I asked, eyeing him warily.

"I loved Camille—but not like this, not like you."

I glanced around. "Stop it, Thomas. No one can hear you."

"Can you?" he asked. When I didn't respond, he let go of my hand. "What? What can I say to convince you?"

"Keep telling me how sad you are to lose Camille. I'm sure that will eventually work."

"You've only heard me say that it's sad. You ignored the part about it being over."

"It's not over," I said, laughing once. "It's never going to be over. You said it yourself. You'll always love her."

He pointed to the other side of the room. "What you saw over there? That was good-bye. She's marrying my brother."

"I also saw you in pain about both."

"Yes! It's painful! What do you want from me, Liis?"

"I want you not to love her anymore!"

The music was in between songs, and everyone turned toward the corner where Thomas and I stood. Camille and Trenton were talking to another couple, and Camille looked just as humiliated as I was. She tucked her hair behind her ear, and then Trenton guided her to the cake table.

"Oh my God," I whispered, covering my eyes.

Thomas glanced behind us and then pulled my hand down, shaking his head. "It's okay. Don't worry about them."

"I don't act this way. This isn't like me."

He puffed out a breath of relief. "I can relate. We tend to have that effect on each other."

Not only was I *not* myself around Thomas, but he also made me feel things I couldn't control. Anger boiled inside of me. If he knew me at all, he would understand that erratic feelings weren't acceptable.

Being with Jackson, I could control my feelings. Yelling at him during a party would never have crossed my mind. He would have been shocked to see me lashing out.

When it came to Thomas, I was all over the place. My head was pulling me in one direction, and Thomas and my heart were pulling me in another. Unpredictable outcomes scared the hell out of me. It was time to bridle my emotions. Nothing was more frightening than being manipulated by my own heart.

When the crowd turned away, I forced a smile, lifting my chin to meet Thomas's eyes.

Thomas's eyebrows pulled in. "What is that? What's the sudden smile about?"

I walked past him. "Told you that you wouldn't be able to tell the difference."

Thomas followed me back to the party. He stood behind me and then wrapped his arms around my middle, resting his cheek in the crook of my neck.

When I didn't respond, he touched his lips to my ear. "The lines are beginning to blur, Liis. Was that just for show?"

"I'm working. Aren't you?" A lump formed in my throat. It was the best lie I'd ever told.

"Wow," he said before releasing me and then walking away.

Thomas stood between Jim and another man. I couldn't be certain, but the man had to be Thomas's uncle. He looked nearly identical to Jim. Clearly, Maddox DNA was dominant, like their family...and their men.

Someone turned down the music and then switched off the lights. It was pitch-dark, and I was standing alone.

The door opened, and after a few seconds of quiet, a man said from the doorway, "Uh…"

The lights flipped on to reveal Travis and who must have been Shepley standing at the door, squinting as their eyes adjusted to the light. Taylor and his twin threw penis confetti into Travis's face, and everyone cheered.

"Congrats, cock-tip!"

"Pussy!"

"Way to go, Mad Dog!"

I studied Travis as he greeted everyone. A lot of shoulder-patting, man hugs, and rough head-rubbing commenced while they all clapped and hooted.

A still scantily clad and shiny Trenton popped and locked, bumped and grinded to the music. Thomas and Jim shook their heads at the sight.

Camille was standing in front of the crowd surrounding Trenton, encouraging him and laughing uncontrollably. Irrational anger came over me. Ten minutes before, she had been draped over Thomas, lamenting over their breakup. I didn't like her. I couldn't imagine why not one but two Maddox men did.

When the song was over, Trenton walked over to Camille and lifted her in his arms, twirling her around in the air. When he lowered her to her feet, she crossed her arms at the back of Trenton's neck and kissed him.

Another song boomed through the speakers, and the few other women present pulled their men onto the modest dance floor. Some of the men joined them, mostly just being silly.

Thomas remained sandwiched between his father and uncle, glancing at me only once in a while. He was angry with me, and he had every right to be. I was giving myself whiplash. I couldn't imagine how he must be feeling.

There I stood, glaring at Camille every time she drew attention to herself, and I hadn't treated Thomas much better. He wasn't just playing a part. He'd expressed interest in me before we had left for the assignment. If anything, I was worse than Camille. At least she didn't jerk around his heart, knowing she was already dealing with broken pieces.

The responsible thing to do would be to keep it professional. One day, I was going to have to choose between Thomas and the Bureau, and I would choose the job. But every time we were alone, every time he touched me, and what I'd felt when I saw him with Camille, I knew that my feelings had become too complex to ignore.

Val had told me to be straight with Thomas, but he wouldn't accept it. My cheeks flushed. I was a strong and intelligent woman. I had broken down the problem, determined the solution, made a decision, and communicated that decision.

I sighed. Then, I'd yelled at him in front of nearly all of his friends and family. He'd looked at me as if I were crazy.

Am I?

He'd told me the picture was gone, but taking a picture off a table wouldn't change feelings. Jim had said Camille was in Thomas's past, and that was true. But I couldn't reconcile that Thomas missed her or that he still loved her.

What I really needed was Thomas's closure, and that solution was reliant on him. Closure wasn't an unreasonable request, but it might be an impossible one. It wasn't up to me. It was up to Thomas.

For the first time in my adult life, I had allowed myself to be involved in a situation that I couldn't control or handle, and my stomach felt sick.

I glanced over at Thomas, and once again, I caught him looking at me. I finally walked over to him, and his shoulders relaxed.

I slipped my hands under his arms and curved them behind his back, pressing my cheek against his lower chest. "Thomas…"

He touched his lips to my hair. "Yes?"

Someone turned down the music, and Trenton walked over to Camille. He took both of her hands, pulling her to the center of the room. He knelt onto one knee and held up a small box.

Thomas pulled away from me and shoved his hands into his pockets, fidgeting for a second or two. Then, he leaned down to whisper in my ear, "I'm sorry." He took a few steps backward and then quietly walked along the back wall, creeping behind the crowd, until he reached the exit.

After one last glance at Camille as she covered her mouth and nodded her head, Thomas pushed open the glass door just enough to slip outside.

Jim looked down and then over at me. "That would be tough for any man."

Everyone cheered, and Trenton stood up to hug his new fiancée. The crowd closed in around them.

"Tough for you, too, I'd imagine," Jim said again, gently patting me on the shoulder.

I swallowed hard and looked to the glass door. "We'll see you at the house, Jim. It was so nice to meet you." I hugged Thomas's father and then hurried out to the parking lot.

My sweater did little to stave off the Midwest's early spring temperatures. I wrapped the knitted fabric tighter around me and crossed my arms, walking along the sidewalk to the back of the hotel.

"Thomas?" I called.

A drunk man appeared from behind a beater Chevrolet that was older than I was. He wiped the vomit from his mouth and stumbled toward me.

"Whoeryou?" he asked, his words melded together.

I stopped and held out my hand. "I'm trying to get to my car. Please step aside."

"Are you stayin' 'ere, sweet thing?"

I raised an eyebrow. His beer gut and stained shirt didn't scream catch, but he clearly didn't see it that way.

"I'm Joe," he said before burping. He smiled, his eyes half-closed.

"It's nice to meet you, Joe. I can see you've had a lot to drink, so please don't touch me. I just want to get to my vehicle."

"Wishesyers?" he asked, turning toward the lot.

"That one." I pointed in a vague direction, knowing it wouldn't matter anyway.

"Wanna dance?" he asked, stumbling to whatever music was in his head.

"No, thank you."

I sidestepped, but he caught my sweater in his fingers.

"Whereyuhgoin' suhfast?"

I sighed. "I don't want to hurt you. Please let go."

He tugged on me once, and I gripped his fingers and pulled them back. He cried out in pain and then fell to his knees.

"Okay, okay!" he pleaded.

I let go of his hand. "The next time a woman tells you not to touch her, you listen. If you only remember one thing from tonight"—I poked his temple and pushed his head—"remember that."

"Yes, ma'am," he said, his breath puffing out in white wisps. Instead of attempting to get up, he got more comfortable on the ground.

I groaned. "You can't sleep here, Joe. It's cold. Get up, and go inside."

He looked up at me with sad eyes. "I don't 'member where m'room is."

"Oh, shit. Joe! You're not harassing this pretty lady, are ya?" Trenton said, taking off his coat. He draped it over Joe's shoulders and then helped him to stand, bearing most of his weight.

"She tried to break my damn hand!" Joe said.

"You probably deserved it, you drunk fucker," he said to Joe. He looked to me. "You all right?"

I nodded.

Joe's knees gave way, and Trenton grunted as he tossed the large man over his shoulder.

"You're Liis, right?"

I nodded again. I was extremely uncomfortable with speaking to Trenton although I wasn't sure why.

"Dad said Thomas came out here. Is he okay?"

"What are you doing out here?" Thomas snapped. He wasn't speaking to me but to his brother.

"I came to check on you," Trenton said, shifting his weight.

"What the hell is going on out here?" Taylor said, staring at Joe hanging over Trenton's shoulder. He sucked on his cigarette and exhaled, the thick smoke swirling into the air.

"She tried to break my damn hand!" Joe said.

Taylor chuckled. "Then, don't put your hands on her, dumbass!"

Thomas looked down at me. "What happened?"

I shrugged. "He touched me."

Taylor doubled over, his whole body trembling with roaring laughter.

Tyler appeared from behind Trenton and Taylor, lighting his own cigarette. "This looks like the real party!"

Taylor smiled. "Did Liis throw you down the first time you touched her, too?"

Thomas frowned. "Shut the fuck up, Taylor. We're ready to go."

Tyler's eyebrows shot up, and he laughed once. "Tommy's Asian beauty knows ca-rah-tay!" He chopped at the air a few times and then kicked forward.

Thomas took a step toward him, but I touched his chest.

Tyler took a step back and held up his hands, palms out. "Just kiddin', Tommy. Fuck!"

All four of Thomas's younger brothers looked very much alike, but it was unsettling how identical the twins were. They even had matching tattoos. Standing next to each other, I couldn't tell who was who until Thomas said their names.

"Well, Joe here is a fat bastard," Trenton said.

"Put me down!" Joe groaned.

Trenton hopped, readjusting Joe on his shoulder. "I'm going to take him to the lobby before he freezes to death."

"You need help?" Thomas asked. "How's the arm?"

"A little stiff," Trenton said. He winked. "I barely notice when I'm drunk."

"See you tomorrow," Thomas said.

"Love you, bro," Trenton said, turning for the entrance.

Thomas's eyebrows pulled in, and he looked down.

I touched his arm. "We're ready," I said to Taylor.

"Okay," Taylor said. "No problem. Travis already left. What a piss biscuit he's turned into."

We returned to the car, and Taylor drove through town, turning down various streets, until he turned into a narrow gravel drive. The headlights illuminated a modest white house with a red porch and a dirty screen door.

Thomas opened my door, but he didn't take my hand. He took all the luggage from Taylor and made his way to the house, glancing back just once to make sure I was following.

"Dad and Trent cleaned up everyone's rooms for the occasion. You can sleep in your old room."

"Great," Thomas said.

The screen door complained when Taylor pulled it open, and then he turned the knob to the front door, walking through.

"Your dad doesn't lock his door when he leaves?" I asked as we followed Taylor into the house.

Thomas shook his head. "This isn't Chicago."

I followed him inside. The furniture was as worn as the carpet, and the air carried a hint of mildew, bacon grease, and stale smoke.

"Good night," Taylor said. "My flight is early. Is yours?"

Thomas nodded.

Taylor hugged him. "See you in the morning then. I'll probably leave around five. Trav said I could take the Camry since he's riding with Shep." He began to walk down the hall and then turned around. "Hey, Tommy?"

"Yeah?" Thomas said.

"It's cool seeing you twice in one year."

He disappeared down the hall, and Thomas looked down and sighed.

"I'm sure he didn't mean to make you feel—"

"I know," Thomas said. He looked up at the ceiling. "We're up there."

I nodded, following Thomas up the wooden stairs. They creaked under our feet, singing a bittersweet song of Thomas's return. Faded pictures hung on the walls, all featuring the same platinum-haired boy I'd seen in Thomas's condo. Then, I saw a picture of his parents, and I gasped. It looked like Travis sitting with a female version of Thomas. He had his mother's eyes. He bore all her features but her jaw and long hair. She was stunning, so young and full of life. It was hard to imagine her being so ill.

Thomas turned into a doorway and then placed our luggage in a corner of the room. The iron-framed full-sized bed was pushed into the far corner, and still, the wooden dresser barely fit. Trophies from Thomas's high school years sat atop shelves on the walls, and pictures from his baseball and football teams hung next to them.

"Thomas, we need to talk," I began.

"I'm going to take a shower. You want to go first?"

I shook my head.

The zipper of Thomas's suitcase made a high-pitched noise as he opened it. He pulled out a toothbrush, toothpaste, a razor, shaving cream, a pair of heather-gray boxer briefs, and navy basketball shorts.

Without a word, he disappeared into the bathroom and began to close the door, but it was off the track. He sighed and set his things on the sink, and then he jostled the door until it sat straight in the doorway.

"You need some help?" I asked.

"Nope," he said before sliding the door closed.

I sat on the bed in a huff, unsure how to fix the mess I'd made. On one hand, it was fairly simple. We worked together. We were on assignment. Worrying about feelings seemed asinine.

On the other hand, the feelings were there. The next couple of days would be tough on Thomas. I'd pretty much stomped all over his heart because I was angry about another woman, who had coincidentally also stomped all over his heart.

I stood up and took off my sweater, staring at the broken door. From beneath the space at the bottom, light glowed into the dark bedroom, and the pipes whined as the shower spit and then shot out water in a steady stream. The shower door opened and then closed.

I shut the bedroom door and then pressed my palm and ear against the sliding door. "Thomas?"

He didn't answer.

I slid open the door, and a gust of steam poured out. "Thomas?" I said again into the foot-wide space.

He still didn't answer.

I slid the door open all the way and then closed it behind me. The shower door was fogged over, only showing Thomas's vague form. The sink was in desperate need of a good scrub with limescale remover, and the peach linoleum was peeling up at the corners.

"It wasn't for show," I said. "I was jealous and angry, but mostly, I'm just scared."

He still didn't answer, instead scrubbing his face with soap.

"I didn't enjoy being with Jackson. Almost from the beginning, I knew this was different. I can see it and feel it, but it still doesn't seem right to me to jump back into something when I've been looking forward to being alone for so long."

Still nothing.

"But if I do, I need you to be totally over her. I don't think that's entirely unreasonable. Do you?" I waited. "Can you hear me?"

Silence.

I sighed and leaned against the vanity with its chipped Formica and rusted drawer pulls. The faucet leaked, and over the years, a black drip stain had formed just above the chrome ring of the drain.

The tip of my thumb was at my mouth, and I nibbled at the skin around my nail, trying to think of what to say next. Maybe he didn't want to hear anything I had to say.

I stood up and slipped my blouse over my head and then pulled off my tall boots. It took some effort to remove my skinny denim jeans, but the socks slipped off without effort. Thank God I'd thought to shave that morning. The long black strands of my hair fell over my breasts, so I didn't feel quite so vulnerable, and I took the two steps toward the shower door.

I tugged once and then again. By the time it opened, Thomas was facing my direction with his eyes closed, lathered shampoo running down his face. He wiped the soap away and glanced at me, and then he quickly rinsed his face and looked again, his eyebrows pushing toward his hairline.

I shut the door behind me. "Are you listening?"

Thomas lifted his chin. "I'll start listening when you do."

"We can talk later," I said, closing my eyes and pulling his face down so that my lips could reach his.

He grabbed my wrists and held me at bay. "I realize what our predicament is this weekend, but I'm done playing games with you. I don't want to pretend anymore. I just want you."

"I'm standing right in front of you." I pressed my body against his, feeling his impressive erection against my stomach.

His breath faltered, and he closed his eyes, the water pouring from his hair down to his face before falling from his nose and chin.

"But will you stay?" He looked down at me.

I frowned. "Thomas…"

"Will you stay?" he asked again, emphasizing the last word.

"Define stay."

He took a step back, the spell gone. He reached over and pulled the lever down, and ice-cold water began to pour over us. Thomas flattened his palms against the wall under the spout, letting his head fall, and I squealed, clawing at the door to escape.

I pushed out and slipped, falling to the floor onto my knees.

Thomas burst out of the door, reaching for me. "Christ! Are you okay?"

"Yeah," I said, rubbing my elbow and then my knee.

Thomas grabbed a towel that was folded over the top of the shower door and draped it over my shoulders, and then he ripped another off the rack and wrapped it around his waist.

He shook his head. "Are you hurt?"

"Just my pride."

Thomas sighed and then lifted my arm to take a look. "Your knee?" he asked, leaning down.

I held out the one that had crashed against the floor, and he inspected it.

"I am a grade-A fuck-up," he said, rubbing his wet hair.

"I'm not giving you much to work with." I let my cheeks fill with air, and then I exhaled.

After several seconds of uncomfortable silence, I left him alone in the bathroom to retrieve my toothbrush, and then I returned. Thomas unscrewed the cap off of the tube of toothpaste. I held out my brush, and he squeezed out a short line onto the bristles and then did the same for his.

We held our brushes under the water and then stared into the mirror of his high school bathroom, wearing thin floral towels, while brushing our teeth together over the same sink. It felt like such a domestic thing to do, and at the same time, the past ten minutes had been so awkward that it was hard to enjoy it.

I leaned over to rinse and spit, and Thomas did the same. He chuckled and used his finger to wipe a speck of toothpaste from my chin, and then he gently cupped his hands on my cheeks. His smile faded.

"I admire your ability to scrutinize every detail, but why do you have to dissect this?" he asked, unhappy. "Why can't we just try?"

"You're not over Camille, Thomas. You made that clear tonight. And you just asked me to promise to stay with you in San Diego. That's a promise we both know I can't and won't keep. It's completely reasonable for you to want something stable after what happened to you, but I can't promise that I won't continue to work my way up the federal ladder."

"What if I give you assurances?" he asked.

"Like what? And don't tell me it's love. We met last month."

"We're not like everyone else, Liis. We spend every day together—sometimes, all day and then evenings and even weekends. If we're keeping track, we've put in the time."

I thought about that for a moment.

"*Stop* overthinking it. You want assurances? This is not guesswork for me, Liis. I loved someone before, but the way I feel about you...it's that feeling, a thousand times over."

"I have feelings for you, too. But feelings aren't always enough." I chewed on my lip. "I'm worried that if we don't work out, the job will be miserable. That's impossible for me to accept, Thomas, because I *love* my job."

"I love mine, too, but being with you is worth the risk."

"You don't know that."

"I know that it won't be boring. I know that I'll never begrudge you a promotion even if it'll take you elsewhere. Maybe I'll get tired of San Diego. I like DC."

"You would come to DC," I deadpanned.

"That's a long time from now."

"That is why I can't promise that I'll stay."

"I don't want you to promise to stay in San Diego. I just want you to stay with *me*."

I swallowed. "Oh. Then…I could…probably do that," I said, my eyes flitting around the tiny room.

"Pretending is over, Liis." Thomas took a step toward me and gently pulled at my towel. It fell to the floor, and then he tugged at his own. "Say it," he said, his voice low and controlled. He cupped each side of my face in his hands. He leaned down but stopped less than an inch from my lips.

"Okay," I whispered.

"Okay what?"

He pressed his mouth against mine. His fingers tangled in my hair as he jerked me against his body. He took a step, guiding me backward, until my back collided with the wall. I gasped, and his tongue slid through my parted lips, brushing gently against mine as if he were searching for the answer. He pulled away, leaving me breathless and craving another taste.

"Okay," I breathed, unashamed of the begging in my voice. "We can stop pretending."

He lifted me, and I wrapped my legs around his backside. He held me just high enough that I could feel the tip of his hardness against the tender pink skin between my thighs.

I sank my fingers into his shoulders, bracing myself for the same overwhelming feeling he'd sent through my body the first night we met. Just lowering me another inch, he would satisfy every fantasy I'd had for the last three weeks.

But he didn't move. He was waiting for something.

I touched my lips to his ear, biting my lip at the anticipation of what I was about to say and what it would lead to. "We can stop pretending, sir."

Thomas relaxed, and then in a slow, controlled movement, he lowered my body down. I moaned the moment he entered me, letting the soft hum escape my lips until his length completely filled me. I pressed my cheek hard against his as my nails bit into the flesh of his thick shoulders. With little effort, he lifted me and then pulled me down again, groaning in reaction.

"Fuck," he said simply, his eyes closed.

Each thrust became more rhythmic, sending flashes of the most wonderful, overwhelming pain through every nerve in my body. He struggled to keep quiet, his muffled grunts getting louder with each passing minute.

"We've gotta...damn it," he breathed.

"Don't stop," I begged.

"You feel too good," he whispered, setting me down on my feet.

Before I could protest, he flipped me around and pushed me toward the wall. My chest and palms were flat against the paint, and I grinned.

Thomas put his hand on my cheek, and I turned just enough to kiss his fingertips. Then, I opened my mouth, letting him slip a finger inside. I pulled back, sucking lightly, and he sighed.

He gently ran his thumb down the line of my jaw, my neck, and then my shoulder. From there, he slid his palm down the length of my spine, over the curves of my backside, and then settled between my thighs. He put gentle pressure on one of my legs, guiding it away from the other. I gladly spread them apart and then placed my palms on the wall, bracing myself, as he yanked my hips back.

With his hand, he slowly guided himself inside me. He didn't pull out. Instead, he moved his hips in a subtle circular motion, savoring the warm sensation of my embrace.

He gripped my hip with one hand and reached around with the other, touching the most sensitive parts of my skin. He moved his middle finger in small circles, and then he pulled back his hips. He groaned as he rocked against me.

I bent over, pressing my backside against him, allowing Thomas to sink himself as deeply as he wanted.

With every thrust, his thick fingers dug into my thighs, guiding me to the very edge of pleasure. I bit my lip, forbidding myself to cry out, and just as a thin sheen of sweat formed on my skin, we tumbled over together.

CHAPTER EIGHTEEN

I REACHED ACROSS THOMAS'S BARE CHEST to turn off the obnoxious noise coming from his cell phone. The movement made evident the soreness and swelling between my legs from the hours of sex the night before, and I rested my head on his rippled abdomen, smiling at the memories flashing in my mind.

Thomas stretched, his legs too long for the bed. The sheets rustled as he stirred, and I ran my fingers over his soft skin, surrounded by the trinkets and trophies of his childhood.

With sleepy eyes, he took one look at me and smiled. He tugged on me until we were face-to-face, and then he wrapped both of his arms around my shoulders, burying his face in the crook of my neck.

I kissed the crown of his head and hummed in total satisfaction. No one had ever made me feel so right about being wrong.

"Morning, baby," Thomas said, his voice sounding strained and hoarse. He rubbed his feet on mine as he carefully raked my ratted hair away from my face. "I probably shouldn't assume, but being a woman married to her career…"

"Yes," I said. "Birth control is in place and good for five years."

He kissed my cheek. "Just checking. I might have gotten a little carried away last night."

"I'm not complaining," I said with a tired smile. "Flight leaves in four hours."

He stretched again, still keeping one arm hooked around my neck. He pulled me to him and kissed my temple. "If this weekend wasn't so important, I'd make you stay in bed with me all day."

"We can do that when we get back to San Diego."

He squeezed me. "Does that mean you're finally available?"

I hugged him back. "No," I said, smiling at his reaction. "I'm with someone."

Thomas pressed his head back against his pillow to look me in the eyes. "Last night, I realized when I was talking to Camille…those relationships didn't work out, but it wasn't because of the job. It's because we weren't invested enough in them."

I eyed him, feigning suspicion. "Are you invested in me?"

"I'm pleading the fifth but only in the interest of not scaring you off with the answer."

I shook my head and smiled.

He touched my hair. "I like this look on you."

I rolled my eyes. "Shut up."

"I'm completely serious. I've never seen you so beautiful, and that's saying something. The first time I saw you…I mean, the very moment I looked over from my barstool and saw your face, I panicked, wondering how in the hell I was going to get your attention and then worrying how I would keep it when I did."

"You got my attention at work the next day."

Thomas looked ashamed. "I don't get surprised very often. I was probably more of an asshole than normal, trying to keep everyone from knowing, and then when it hit me that I'd put you in danger—"

I touched his lips with my finger, and then I realized I could kiss them if I wanted. Immediately, I took the opportunity. They were soft and warm, and I had trouble pulling away, but even when I tried, Thomas placed his hand on my cheek, holding me while he caressed my tongue with his.

My God, he was perfection. I silently scolded myself for waiting that long to allow myself to enjoy him.

When he finally released me, he only pulled away a few centimeters, brushing his lips against mine. "I've always been a morning person, but I have no idea how I'm going to get out of this bed with you in it."

"Tommy!" Jim yelled from downstairs. "Get your ass down here and make your mom's omelets!"

Thomas blinked. "The idea just came to me."

I pulled on a loose-fitting tank top and maxi skirt. Thomas pulled a white V-neck T-shirt over his head and then slipped on a pair of khaki cargo shorts.

He rubbed his hands together. "Holy shit, it's cold," he said, sliding his arms into his sport coat. "But I don't want to sweat my ass off when we get off the plane in Charlotte Amalie."

"I had the same idea," I said, pulling on my sweater.

"I might have a..." He opened his closet and pulled something off a hanger before tossing it to me.

I held up the gray hoodie with navy writing that read ESU WILDCATS. It was a men's medium. "When did you wear this? As a toddler?"

"As a college freshman. You can have it."

I took off my sweater and pulled his hoodie over my head, feeling extremely foolish about how giddy it made me.

We packed the few things we'd removed from our luggage, and then Thomas carried our luggage downstairs while I brushed the sex tangles from my hair. I made the bed and gathered the dirty laundry, but before leaving, I took one last longing look at the room. This was the site of the beginning of what was to come, whatever that was.

I descended the stairs, grinning at Thomas standing in front of the stove, his father holding the salt and pepper.

Jim shrugged. "No one else but Tommy can make omelets like Diane, so I get them when I can."

"I'm going to have to try it one day," I said, grinning even wider when Thomas turned to wink at me. "Where is the laundry room?"

Jim put the spices on the counter and walked over to me with his arms open. "Let me."

I felt weird about handing Jim those towels, mostly because it was the last thing Thomas and I had each worn before having the best sex of my life, but I didn't want to argue or explain, so I handed them over.

I walked over to Thomas and slipped my arms around his middle. "If I'd known you could cook, I would have spent more time upstairs."

"We can all cook. Mom taught me. I taught the boys."

The butter in the pan popped, striking my hand. I yanked it back and then shook it. "Ow!"

Thomas dropped the spatula on the counter. He took my hand in both of his and inspected it. "You okay?" he asked.

I nodded.

He lifted my knuckles to his lips, tenderly kissing all four of them. I watched him, in awe of how different he was here than the man he was at the office. No one would believe it if they saw him standing in his dad's kitchen, cooking and kissing the hurt from my hand.

"You're one of the boys, too," I said when he turned to check the progress of the omelet.

"I've tried telling him that for years," Jim said, returning from the hall. "You should have seen him dressing Trenton for his first day of kindergarten. He made sure to fuss like their mom would have."

"I gave him a bath the night before, and he woke up dirty." Thomas frowned. "I had to clean his face four times before he got on the bus."

"You've always taken care of them. Don't think I didn't notice," Jim said, a tinge of regret in his voice.

"I know you did, Dad," Thomas said, clearly uncomfortable with the conversation.

Jim crossed his arms over his protruding belly, pointed once at Thomas, and then touched his finger to his mouth. "Do you remember Trav's first day? You all beat the stuffing out of Johnny Bankonich for making Shepley cry?"

Thomas puffed out a laugh. "I remember. Too many kids got their first black eyes from one of the Maddox brothers."

Jim wore a proud smile. "Because you boys protected each other."

"That we did," Thomas said, folding over the omelet in the pan.

"Together, there wasn't anything you couldn't figure out," Jim said. "You'd beat the tar outta one of your brothers, and then you'd beat the tar outta someone else for laughing about you kicking your brother's ass. There's nothing none of you can do that would change how much you mean to each other. Just remember that, son."

Thomas looked at his father for a long time and then cleared his throat. "Thanks, Dad."

"You got a pretty girl there, and I think she's smarter than you. Don't forget that either."

Thomas put Jim's omelet on the plate and handed it to him.

Jim patted Thomas on the shoulder and took his plate to the dining room.

"You want one?" Thomas asked.

"I think I'll just get coffee at the airport," I said.

Thomas smirked. "Are you sure? I make a mean omelet. Don't you like eggs?"

"I do. It's just too early to eat."

"Good. That means I'll get to make you one of these sometime. Camille hated eggs…" He trailed off, instantly regretting his words. "I don't know why the fuck I just said that."

"Because you were thinking about her?"

"It just popped into my head." He looked around. "Being here does weird things to me. I feel like I'm two people. Do you feel different when you're at your parents' house?"

I shook my head. "I'm the same everywhere I go."

Thomas considered that and then nodded, looking down. "We should probably get on the road. I'll go check on Taylor."

He kissed my cheek and then turned left down the hallway. I ambled into the dining room, pulling out a chair next to Jim. The walls were decorated with poker chips along with pictures of dogs and people playing poker.

Jim was enjoying his omelet in silence with a sentimental look on his face. "It's strange how food can remind me of my wife. She was a damn good cook. Damn good. When Thomas makes me one of her omelets, it's almost like she's still here."

"You must miss her, especially during times like today. When is your flight scheduled to leave?"

"I'm leaving later, sis. I'm catching a ride with Trent and Cami. Tyler is, too. We're on the same flight."

Cami. I wondered why Thomas didn't call her that.

"That's good that we can all carpool to the airport."

Thomas and Taylor stood near the front door.

"Are you coming, baby?" Thomas called.

I stood. "See you this evening, Jim."

He winked at me, and I hurried to the door. Thomas held it open for Taylor and me, and then we walked out to Travis's car.

Dawn was two hours away, and the whole town of Eakins seemed to still be asleep. The only sounds were our shoes crunching the frozen dew on the grass.

I stuffed my hands into the front pocket of the hoodie and shivered.

"Sorry," Taylor said, pushing the key remote to unlock the doors and then again to pop the trunk.

Thomas opened the back door for me and then walked the bags to the trunk.

"I should have warmed up the car," Taylor said, standing next to his open door.

"Yeah, that would have been nice," Thomas said, loading our bags and then Taylor's.

"I couldn't sleep last night. I'm freaking out that Falyn's not going to show."

Taylor sat behind the wheel and then waited for Thomas to get in.

He started the car, but he waited to switch on the lights until he backed out of the driveway, so they wouldn't shine into his dad's house. I smiled at the unconsciously sweet gesture.

The dashboard lights made Thomas's and Taylor's faces glow a dim green.

"She'll show," Thomas said.

"I think I'm going to tell her about the chick at the bar," Taylor said. "It's been eating at me."

"Bad idea," Thomas said.

"You don't think he should tell her?" I asked.

"Not if he wants to keep her."

"I didn't cheat on her," Taylor said. "She dumped me."

Thomas looked at him, impatient. "She doesn't care that she broke up with you. You were supposed to be sitting at home, thinking of ways to get her back."

Taylor shook his head. "I was, and then I started feeling like I was going to go crazy, so I bought a plane ticket to San Diego."

Thomas shook his head. "When are you dumbasses going to learn that you can't go off and sleep with someone the second you're rejected? It's not going to make you feel better. Nothing will make you feel better but time."

"Is that what made you feel better?" Taylor asked.

My breath caught.

Thomas craned his neck and glanced back at me. "Maybe now isn't the best time, Taylor."

"Sorry. I just…I need to know—in case she doesn't show. I can't feel like that again, man. It feels like death. Liis, do you know how to get over someone?"

"I, um…I've yet to have my heart broken."

"Really?" Taylor asked, looking at me in the rearview mirror.

I nodded. "I didn't date much in high school, but it's avoidable. One can analyze behaviors and observe markers that tip off the end of any relationship. It's not that hard to calculate risk."

"Whoa," Taylor said, looking to Thomas. "You've got your hands full with this one."

"Liis has yet to figure out that it's not about math," Thomas said with a smile. "Love isn't about predictions or behavioral markers. It just happens, and you have no control."

I frowned. In the last three weeks, I'd had a glimpse of what Thomas described, and it was becoming obvious that it was going to be something I would have to get used to.

"So, you've only dated guys who didn't make you feel too much," Taylor said.

"Definitely no one I was…invested in."

"Are you invested now?" Taylor asked.

Even from the back, I could see the grin on Thomas's face.

"You're going to let your little brother do your dirty work?" I asked.

"Just answer the question," Thomas said.

"I'm invested," I said.

Taylor and Thomas traded glances.

Then, Thomas turned to me. "If it makes you feel better, I've run the numbers. I'm not going to break your heart."

"Oh," Taylor said, "intellectual foreplay. I don't know what the fuck y'all are talking about, but I'm feeling a little uncomfortable right now."

Thomas smacked the back of Taylor's head.

"Hey! There will be no molesting the driver on this trip!" Taylor said, rubbing the sting from the back of his head.

The plane left the runway just after sunrise. Flight was an amazing thing. In the morning, we could see our breath, and just being outside had hurt our skin. In the afternoon, we were peeling off layers and putting on sunscreen to shield our faces from the bright Caribbean sun.

Thomas opened the sliding glass door and stepped out onto the balcony of our second-floor room at The Ritz-Carlton where Travis and Abby were getting married—again.

I followed Thomas, resting my hands on the railing and scanning the scenery below. The grounds had been meticulously kept, and there were so many colors and sounds. The birds were calling to each other, but I couldn't see them. The muggy air made taking a breath feel like effort, but I loved it.

"It's beautiful," I said. "Look through the trees. You can see the ocean. I would live here in a heartbeat if the Bureau had an office here."

"We could always retire here," Thomas said.

I looked up at him.

He cringed. "Too honest?"

"Is that what that was?"

He shrugged. "Just thinking out loud." He bent down to peck my cheek and then returned to the room. "I'm going to hop in the shower. Wedding is in ninety minutes."

I turned to take in the scenery again, breathing in the salty thick air. I had just agreed to try a relationship with him, and he was talking about the rest of our lives.

I followed Thomas into the room, but he was already in the shower. I knocked on the door and then opened it.

"Don't say it," Thomas said, scrubbing his hair.

"Say what?"

"What you're about to say. You're overanalyzing."

I frowned. "That's part of who I am. That's why I'm good at my job."

"And I accept that. What I won't accept is you using it to push me away. I know what you're doing."

Anger, humiliation, and devastation hit me at once. "And I accept that you're gifted at seeing people for who they really are but not when you point it in my direction and avoid using that talent on yourself."

He didn't respond.

"Thomas?"

"We've already been over this."

"What Taylor said this morning, about how to get over someone—"

"No, Liis."

"You don't even know what I'm going to ask."

"Yes, I do. You want to know if I am using you to get over Camille. The answer is no."

"Then, how did you get over her? You weren't over her before."

He was quiet for a moment, letting the water run forward over his scalp and down his face. "You can't just stop loving someone. I don't know how to explain it to you if you've never been in love."

"Who said I've never been in love?"

"You did—when you said you've never had your heart broken."

"A lot of people on this earth have been in love and haven't had their hearts broken."

"But you're not one of them."

I winced. "Are you over her?"

He hesitated. "It's hard to explain."

"It's a yes or no question."

He wiped his face and opened the door. "Baby, for the tenth time…I don't want to be with her. I want you."

"Would you still be with her if Trent hadn't come along?"

He puffed out a frustrated sigh. "Probably. I don't know. It depends on if she would have moved out to California like we'd talked about."

"You talked about moving in together?"

He sighed. "Yes. Evidently, we need to talk more about this until you're clear and you feel better about certain things, but right now, we have to get ready for the ceremony. Okay?"

"Okay. But…Thomas?"

"Yeah?"

"I'm never going to be okay with unresolved feelings."

He looked at me with sad eyes. "Don't do that. I'm sorry I talked about retiring here. It's too soon. I freaked you out. I get it."

"That's not what I'm doing. This has been an ongoing conversation."

"I'm aware."

I glared at him.

"Liis…" He pressed his lips together, stopping himself from whatever he was about to say. After a few moments, he spoke again, "We'll figure it out. Just hang in there with me."

I nodded, and then he offered a small smile before pulling the shower door closed.

"Thomas?" I said.

He opened the door again, aggravation darkening his face.

"I just…I don't want to hurt you."

His eyes turned soft. He looked wounded. "You don't want to get hurt."

"Does anyone?"

"You have to weigh the joy against the risk."

I nodded and then left him to finish his shower. The foliage and ocean were visible even from the middle of the room, and I tried to forget about my present worries and our future and everything in between.

I fell onto the bed, bouncing twice. It was unsettling being with someone with such a strong bullshit shield. Thomas had called me out on making excuses to run before I'd even realized what I was doing.

There was a knock on the door. I looked around, not sure if we had even told anyone which room we were in. I crept over to the door and used the peephole. My blood ran cold and boiled at the same time.

Oh. My. God.

CHAPTER NINETEEN

I DIDN'T KNOW WHAT ELSE TO DO, so I slid the chain and then yanked the door open with a smile. "Hi."

Camille hesitated. Her navy strapless cocktail dress had the tiniest bit of sparkle in the threading. When she made the slightest shift, the fabric would catch the light, emphasizing her every movement. I imagined she had to stick to simple clothing to avoid clashing with the busy color-by-numbers on her arms.

"The, uh...the guys are all getting ready in Shepley and America's room. They're taking pictures, too."

"Okay," I said, slowly pushing the door shut. "I'll let him know."

Camille put her hand on the door, stopping it from closing. I shot her a look, and she immediately snapped her hand back, protectively holding it. With her arms and even her knuckles tattooed, the fact that she worked in a bar at least gave the impression that a dirty look wouldn't have an effect on her. Camille stood a whole head taller than me, so her acting intimidated didn't make sense.

"Fuck, I'm sorry," she said. "I just..."

She knows something. "You came here to see him?" I asked.

"No! I mean, yes, but it's not like that." She shook her head, and the ends of her razor-cut strands trembled as if they were nervous, too. "Is he here?"

"He's in the shower."

"Oh." She bit her lip and looked everywhere but at me.

"Would you like to come back?"

"I'm...in the other building on the opposite side of the property."

I watched her for a moment in disbelief. Begrudgingly, I extended the last invite I wanted to give. "Would you like to come in?"

She smiled, looking sheepish. "If it's all right. I don't want to impose."

I opened the door wide, and she stepped through. She sat on the exact spot of the bed where I had just been, and the fires of hell burned in my chest. I hated that she could get under my skin without even trying.

The shower shut off, and almost immediately, the bathroom door opened. A puff of steam preceded Thomas, who was covered only by the white towel he held loosely at his waist. "Baby, have you seen my…" He saw Camille first, and then his eyes searched for me. "Razor?"

I nodded. The shock and discomfort on his face when he had seen Camille gave me a tiny bit of satisfaction, as did her hearing that term of endearment. In the same moment, I felt foolish for being so juvenile.

"You put it in the inside pocket of your luggage this morning." I walked the few steps to his suitcase and rummaged through it.

"Could you hand me a T-shirt and shorts, too?" he asked.

He closed the door, and once I located the items, I joined Thomas in the bathroom.

Thomas took the shirt, shorts, and razor from me, and then he leaned down. "What is she doing here?" he quietly hissed.

I shrugged.

He looked at the wall in the direction of where Camille was sitting. "She didn't say anything?"

"She said the guys were getting ready in Shepley's room, and then you all have pictures."

"Okay…but why is she still here?" The disgusted look on his face made me feel even more validation.

"She didn't say. She just wanted to come in."

Thomas nodded once and then bent down to kiss my cheek. "Tell her I'll be out in a minute."

I turned and grabbed the knob, but then Thomas spun me around, grabbed my cheeks, and attacked my lips with his.

When he let me go, I was breathless and disoriented. "What was that?" I asked.

He huffed, "I don't know what she's going to say. I just don't want you to be upset."

"Why don't you take it outside?" I offered.

He shook his head. "She knew we were sharing a room. If she wants to talk to me, she can say it in front of you."

"Just...stop fidgeting. You look terrified."

He dropped his towel and then pulled his T-shirt over his head.

I returned to the room. "He'll be out in a minute."

Camille nodded.

I sat in the chair in the corner and reached for the closest reading material.

"This is a nice room," Camille said.

I glanced around. "Yes, it is."

"Did they tell you they had the tuxes delivered? His should be in the closet."

"I'll let him know."

When Thomas came out of the bathroom, Camille immediately stood.

"Hi," he said.

She smiled. "Hey. The, uh...the guys are in Shep's room."

"I heard," Thomas said simply.

"And your tux is in the closet."

"Thank you."

"I was, um...hoping we could chat for a minute," she said.

"About what?" he asked.

"Last night...and other things." She looked as terrified as he had.

"We talked about it last night. You have more to say?" Thomas asked.

"Can we..." She gestured to the hall.

"I think it's more respectful to Liis if we don't."

Camille glanced at me, sighed, and then nodded, picking at her metallic black nail polish.

"You look really happy," she said, looking down. "Your brothers want you home, T.J." When Thomas didn't respond, she looked up at him. "I don't want things to be awkward. I don't want you to stay away. So, I was hoping...since you seem so happy now...that you would consider visiting more often. Abby, Liis, Falyn, and I need to be a united front." She chuckled nervously.

"You Maddox boys are a lot to handle, and I just…want to get along."

"Okay," Thomas said.

Camille's face turned bright red, and I silently cursed myself for the empathy I felt.

"You're different, T.J. Everyone can see it."

Thomas began to speak, but she cut him off, "No, I'm glad. We're all glad. You're the man you were meant to be, and I don't think you could have done that if you were with me."

"What are you getting at, Camille?" Thomas asked.

Camille winced. "I know Liis doesn't work at the university." She held up her hand to me when my mouth fell open. "It's okay. It won't be the first secret I've kept." She walked toward the door and turned the knob. "I'm just so damn glad for you both. You're exactly who he needed. I just…I heard your discussion at the party last night, and I thought it would be best if we at least had a conversation. We need to put this behind us, T.J., as a family, and Liis is a big part of that."

Thomas stood next to me and smiled. "Thank you for stopping by. We'll make more of an effort to visit—as our jobs allow."

I shot Thomas a look.

"Okay. See you at the ceremony," she said before closing the door behind her.

"Is she going to talk?" I asked, panicked.

"No. I trust her."

I sat down and covered my face, feeling tears burning my eyes.

"What?" Thomas said, kneeling in front of me and touching my knees. "Talk to me. Liis?" He paused when he saw my shoulders trembling. "Are you…crying? But you don't cry. Why are you crying?" he spoke the words in staccato, flustered at the sight of me.

I looked up at him with wet eyes. "I'm a terrible undercover agent. If I can't play the part of your girlfriend when I *am* your girlfriend, I am officially a failure."

He chuckled and touched my cheek. "Jesus Christ, Liis. I thought you were going to say something completely different. I have never been so scared in my life."

I sniffed. "What did you think I was going to say?"

He shook his head. "Doesn't matter. The only reason Camille knows you're an agent is because she knows I'm an agent."

"Anthony knew."

"Anthony serves agents every night of the week. The locals call that neighborhood the Eagle's Nest because of the concentration of federal agents." He used his thumbs to wipe the tears from my cheeks, and then he touched his lips to mine. "You're not a failure. I would never fall this hard for a failure."

I blinked. "You're falling for me?"

"Already at the bottom. Splat."

I quietly giggled, and the green in his hazel eyes sparked.

He touched my bottom lip with his thumb. "I wish I didn't have to go. I would love to lie in a hammock on the beach with you."

Camille was right. He was different, even from the man I'd met at the bar. The darkness in his eyes was completely gone.

"After the reception?"

Thomas nodded and then kissed me good-bye, his lips lingering on my mouth.

"It's a date," he whispered. "I won't see you until the wedding, but Dad is going to save you a seat in the front row. You'll be sitting with Camille, Falyn, and Ellie."

"Ellie?"

"Ellison Edson. She's Tyler's friend. He's been chasing her forever."

"Forever? I should have made you chase me a little longer. I think I made it too easy for you."

Thomas's eyes turned mischievous. "Feds don't chase. They hunt."

I smiled. "You'd better go."

He hopped up and walked across the room. After stuffing socks in a pair of shiny black dress shoes, he grabbed the plastic-covered tux hanging in the closet. He swung the hanger over his shoulder. "See you soon."

"Thomas?"

He stood with his hand on the door, turning his head to the side, while he waited for me to speak.

"Do you feel like we're going a hundred miles per hour?"

He shrugged, the things in his hands pulling up as his shoulders did. "I don't care. I'm trying not to think too hard about it. You're doing that for both of us."

"My head is telling me that we should tap on the brakes. But I don't really want to."

"Good," he said. "I don't think I could have agreed to that." He smiled. "I've done a lot of things wrong, Liis. Being with you isn't one of them."

"See you in an hour," I said.

He twisted the knob and closed the door behind him. I sat back in the chair and slid down, taking a deep breath and refusing to overanalyze the situation this time. We were happy, and he was right. It didn't matter why.

Travis pulled Abby into his arms and leaned her back a bit as he kissed her. We all clapped, and Thomas caught my eyes and winked.

Abby's veil blew in the Caribbean breeze, and I held up my cell phone to snap a picture. Camille, on one side of me, and Falyn, on the other, were doing the same.

When Travis finally righted Abby, the Maddox brothers and Shepley all broke into cheers. America was standing next to Abby, holding the bride's bouquet with one hand and wiping her eyes with the other. She pointed and laughed at her mother, who was dabbing her eyes, too.

"I present to you Mr. and Mrs. Travis Maddox," the pastor said, his voice straining over the wind, ocean waves, and the celebration.

Travis helped Abby descend the steps of the gazebo, and they walked down the aisle before disappearing behind a wall of trees and shrubs.

"Mr. and Mrs. Maddox ask that you join them at the restaurant Sails for dinner and the reception. I speak for them when I say thank you for being present on this most special day."

He nodded, and everyone stood, gathering their things.

Thomas joined me with a wide grin, seeming relieved that the ceremony was over.

"Say cheese!" Falyn said, holding up her camera phone.

Thomas wrapped me in his arms and kissed my cheek. I smiled.

Falyn smiled, too, showing us the picture when she was finished. "Perfect."

Thomas squeezed me. "She is."

"Aw, cute," Falyn said.

Taylor tapped her shoulder, and she turned to hug him.

A palpable tension overwhelmed the space around us when Trenton pulled Camille into his arms and kissed her.

Jim clapped his hands and rubbed them together. "Grab your ladies, boys. I'm starved. Let's eat."

Thomas and I walked, hand in hand, following Jim with Trenton and Camille. Taylor and Falyn, and Tyler and Ellison were not far behind.

"Taylor looks relieved," I whispered.

Thomas nodded. "I thought he was going to pass out when she texted him, saying her plane had landed. I don't think he believed she was coming until then."

We walked to the outdoor restaurant. Large white canvases shaded the tables from the glow of the sunset. Thomas led me to a table where Shepley and America were sitting with who I recognized as Jack and Deana from my research prior to the trip. We had barely sat down when the server approached, asking for our drink orders.

"I'm so glad to see you, sweetheart," Deana said. Her long lashes blinked once over her hazel-green eyes.

"It's good to see you, too, Aunt Deana," Thomas said. "Have you met Liis?"

She shook her head and then reached across Thomas. "We didn't get a chance to meet before the ceremony. Your dress is absolutely stunning. That violet is so vivid. You're practically glowing. It's perfect with your skin and hair."

"Thank you," I said, shaking her hand once.

She and Jack turned to give their drink orders.

I leaned into Thomas's ear. "She looks so much like your mother. If I hadn't read up on it before, I would have been very confused. You and Shepley could be brothers."

"It throws people off all the time," he said. "She's right, by the way. You're stunning. I didn't get a chance to tell you, but when you walked around the corner, I had to force myself to stay in the gazebo."

"It's just a purple maxi dress."

"It's not the dress."

"Oh," I said, my lips curving upward.

Abby and Travis walked in, and the hostess announced their arrival over the PA system. A rock ballad came over the speakers, and Travis pulled Abby out to dance.

"They are so sweet," Deana said, her bottom lip trembling. "I wish Diane could have been here to see it."

"We all do, baby," Jack said, curling his arm around his wife's shoulder and squeezing her to his side.

I looked over at Jim. He was sitting and chatting with Trenton and Camille. When Jim watched Travis and Abby dancing, he had that same sentimental smile on his face. I knew he was thinking about Diane, too.

The sun fizzled into the ocean while the not-so-new newlyweds danced to their song. When they finished, we all clapped, and the first course was brought out.

We ate and laughed as the brothers teased each other and told stories from their tables.

After dessert, Shepley stood up and tapped his glass with his fork. "I've had a year to write this speech, and I wrote it last night."

Laughter rumbled across the patio.

"As the best man and the best friend, it's my duty to both honor and embarrass Travis. Starting with a story from our childhood, there was one time when I set my bean burrito on the bench, and Travis chose that moment to see if he could jump over the back and sit beside me."

America cackled.

"Travis isn't just my cousin. He's also my best friend and my brother. I'm convinced that, without his guiding hand while we were growing up, I would have been half the man I am today...with half as many enemies."

The brothers all covered their mouths with their fists and guffawed.

"This time should be spent musing over how he met Abby, and I can do that because I was present when it happened. Even though I might not have always been their biggest cheerleader, Travis didn't need me to be. From the beginning, he knew that he

belonged to Abby and that she belonged to him. Their marriage
has reinforced what I've always thought and lived by—that
stalking, harassment, and inflicting general misery on a woman will
eventually pay off."

"Oh, good Lord, Shepley Maddox!" Deana wailed.

"I'm not going to use this time for any of that. Instead, I'll just
raise my glass to Mr. and Mrs. Maddox. From the beginning and
through all their highs and lows and through the last year while
everyone told them that they were crazy and that it wouldn't work,
they loved each other. That has always been the constant, and I
know it always will be. To the bride and groom."

"Hear, hear!" Jim yelled, raising his glass.

We raised our drinks as we chanted the same and then clapped
while Travis and Abby kissed. He looked into her eyes with such
affection. It was a familiar affection—the same way Thomas
looked at me.

I rested my chin on my palm, watching the sky bruise with
pinks and purples. The lights hanging from the edges of the white
canvas ceiling were blowing in the gentle breeze.

After America gave her speech, the music began to play. At
first, no one danced, but after the third round of drinks, almost
everyone was on the dance floor. The brothers, including Thomas,
were teasing Travis with their own Travis-like dance moves, and I
was giggling so hard that tears were streaming down my face.

Abby strolled across the room and sat next to me, watching the
boys from her new seat. "Wow," she said. "I think they're trying to
scare poor Cami off."

"I don't think that's possible," I said, wiping my cheeks.

Abby watched me until I looked at her. "She's going to be my
sister-in-law soon, I hear."

"Yes. The proposal was quite entertaining."

She turned her head to the side a bit and clicked her tongue.
"Trent always is. So, you were there?"

"I was." I wished Thomas had never warned me about how
smart she was. Her calculating eyes made me want to sink back
into my seat.

"For the entire thing?" she asked.

"For most of it. Travis was the first to leave."

"Were there strippers?"

I sighed in relief. "Just Trenton."

"Dear Jesus," she said, shaking her head.

After a few moments of uncomfortable silence, I spoke up, "It was a beautiful ceremony. Congratulations."

"Thank you. You're Liis, right?"

I nodded. "Liis Lindy. Nice to finally meet you. I've heard a lot about you. Poker phenom? So impressive," I said without an ounce of condescension.

"What else did Thomas tell you?" she asked.

"He told me about the fire."

Abby looked down and then to her husband. "A year ago today." Her mind drifted off to somewhere unpleasant, and then she snapped back to reality. "We weren't there, thank God. We were in Vegas. Obviously. Getting married."

"Was Elvis there?"

Abby laughed. "He was! He was. We were married in the Graceland Chapel. It was perfect."

"You've got family out there, right?"

Abby's shoulders relaxed. She was as cool as ice. I wondered if even Val could get a read on her.

"My dad. We don't speak."

"So, I guess he didn't go to the wedding."

"No. We didn't tell anyone."

"Really? I thought Trent and Cami knew. But that can't be right because he was at the fight that night, right? Christ, that's scary. We're lucky we're looking at him making an ass of himself right now."

Abby nodded. "We weren't there. People say"—she chuckled—"that we ran off to Vegas to get married to give Travis an alibi. I mean, how ridiculous."

"I know," I said, trying to sound disinterested. "That would be crazy. And you obviously love him."

"I do," she said with conviction. "They say that I married him for something other than love. Even if it were true—and it's not—that's just...well, it's fucking moronic. If I had whisked him off to Vegas to marry him for an alibi, it would have been out of love, right? Wouldn't that have been the goddamn point? Wouldn't that have been the ultimate act of love for someone? To go against your own rules because you love that person too much?"

The more she talked, the angrier she became.

"Absolutely," I said.

"If I did save him, it was because I loved him. There is no other reason to do that for someone, is there?"

"I don't know of any," I said.

"But I wasn't saving him from the fire. We weren't even there. That's what pisses me off the most."

"No, I totally get it. Don't let them ruin your night. If they want to hate on everything, let them. You get to determine how this plays out. This isn't their story to tell."

She offered a smile, shifting nervously in her seat. "Thank you. I'm glad you came. It's nice to see Thomas happy again. It's nice to see Thomas at all." She smiled and sighed, content. "Promise me you'll have your wedding here, so I have an excuse to come back."

"Pardon?"

"It's still new with Thomas and you, right? And he brought you to a wedding. That's a very non-Maddox thing for him to do if he's not head over heels, which I'm willing to bet that he is." She turned to watch the dance floor, satisfied. "And I never lose a bet."

"He didn't want to be the only one without a date."

"Bullshit. You two are as thick as thieves. You've got it bad. I can tell," she said with a mischievous grin. She was trying to make me squirm and enjoying the hell out of it.

"Is this your version of an initiation?" I asked.

She laughed and leaned over, touching her bare shoulder to mine. "You caught me."

"What are you doing, bitches?" America said, shimmying over to us. "This is a fucking party! We're dancing!"

She tugged on Abby's hand and then mine. We joined the mob on the dance floor. Thomas grabbed my hand, twirled me around, pulled me until my back was against him, and then folded his arms across my middle.

We danced until my feet hurt, and then I noticed Abby and America hugging America's parents good night. Then, Jack and Deana left, and we all hugged Jim before he left for his room.

Travis and Abby were eager to be alone, so they thanked us all for coming, and Travis carried her away into the night.

We said our good-byes, and then Thomas pulled me along the dimly lit curved sidewalk until we were at the beach.

"Hammock," he said, pointing to a dark form twenty yards from the water.

I pulled off my shoes, and Thomas did the same before we strolled through the white sand. Thomas sat down on the woven ropes first, and then I joined him. It rocked as we struggled to navigate the hammock without falling out.

"This should be easier for us," Thomas teased.

"You should probably—"

The hammock jerked. We held on to each other and froze, our eyes wide. Then, we both burst into laughter.

As soon as we were settled, a drop of rain hit my cheek.

More drops fell, and Thomas wiped his eye. "You have got to be kidding me."

The rain began to fall in big warm drops, tapping at the sand and the water.

"I'm not moving," he said, squeezing me in his thick arms.

"Then, neither am I," I said, nuzzling my cheek against his chest. "Why did Toto's babysitter and Camille both call you T.J.?"

"It was how they talked about me without letting anyone know it was me."

"Thomas James," I said. "Clever. Is the other girl an ex, too?"

He chuckled. "No. She was Camille's roommate."

"Oh."

Thomas anchored his foot on the sand and then pushed off, rocking us a bit.

"This is incredible. I could definitely retire here. It feels so…I can't even describe it."

He kissed my temple. "This feels a lot like falling in love."

The rain clouds had snuffed out the moon, making the sky pitch-black. The muffled music still playing at Sails sounded a mile away, and hotel guests were running to get out of the rain. We might as well have been on a secluded island, away from everyone else, lying together in our small but quiet section of the beach.

"Splat?" I asked.

"Obliteration," he said.

I squeezed him, and he took in a deep breath through his nose.

"I hate myself for saying this, but we should probably turn in. We've got an early morning."

I looked up at him. "It's going to be okay, you know. Travis will be fine. We'll get rid of Grove. It's all going to work out."

"I just want to think about you tonight. Tomorrow is going to be tough."

"I'll do my best to keep your attention." I wiggled out of the hammock and got to my feet. I helped him out, and I pulled his lips down to meet mine, sucking his bottom lip as I drew back.

He hummed. "I have no doubt. You've been an impeccable distraction."

My heart sank.

"What?" he asked, seeing the hurt in my eyes.

"Why don't you just admit it? Just say it out loud. You're using me to stop thinking about her. That's not closure. It's stalling."

His face fell. "That's not what I meant."

"This isn't falling in love, Thomas. You said it perfectly. I'm running interference."

Above us, motion caught my eyes, and Thomas looked up, too. Trenton was twirling Camille on the balcony of Sails, and then he brought her into his arms. She squealed in delight, they both laughed, and then they disappeared from our view.

Thomas looked down and rubbed the back of his neck. His eyebrows pulled in. "Being with her was a mistake. Trenton has loved her since they were kids, but I didn't think he was serious enough about her. I was wrong."

"Then, why can't you just let her go?"

"I'm trying."

"Using me to do it doesn't count."

He breathed out a laugh. "I'm running out of ways to explain this to you."

"Then, stop. I need a different answer, and you don't have one."

"You act as is loving someone can just be flipped off like a light switch. We've had this conversation a dozen times. I want *you*. I'm with *you*."

"While you're missing her, wishing you were with her. And you want me to change everything I trust for that?"

He shook his head in disbelief. "This is an impossible situation. I thought we were perfect because we're the same, but maybe we're too alike. Maybe you're my payback instead of my redemption."

"Your payback? You've made me believe all weekend that you were falling for me!"

"I am! I have! Jesus Christ, Camille, how can I get that through your head?"

I froze, and once Thomas realized his mistake, he did, too.

"Goddamn it. I am so sorry," he said, reaching out for me.

I shook my head, and my eyes burned. "I am so...stupid."

Thomas let his hands fall to his thighs. "No, you're not. That's why you've held back. Even from the first night, you knew to keep your distance. You're right. I can't love you the way you need me to. I don't even love myself." His voice broke on the last sentence.

My lips pressed into a hard line. "I can't redeem you, Thomas. You'll have to come to terms with what you did to Trent on your own."

Thomas nodded and then turned toward the sidewalk. I stayed behind, watching the dark ocean roll onto the sand, with the sky crying on my shoulders.

CHAPTER TWENTY

"YOU LOOK NERVOUS," I SAID. "He's going to smell you from a mile away if you don't man up."

Thomas glanced at me, but instead of shooting me the dirty look I had expected, he used amazing restraint, simply looking away.

A knock on the door jolted us both to the matter at hand, and I went to the door, opening it.

"Good morning, Liis," Travis said, a euphoric glow on his face.

"Come on in, Travis." I stepped to the side, letting him pass, as I tried to keep the heavy guilt I felt from weighing down my Oscar-worthy smile. "How was your night? I don't need details. I'm just being polite."

Travis chuckled and then noticed the folded sheets, blanket, and pillow on the couch. "Oh," he said, rubbing the back of his neck. "Better than your night, brother. Should I, uh...should I come back? The front desk left me a note, saying you needed me to come here at six."

"Yeah," Thomas said, shoving his hands in his pockets. "Have a seat, Trav."

Travis walked over to the couch and sat down, looking up at us with wary eyes. "What's going on?"

I sat down on the corner of the bed, keeping my shoulders relaxed and trying to seem generally nonthreatening. "Travis, we need to talk to you about your involvement in the March nineteenth ESU fire."

Travis furrowed his brow, and then he laughed once without humor. "What?"

I continued, "The FBI has been investigating the case, and
Thomas has been able to strike a deal in your favor."

Travis clasped his hands together. "The FBI? But he's an ad
exec." He gestured to his brother. "Tell her, Tommy." When
Thomas didn't respond, Travis's eyes narrowed. "What is this?"

Thomas looked down and then back at his brother. "I'm not in
advertising, Trav. I'm a Special Agent of the FBI."

Travis stared at his brother for a full ten seconds and then
cackled. "Oh my God, dude! You were beginning to freak me out.
Don't do that to me! What do you really need to talk to me about?"
His laughter faded when Thomas didn't crack a smile. "Tommy,
knock it off."

Thomas shifted. "I've been working with my boss for a year
now, Travis, trying to negotiate a deal for you. They know you
were in Eakins. Abby's plan didn't work."

Travis shook his head. "What plan?"

"For the wedding in Vegas to provide you with an alibi to keep
you out of prison," Thomas said, trying to keep his expression
relaxed.

"Abby married me to keep me out of prison?"

Thomas's eyes fell, but he nodded. "She doesn't want you to
know."

Travis jumped up, grabbed Thomas's shirt, and shoved him all
the way to the other side of the room against the wall. I stood, but
Thomas held out his hand, warning me away.

"C'mon, Travis, you're not stupid. I'm not telling you anything
you don't know," Thomas grunted.

"Take it back," Travis seethed. "Take back what you said
about my wife."

"She was nineteen, Travis. She didn't want to get married until
you were at risk for going to prison for organizing the fight."

Travis took a swing at Thomas, but he ducked. They scuffled,
and then Thomas got the upper hand, pinning his younger brother
to the wall with his forearm.

"Knock it off! Goddamn it! She loves you! She loves you so
much that she did something she had no intention of doing for
years down the line just so she could save your stupid ass!"

Travis was breathing hard, and he held up his hands in
surrender.

Thomas let him go, taking a step back, and then Travis swung, catching Thomas hard in the jaw. Thomas gripped his knee with one hand and clenched his jaw with the other, trying to harness his temper.

Travis pointed at him. "That's for lying to Dad."

Thomas stood upright and then held up his index finger. "That's your one. Don't make me beat your ass. I feel bad enough."

Travis looked at me, sizing me up. "You're really FBI?"

I nodded, eyeing him warily. "Don't make me beat your ass either."

Travis laughed once. "I'd have to let you. I don't hit girls."

"I hit boys," I said, still on guard.

Thomas rubbed his cheek and raised his eyebrows. "You hit harder than you used to."

"That wasn't even full power, dickhead," Travis sneered.

Thomas worked his jaw back and forth. "Abby gets points for creativity, Trav, but the records show that you purchased the tickets on your credit card well after the fire started."

Travis simply nodded. "I'm listening."

"I've also been working on a case involving a money-laundering and drug-smuggling ring in Vegas. It's run by a man named Benny Carlisi."

"Benny?" Travis asked, clearly confused. "Tommy, are you fuckin' serious right now? You're in the motherfucking FBI."

"Focus, Travis. We don't have much time, and this is important," Thomas snapped. "You're in a lot of trouble. My boss is expecting an answer today. Do you understand?"

"What kind of trouble?" Travis sat back down on the couch.

"You're looking at the same counts of manslaughter that Adam was charged with. You're looking at prison time."

"How long?" Travis asked. He seemed like a scared little boy when he looked up with his big brown eyes at his brother.

"Adam has ten years," Thomas said, trying to retain his stoic expression. "I don't see your sentence having a different outcome. The media has been all over this. They want retribution."

Travis looked down, and his hands touched his head. "I can't be away from Abby that long."

His words tugged at my heart. He didn't care about going to prison. He just didn't want to be separated from his wife.

"You won't have to go to prison, Travis," I said. "Your brother has spent a lot of time and effort making sure that won't happen. But you have to agree to something first."

Travis glanced to Thomas and then back at me. "Like what?"

Thomas returned his hands to his pockets. "They want to recruit you, Trav."

"The mob?" he asked. He shook his head. "I can't fight for Benny. Abby will leave me."

"Not the mob," Thomas said. "The FBI."

Travis laughed once. "What do they want with me? I'm a college kid…a fucking part-time personal trainer."

"They want you to use your previous contact with Mick and Benny to gain intelligence on the inner workings of their illegal operations," I said.

"They want you to work undercover," Thomas clarified.

Travis stood and began to pace. "He'll want me to fight for him, Tommy. I can't do that. I'll lose my wife."

"Then, you'll have to lie," I said matter-of-factly.

Travis looked at me and then at his brother, crossing his arms. "Fuck you both. I won't do it."

"What?" Thomas said.

"I won't lie to Pigeon."

Thomas narrowed his eyes. "You don't have a choice. You can either lie to Abby and keep her or go to prison and lose her."

"I won't lie. Can't I tell her? She grew up around men like Benny. She won't blab."

Thomas shook his head. "You'll put her in danger."

"She'll be in danger if I fuck with these guys! You think they'll shoot me in the head and be done with it? People like that take out your entire family. We'll be lucky if they stop with Abby. They'll probably move on to Dad and Trent, Taylor, and Tyler, too! What the fuck have you done, Tommy?"

"Help me take them down, Travis," Thomas said.

"You sold us out. For what? A goddamn promotion?" Travis shook his head.

I inwardly cringed. I knew Thomas was dying inside.

"Dad told us we couldn't go into law enforcement. Mom didn't want it!"

Thomas sighed. "Says the guy who's majoring in criminal justice. You're wasting time, Travis. Abby will be awake soon."

"You fucked us all! You son of a bitch!" Travis screamed, punching at the air.

"Are you finished?" Thomas asked, his voice even.

"I won't lie to Abby. If I have to lie to her, it's a deal-breaker."

"So, you're not taking the deal?" Thomas asked.

Travis laced his hands on top of his head, looking distraught. "I can't lie to my wife." His arms fell to his sides, and his eyes glossed over. "Please don't make me do this, Tommy." His bottom lip quivered. "You're my brother."

Thomas stared him in the eyes, speechless.

I shifted to my other leg, keeping a confident stare. "Then, maybe you shouldn't have engaged in an illegal activity that caused the deaths of a hundred and thirty-two college kids."

Travis's face crumbled, and then his head fell forward. After a full minute, he rubbed the back of his neck and looked at me. "I'll think about it," he said, walking toward the door.

"Travis," Thomas said, taking a step.

"I said I'll think about it."

I touched Thomas's arm and then startled when the door slammed.

Thomas grabbed his knees, gasping for air, and then he collapsed onto the floor. I sat on the floor beside him, tightly holding him, while he quietly sobbed.

I nodded to Anthony again, insisting that he pour Thomas another drink. He hadn't spoken after Travis agreed to recruitment or when we drove from the hotel to the airport. He hadn't spoken a word during the plane ride. He'd merely gestured that we share a cab for the short ride to our building.

I hadn't asked, but I'd told him that we were going to Cutter's. It had been easy to convince him of things when he refused to protest.

"Jesus," Val said quietly as she maneuvered her purse off her shoulder. She sat down. "He looks like hell."

Marks sat on the other side of Thomas, allowing his friend to get drunk in peace. He popped a few peanuts into his mouth and stared at the television.

"He'll be okay," I said. "How's Sawyer?"

Val made a face. "How would I know?"

"Really?" I deadpanned. "Are you really going to try to lie to me?"

She glared at the back of Thomas's head. "Maddox told you?" she hissed.

"Yes, and he's had a shitty weekend, so you can't be mad at him. I, however, can be extremely pissed at you for holding back something so monumental when you've insisted on knowing every morsel of information about me."

Val pouted. "I'm sorry. I didn't want you to know. I don't want anyone to know. I wish it never happened."

"It might help you to forget if you didn't live with him," I said.

"He won't sign the divorce papers, and if I move out, I lose the condo."

"So?"

"I lived there first!"

"Move in with me," I said.

"Really?" she asked, her eyes softening. "You would do that for me?"

"Yes. What a nightmare. And besides, it would be nice to share the bills. I could buy a car, and until then, ride with you to work."

"I appreciate that," Val said, tilting her head to the side. "I really do, but I'm not losing the condo. It's mine, and his ass is moving, not me."

"Why don't you want to ride to work with me anymore?" Thomas slurred.

It was the first time he'd spoken in hours, and the sound of his voice surprised me as if he'd just shown up.

"I do," I said. "I just meant that if Val moved in, it would be a good trade."

His shirtsleeves were rolled almost to his elbows, and his tie was loose and hanging haphazardly from his neck. He'd had so much to drink that his eyes were half closed.

"What's wrong with riding with me?"

"You're moving in with Liis?" Marks asked, leaning backward to look at Val.

"No," Val said.

"Why not?" Marks asked. "She offered, and you said no? Why would you say no?"

"Because it's my condo, and I'm not giving it to Charlie!"

Marks opened his mouth to speak.

Before he could say anything, Thomas leaned closer to me. "You're too good for my carpool now?"

I rolled my eyes. "No." I looked to Val. "Who is Charlie?"

"Sawyer," she sneered.

"Oh, I think you are," Thomas said. "I think you think you're too good for a lot of things."

"Okay," I snipped, my voice dripping with sarcasm. I used to do that to my mother, and it had driven her absolutely insane. She would cuss at me in Japanese, which she never, ever did, unless it was in response to that single two-syllable word. In her eyes, nothing was more disrespectful. "Just get drunk, Thomas, so we can take you home, and Marks can tuck you in."

"It's Agent Maddox to you."

"Fine. I'll call you that when you're not slobbering drunk."

"You forget you brought me here," he said before taking a gulp.

Val and Marks traded glances.

"Would you like another drink?" I asked Thomas.

He looked offended. "No. It's time for us to go home."

I raised an eyebrow. "You mean, it's time for *you* to go home."

"So, everything you said this weekend was bullshit?" he asked.

"No, I recall being very truthful."

His nose wrinkled. "You came home with me the last time we had drinks here together."

Marks winced. "Hey, Thomas, maybe we should—"

"No, *you* came home with *me*," I said, trying very hard not to get defensive.

"What does that even mean?" Thomas asked. "Speak English!"

"I'm speaking English. I just don't speak drunk," I said.

The disgusted look on his face only grew more severe. "That's not even funny." He looked at Marks. "She's not even funny. And that's bad because I'm drunk," he said, pointing at himself. "I think everything's funny."

Anthony held up his hand, a blue rag hanging from it. "I don't mean to poke the bear, but I've got one nerve left, and Maddox is dry-humping it. So, could you all move it along?"

Thomas threw back his head and laughed, and then he pointed at Anthony. "Now, that's funny!"

I touched Thomas's arm. "He's right. C'mon. I'll walk you to your condo."

"No!" he said, pulling his arm away.

I held out my hands. "Do you want me to walk you or not?"

"I'm asking my girlfriend to come home with me!"

Val's mouth fell open, and Marks's eyes bounced between Thomas and me.

I slightly shook my head. "Thomas, we're back in San Diego. The assignment is over."

"So, that's it then?" He stood up, weaving.

Marks stood with him, readying his hands to catch Thomas if he fell.

I stood up, too, motioning to Anthony that we needed the check. He had already printed it out, so he grabbed it from beside the register and placed it on the counter.

I scribbled my name and reached for Thomas's arm. "Okay, let's go."

Thomas pulled his arm away. "You're dumping me, remember?"

"Fine. Can Marks walk you?" I asked.

Thomas pointed at me. "No!" He chuckled, reached for Marks's shoulder, and they walked toward the door.

I blew my hair from my face.

"I want to hear more about this weekend," Val said. "But I'll let it go this time."

We joined the boys on the sidewalk, and then we watched as Marks struggled to keep Thomas walking in a straight line. The four of us took the elevator to the sixth floor, and Val and I watched as Marks fished Thomas's keys out of his pocket and opened his door.

"Okay, buddy. Tell the girls good night."

"Wait." Thomas grabbed the doorjamb while Marks pulled at his middle from inside the condo. "Wait!"

Marks released him, and Thomas nearly fell forward. I reached for him and helped him to stand upright.

"You promised you'd stay with me," he said. The misery in his eyes was unbearable.

I glanced at Val, who was quickly shaking her head, before I turned back to Thomas.

"Thomas…" I began. Then, I looked to Val and Marks. "I've got him. You guys should head home."

"You sure?" Marks asked.

I nodded, and after a few glances over her shoulder, Val took the elevator with Marks to the lobby.

Thomas hugged me, desperately pulling on me. "I'll sleep on the floor. I just feel like a piece of shit. My whole family hates me, and they should. They should."

"C'mon," I said, walking him inside. I kicked the door shut, reached back to lock the bolt, and then helped Thomas to his bed.

He fell onto his back and covered his eyes with his hands. "The room is spinning."

"Put your foot on the floor. That helps."

"My feet are on the floor," he slurred.

I yanked him down and then placed his feet on the rug. "Now, they are."

He began to laugh, and then his eyebrows pulled in. "What did I do? What the fuck did I do, Liis?"

"Hey," I said, climbing into the bed next to him. "Just go to sleep. It will be different tomorrow."

He turned, burying his face into my chest. I reached up for a pillow, propping my head. Thomas sucked in a breath, and I hugged him tight.

"I fucked up," he said. "I really fucked up."

"We'll make it right."

"How can we make it right if you're done with me?"

"Thomas, stop. We'll fix everything tomorrow. Just sleep."

He nodded and then took a deep breath before exhaling slowly. When his breathing evened out, I knew he was asleep. I lifted my hand to glance at my watch, and I rolled my eyes. We would both be exhausted in the morning.

I hugged him again, and then I leaned down to kiss his cheek before slowly drifting off to sleep.

CHAPTER TWENTY-ONE

I TAPPED MY NAILS ON THE COMPUTER as I listened to the recorded conversation coming through my headphones. The Japanese was broken, mostly slang, but Agent Grove had gotten the numbers wrong again. This time, he had even falsely identified a location as a supposed vacant building next to a hospital when it was actually next to a medical professional building seven miles away.

I picked up the receiver of my landline and hit the first speed-dial button.

"Office of the Assistant Special Agent in Charge. Constance speaking."

"Agent Lindy for Agent Maddox, please."

"I'll put you through," Constance said.

Her reply took me off guard. She usually at least checked with him first.

"Liis," Thomas answered. His voice was soft and tinged with surprise.

"I'm listening to these Yakuza recordings. Grove"—I glanced over my shoulder and then away from my open door—"is getting brazen, almost sloppy. He's falsely identifying locations. I feel like something is getting ready to go down."

"I'm working on it."

"We have to remove him before he gets wind of Travis's recruitment anyway. What are we waiting for?"

"A staged accident. That's the only way Tarou won't know we're onto him and Benny. Otherwise, we could jeopardize the entire operation."

"I see."

"What are you doing for lunch?" he asked.

"I, uh…Fuzzy's with Val."

"Okay." He chuckled nervously. "What about dinner?"

I sighed. "I'm playing catch-up. I'll be working late tonight."

"Me, too. I'll take you home, and we can grab take-out on the way."

I looked out the wall of windows to the squad room. Val was on the phone, having no clue that we now had plans for lunch.

"I'll let you know," I said. "The odds of us finishing at the same time are slim."

"Just let me know," Thomas said before the line clicked.

I placed the receiver on its base and sank back into my throne.

Once again, the headphones covered my ears, and I pressed Play on the keyboard.

The morning had felt like any other, except I'd felt tired and woken up alone in Thomas's bed. He had knocked on my door as I was getting dressed for work. When I had opened the door, he'd given me a bagel and cream cheese with a coffee.

The ride to work had been awkward, and my thoughts had led to researching car dealerships and dreading the possibility that I might have to resort to flying back to Chicago and driving my Camry all the way to San Diego.

Just as the recording was getting interesting, my door flew open and then slammed shut. Thomas flicked back the side of his suit jacket and put a hand on his hip, desperately trying to think of something to say.

I yanked off my headphones. "What?" My mind raced with different awful scenarios, all leading back to Thomas's family.

"You're avoiding me, and Constance said you were on the phone with a car dealership when she walked by. What's going on?"

"Uh…I need a car?"

"Why? I drive you to and from work."

"I do go to other places besides work, Thomas."

He walked to my desk and put his palms flat on the smooth wood, looking me in the eyes. "Be straight with me."

"You said you were going to explain more about Camille. How about now?" I asked, crossing my arms.

He looked behind him. "What? Here?"

"The door is closed."

Thomas sat in a chair. "I'm sorry I called you Camille. We were talking about her, tensions were high, and I could hear her and Trent laughing. It was an honest mistake."

"You're right, Jackson. I forgive you."

Thomas's cheeks flushed. "I feel terrible."

"You should."

"You're not really done, Liis, not after one stupid mistake."

"I don't think we ever really got started, did we?"

"I have some pretty strong feelings here. I think you do, too. I know you don't like to be out of your comfort zone, but this is just as frightening for me. I assure you."

"I'm not afraid anymore. I took the leap. You just didn't go with me."

His expression changed. He was looking inside of me, into the depths I couldn't hide. "You're running. I scare the hell out of you."

"Stop."

His jaw muscles danced under his skin. "I won't chase you, Liis. If you don't want me, I'll let you walk."

"Good," I said with a relieved smile. "Saves us both a lot of time."

He begged me with his eyes. "I didn't say I wanted you to."

"Thomas," I said, leaning forward, "I'm busy. Please let me know if you have any questions about my FD-three-oh-two. I'll leave it with Constance by end of day."

He stared at me in disbelief and then stood, turning for the door. He twisted the knob but hesitated, looking over his shoulder. "You can still catch a ride with me to and from work until you figure out the car situation."

"Thank you," I said. "But I've got something worked out with Val."

He shook his head and blinked, and then he opened the door before closing it behind him. He turned right instead of left toward his office, and I knew he was going to the fitness room.

In the time it took Thomas to clear the security doors, Val scurried into my office and sat down. "That looked ugly."

I rolled my eyes. "It's done."

"What's done?"

"We…kind of had a thing over the weekend. It's over."

"Already? He looks miserable. What did you do to him?"

"Why is it automatically my fault?" I snapped. When Val arched an eyebrow, I continued, "I agreed to try something similar to a relationship, and then he admitted to still being in love with Camille. Then, he called me Camille, so…" I played with the pencils in their holder, trying to keep from getting angry about it all over again.

"He called Camille?" she asked, confused.

"No, he called *me* Camille—as in, called me by her name by mistake."

"In bed?" she shrieked.

"No," I said, my face twisting into disgust. "On the beach. We were arguing. I'm still not sure about what."

"Oh, this sounds promising. I guess we should have known two control freaks weren't going to get along."

"That's what he said, too. Oh, by the way, you and I have a lunch date."

"We do?"

"That's what I told Thomas, so yes."

"But I have plans with Marks."

"Oh no, you owe me."

"Fine," she said, resting her elbow on my desk and then pointing at me. "But you're going to give details about the whole weekend."

"Sure. Right after you tell me all about your marriage."

She rolled her eyes. "No!" she whined. "See? This is why I didn't want you to know."

"Realizing that not everyone wants to spill their every thought, feeling, and secret is a good lesson for you to learn. Glad I finally have some leverage."

She glared at me. "You're a bad friend. See you at lunch."

I smiled at her, situating my headphones back onto my ears, and Val returned to her desk.

The rest of the day went on as usual as did the day after that.

Val would wait for me every morning, right outside the building. The better days were when I wouldn't catch Thomas in the elevator. For the most part, he would be polite. He stopped coming to my office, instead directing me through emails from Constance.

We collected evidence against Grove, and in turn, used Tarou's trust in him to gain intelligence. The answers hid within the small talk and smug comments between Grove and Tarou and his associates, like how gullible the Bureau was and how easy our system was to get around if one knew the right person.

Exactly two weeks after Thomas and I had given Polanski the disputably good news about Travis, I found myself in Cutter's alone, bantering with Anthony.

"So, I told him, 'Bitch, you don't even know me,'" he said, cocking his head to one side.

I offered a weak clap and then held up my glass. "Well done."

"Sorry that I got ratchet for a second, but that is what I told him."

"I think you handled it well," I said before taking another sip.

Anthony leaned over and jerked up his head once. "Why don't you come in here with Maddox anymore? Why doesn't Maddox come in here at all anymore?"

"Because the women of the world are systematically ruining his favorite places for him."

"Oh, that's lame. And they say I'm a drama queen." His eyes widened for a beat.

"Who are *they*?"

"You know," he said, dismissively waving his hand. "They." He pointed at me. "You all need to fix it. It's screwing with my tips." He glanced up and then back down. "Uh-oh, Aqua Net, eleven o'clock."

I didn't turn. I didn't need to. Sawyer was breathing in my ear in much less time than it should have taken him to walk to my chosen stool.

"Hey, beautiful."

"They won't take your money at the strip club?" I asked.

He grimaced. "You're in a shitty mood. I know you're not teacher's pet anymore but no need to project your anger."

I took a drink. "What do you know about being teacher's pet? No one likes you."

"Ouch," Sawyer said, offended.

"I'm sorry. That was harsh. But in my defense, you would make at least one friend if you signed your damn papers."

He blinked. "Wait—what are we talking about?"

"Your divorce papers."

"I know, but are you saying we're not friends anymore?"

"We are not," I said before taking another drink.

"Oh, for fuck's sake, Liis. You spend one weekend with Maddox, and you're drinking the Kool-Aid." He shook his head and took a swig from the beer bottle Anthony had set down in front of him. "I'm disappointed."

"Just sign the papers. How hard is that?"

"Contrary to popular belief, ending a marriage is hard."

"Really? I thought it would be easier for a cheater."

"I didn't cheat!"

I arched an eyebrow.

"Her"—he gestured to his eyes and head—"thing was driving me nuts. Do you have any idea what it's like to be with someone and not be allowed to have any secrets?"

"Then, why would you cheat on her? You were basically asking for a divorce, and now, you won't give her one."

He laughed once, chugged his beer, and then set it on the bar. "Because I thought she'd stay out of my head after that."

"That," I said, nodding to Anthony when he set down a fresh Manhattan, "makes you sound like an idiot."

He fingered his bottle. "I was. I was an idiot. But she won't let me fix it."

I craned my neck at him. "You're still in love with Val?"

He kept his eyes on his beer. "Who do you think gave her the bunny on her desk for her birthday? Damn sure wasn't Marks."

"Oh, shit," Anthony said. "I had a bet going with Marks that you were gay."

"Your gaydar is off," I said.

One side of Anthony's mouth curved up. "I bet that he was straight."

Sawyer's nose wrinkled. "Marks thinks I'm gay? What the fuck?"

I cackled, and just as Anthony leaned over to speak, Thomas sat in the stool next to me.

"Anthony needs to tell you that I'm here," Thomas said.

My back stiffened, and my smile faded. "Maddox," I said, greeting him.

"No shade, Maddox," Anthony said. "I just promised I'd have her back from now on."

Thomas looked confused.

"He means, *no offense*," I said.

"Oh," Thomas said.

"The usual?" Anthony asked, seeming annoyed that I'd had to translate.

"I'll have a Jack and Coke tonight," Thomas said.

"You got it."

Sawyer leaned forward. "Bad day, boss?"

Thomas didn't answer. Instead, he stared at his hands clasped in front of him on the bar.

Sawyer and I traded glances.

I continued our conversation, "Does she know?"

"Of course she knows. She knows everything," Sawyer said with a grimace.

"It might just be time to move on."

A couple of young guys pushed through the door. I'd never seen them here before, but they walked with their chests puffed out and their arms swinging. I began to turn around as one of them gave me a once-over.

"Nice blazer, Yoko," he said.

Sawyer put his foot on the ground and began to stand, but I touched his arm.

"Ignore them. The Casbah had a rock concert tonight. They're probably coming from there and looking for a fight. Look at the big one's shirt."

Sawyer quickly glanced in the pair's direction, pointing out the two-inch long rip around the collar of the man's T-shirt. We ordered another round. Thomas finished his drink, tossed a bill on the bar, and left without a word.

"That was weird," Sawyer said. "He hasn't been in here in how long?"

"Over two weeks," Anthony said.

Sawyer spoke, "And he shows up, has one drink, and leaves."

"Doesn't he usually only have one drink?" I asked.

Anthony nodded. "But never when he has that look on his face."

I turned toward the door, seeing the ripped T-shirt guy and his friend leaving. "That didn't last long."

"I heard them say they were bored. Apparently, the service was too slow," Anthony said with a wink.

"You're brilliant," I said with a grin.

"You should talk to Val one more time, Sawyer. Lay it all out on the table. If she doesn't go for it though, you need to move out, and you need to sign those papers. You're not being fair to her."

"You're right. I hate you, but you're right. And no matter what you say, Lindy, we're still friends."

"Fine."

Sawyer and I tabbed out, said good-bye to Anthony, and then walked across the dark room, pushing out the door. The sidewalk was well lit, traffic was normal, but something was off.

Sawyer touched my arm.

"You, too?" I asked.

We carefully approached the corner, and someone groaned.

Sawyer meant to take a quick peek around, but he stared, and his mouth fell open. "Oh, shit!"

I followed him and immediately pulled out my cell phone. The two men from the bar were lying in matching puddles of blood.

"Nine-one-one. What is your emergency?"

"I have two males, early to mid-twenties, badly beaten on the sidewalk in Midtown. They're both going to need an ambulance on the scene."

Sawyer checked them both. "This one's unresponsive," he said.

"They're both breathing. One is unresponsive."

I gave her the address and then pressed End.

Sawyer glanced around. A middle-aged couple was walking in the opposite direction on the next block, but other than them and a homeless man digging in the trash on the corner to the north, the block was empty. I saw no one who looked suspicious.

Sirens echoed in the distance.

Sawyer shoved his hands in his pants pockets. "I guess they found the fight they were looking for."

"Maybe it was the people they had a run-in with earlier?"

Sawyer shrugged. "Not my jurisdiction."

"Funny."

A police cruiser arrived within minutes, followed soon after by an ambulance. We told them what we knew, and once we offered them credentials, we were free to leave.

Sawyer walked me to the lobby and gave me a hug.

"Sure you don't want me to walk you home?" I asked. "Whoever did that could still be out there."

Sawyer chuckled. "Shut up, Lindy."

"Good night. See you tomorrow."

"Nope. I'll be out."

"Oh, right. The, uh…the thing," I said. My head was fuzzy. I was glad we'd decided to leave the bar when we did.

"I'm tailing one of our Vegas sources, Arturo."

"Benny's guy? Why is he in San Diego?" I asked.

"Benny sent him to visit his new Eastern family. I'm making sure he stays on the straight and narrow. I don't want the Yakuza guys to scare him into disclosing or alerting them to our interest."

"Sounds very official."

"It always is. Night."

Sawyer pushed out of the lobby doors, and I turned to press the elevator button. It was smudged with fresh blood. I glanced around and then used the inside of my blazer to clean it.

The doors slid open, the chime pleasant and welcoming, but when I stepped inside, my heart sank. The button for the sixth floor was smeared with blood as well.

Again, I used my blazer to hide the evidence, and then I waited impatiently for the doors to open. I stomped out and walked straight to Thomas's door, banging on the metal. When he didn't answer, I banged again.

"Who is it?" Thomas asked from the other side.

"Liis. Open the fuck up."

A chain rattled, the bolt lock clicked, and then Thomas opened his door. I pushed through, shouldering past him, and then twirled around, crossing my arms.

Thomas had an ice pack on his right hand and a bloody bandage on his left.

"Christ! What did you do?" I said, reaching for his bandage.

I carefully peeled it away from his weeping raw knuckles and then looked up at him.

"The racist bastards insulted you."

"So, you tried to beat them to death?" I shrieked.

"No, that came after I heard them casually mention that they hoped your route home included a dark alley."

I sighed. "C'mon. I'll clean you up."

"I got it."

"Wrapping and icing doesn't constitute cleaning. You're going to get an infection in your joints. Does that sound like fun?"

Thomas frowned.

"Okay then."

Thomas and I went into his bathroom. He sat on the edge of the tub, holding up both of his hands in loose fists.

"First-aid kit?"

He nodded toward the sink. "Underneath."

I pulled out a clear plastic container, unsnapped it, and opened it wide, poking through the various items. "Peroxide?"

Thomas recoiled.

"You can punch two full-grown men until the skin sheds off your knuckles, but you can't handle a few seconds of a fizzy burning sensation?"

"In the medicine cabinet. The mirror pulls open."

"I know. Mine, too," I deadpanned.

"I tried to walk home without—"

"Attacking them?"

"Some people are belligerent, predatory assholes their entire lives until one person comes along and beats the shit out of them. It gives them a new perspective."

"Is that what you're calling it? You think you did them a favor."

He frowned. "I did the world a favor."

I poured the hydrogen peroxide over his injuries, and he sucked air through his teeth as he jerked his hands back.

I sighed. "I just can't believe you lost your shit like that over a stupid insult and an empty threat."

Thomas leaned his face toward his shoulder and used it to wipe his cheek, smearing two small specks of blood.

"You should probably bathe in this," I said, holding up the big brown bottle in my hands.

"Why?"

I grabbed tissue from the toilet paper roll and soaked it in the disinfectant. "Because I'm fairly certain that's not your blood."

Thomas looked up, seeming bored.

"I'm sorry. Would you like me to leave?" I asked.

"Actually, I would."

"No!" I snapped.

"Oh! *That* insults you."

I dabbed at his wounds with a clean cotton ball. "Strangers can't hurt my feelings, Thomas. People I care about can."

His shoulders sagged. He suddenly looked too tired to argue.

"What were you doing at Cutter's?" I asked.

"I'm a regular there."

I frowned. "You haven't been."

"I needed a drink."

"Bad Monday?" I asked, wondering if there was ever a good one.

He hesitated. "I called Travis on Friday."

"April Fools' Day?" I asked. Thomas gave me a few seconds. "Oh! His birthday."

"He hung up on me."

"Ouch."

Right when I said the word, Thomas jerked his hand back.

"Son of a—" He pressed his lips together, the veins in his neck swelling, as he strained.

"Sorry." I flinched.

"I miss you," Thomas said quietly. "I'm trying to keep it professional at work, but I can't stop thinking about you."

"You've been kind of a bear. People are likening it to the days just post-Camille."

He laughed once without humor. "There's no comparison. This is much, much worse."

I concentrated on wrapping his wounds. "Let's just be glad that we didn't let this get too far."

He nodded. "You should definitely be glad. I wasn't that smart."

I let my hands fall to my lap. "What are you talking about? You told me two weeks ago that you couldn't love me."

"Liis...do you have feelings for me?"

"You know I do."

"Do you love me?"

I stared into his desperate eyes for a long time. The more seconds that passed, the more hopeless he looked.

I let out a faltering breath. "I don't want to be in love, Thomas."

He looked down at the bandages on his hands, already dotted red with his blood. "You didn't answer my question."

"No."

"You're lying. How can you have such a strong personality and be so fucking afraid?"

"So what?" I snapped. "You would be scared, too, if I told you I was still in love with Jackson and you were way, *way* out of your emotional comfort zone."

"That's not fair."

I lifted my chin. "I don't have to be fair to you, Thomas. I just have to be fair to me." I stood and took a step backward toward the door.

He shook his head and chuckled. "You, Liis Lindy, are most definitely my payback."

CHAPTER TWENTY-TWO

THE STAIRS SEEMED PREFERABLE to taking the elevator one floor down. I trudged down to my floor and passed my door to walk the few steps to the window at the end of the hallway.

The corner across the street was smeared with blood, but no one seemed to notice. The people who walked by had no idea about the violence that had occurred, not even an hour before, in the space they were passing through.

A couple stopped just a few feet from the largest stain, arguing. The woman looked both ways and then crossed the street, and I recognized her just before she slipped beneath the awning of our lobby. Marks followed her, and I sighed, knowing they would both be stepping off the elevator minutes later.

I went to my door and unlocked it, and then I waited in the open doorway. The elevator chimed, and the doors revealed my friend looking angrier than I'd ever seen her.

She stepped out and then stopped abruptly, elbowing Marks when he ran into her. "Are you leaving?" she asked me.

"No. Just getting home." I held the door open. "Come in."

She passed by, and then Marks paused, waiting for my permission. I nodded, and he followed her to the couch.

I shut the door and turned, crossing my arms. "I am not in the mood to Dr. Phil you two. I can't figure out my own shit." I raked my hair away from my face, and then I walked over to the chair, scooping up the folded throw and holding it in my lap as I sat down.

"You agree with me, don't you, Liis?" Marks asked. "She needs to kick him out."

"He won't leave," Val said, exasperated.

"Then, I'll make him leave," Marks growled.

I rolled my eyes. "C'mon, Marks. You know the law. He is her husband. If the cops came, you would be the one asked to leave."

Marks's jaw worked beneath the skin, and then he looked beyond my kitchen. "You have a second bedroom. You've invited her."

"She doesn't want to lose her condo," I said.

Val's eyes widened. "That's what I've told him."

"I don't want you living with him! It's fucking weird!" Marks said.

"Joel, I'm handling this," Val said. "If you don't want to stick around, I understand."

I narrowed my eyes. "Why are you two here?"

Marks sighed. "I came to pick her up for dinner. He made a big deal. Usually, I wait for her outside, but I thought I'd be a fucking gentleman for once. He made a scene. Who's she pissed at? Me."

"Why do we do this to ourselves?" I asked, mostly to myself. "We're grown adults. Love makes us so stupid."

"He doesn't love me," Val said.

"Yes, I do," Marks said, looking at her.

She slowly turned to him. "You do?"

"I chased you for months, and I'm still chasing you. You think this is a casual fling for me? I love you."

Val's face fell, and her lip jutted out. "I love you, too."

They hugged each other and then began to kiss.

I looked up at the ceiling, contemplating a tantrum.

"Sorry," Val said, fixing her lipstick.

"It's fine," I deadpanned.

"We should probably get going," Marks said. "We barely got a reservation. I don't want to have to drive around looking for a decent meal at nine thirty at night."

I forced a smile and then walked to the door, opening it wide.

"Sorry," Val whispered as she passed.

I shook my head. "It's fine."

I shut the door, walked straight back to my bedroom, and fell face-first onto my bed.

Val and Marks had made finding a solution look so easy, figuring it out even though Val had been sharing a condo with Sawyer for over a year. I was miserable living an entire floor below

Thomas. But our problems seemed more complicated than living with an ex. I loved a man who I couldn't love, who loved someone else but loved me more.

Love could kiss my ass.

The next morning, I was relieved not to see Thomas in the elevator.

As the weeks passed, it became less of a worry and more of a memory.

Thomas would make sure to arrive at work before me and to stay far later. The meetings were short and tense, and if we were given an assignment, Val, Sawyer, and I hated to come back to Constance empty-handed.

The rest of Squad Five kept their heads down, scowling at me when they thought I wouldn't notice. The days were long. Just being in the squad room was stressful, and I had quickly become everyone's least favorite supervisor in the building.

Eight straight days went by without any run-ins with Thomas at Cutter's, and then another week passed.

Anthony had given me the number of a friend who knew someone who shipped vehicles, and once I'd called and mentioned Anthony's name, the price dropped in half.

By May, my Camry had been delivered, and I was able to explore more of San Diego. Val and I went to the zoo, and I began systematically visiting all the beaches, always alone. It became sort of a thing.

It didn't take me long to fall in love with the city, and I wondered if falling quick was going to start being a thing with me, too. That was squashed after several outings with Val as I began to understand that every interaction with a man just reminded me of how much I missed Thomas.

One hot, sticky Saturday night, I pulled into the Kansas City Barbeque parking lot and shoved my keys into my purse. Even in a sundress, I could feel the sweat dripping from under my breasts and down to my stomach. It was a heat only the ocean or a pool could alleviate.

My skin was slick, and my hair was pulled into a loose knot at the top of my head. The humidity reminded me of the island, and I needed to distract myself.

I pushed the door open and froze. The first thing in my line of sight was Thomas standing in front of the dartboard with a blonde, holding her in one arm as he tried to help her aim a dart with the other.

The moment we made eye contact, I turned on my heels and walked quickly to my car. Running was not conducive in wedges. Before I could even clear the front patio, someone rounded the corner, and I plowed into him, getting knocked off my footing.

Before I hit the ground, large hands swooped me up.

"What the hell is your hurry?" Marks said, releasing me once I'd found my balance.

"Sorry. I was just coming in here for a late dinner."

"Oh," he said with a knowing smile. "You saw Maddox in there."

"I, uh…can find somewhere else to eat."

"Liis?" Thomas called from the doorway.

"She doesn't want to eat here since you're here," Marks yelled back, cupping my shoulder.

Everyone dining on the patio turned to look at me.

I pushed Marks's hand away and lifted my chin. "Fuck off."

I stomped toward my car.

Marks called after me, "You've been hanging out with Val too long!"

I didn't turn around. Instead, I reached into my purse for my keys and pressed the keyless entry.

Before I could open the door, I felt hands on me again.

"Liis," Thomas said, breathless from jogging across the parking lot.

I jerked my arm away and yanked the door open.

"She's just a friend. She worked in Constance's position for Polanski when he was the ASAC."

I shook my head. "You don't have to explain."

He pushed his hands into his pocket. "Yeah, I do. You're upset."

"Not because I want to be." I looked up at him. "I'll figure it out. Until then, the avoidance thing is working for me."

Thomas nodded once. "I'm sorry. Upsetting you is the last thing I want to do. You, um…you look gorgeous. Were you meeting someone?"

I made a face. "No, I'm not meeting someone. I'm not dating. I don't date," I snapped. "Not that I don't expect you to," I said, motioning to the restaurant.

I began to sit in the driver's seat, but Thomas gently held my arm.

"We're not dating," he said. "I was just helping her with darts. Her boyfriend is in there."

I glared at him, dubious. "Great. I have to go. I haven't eaten."

"Eat here," he said. He offered a hopeful small smile. "I can teach you how to play, too."

"I'd rather not be one of many. Thank you."

"You're not. You never have been."

"No, just one of two."

"Whether you believe it or not, Liis…you've been the only. There has never been anyone else but you."

I sighed. "I'm sorry. I shouldn't have brought it up. I'll see you at work on Monday. We have an early meeting."

"Yep," he said, taking a step back.

I slid into the driver's seat and then stabbed the ignition with the key. The Camry made a dainty growl, and then I backed up and pulled away, leaving Thomas alone in the parking lot.

The first lit drive-through sign I saw, I pulled in and waited in line. Once I received my non-Fuzzy burger and small fries, I drove the rest of the way home.

My sack crinkled as I shut my car door, and then I walked to the lobby doors, feeling abysmal that my brilliant plan for distraction couldn't have been more of a failure.

"Hey!" Val called from across the street.

I looked over at her, and she waved.

"You're a hot bitch! Come to Cutter's with me!"

I lifted my sack.

"Dinner?" she yelled.

"Kind of!" I called back.

"Fuzzy's?"

"No!"

"Gross!" she yelled. "Liquor will be more satisfying!"

I sighed and then glanced each way before crossing the street. Val hugged me, and then her smile faded when she noticed my expression.

"What's wrong?"

"I went to KC Barbeque. Thomas was there with a very tall and pretty blonde."

Val pursed her lips. "You're way better than her. Everyone knows she's a total skank."

"Do you know her?" I asked. "She is Polanski's assistant."

"Oh," Val said. "No, Allie is super sweet, but we're going to pretend she's a skank."

"*Allie?*" I whined, puffing out a breath like the wind had been knocked out of me. The name sounded exactly like the perfect girl who Thomas could fall in love with. "Kill me now."

She hooked her arm around me. "I'm packing heat. I can if you want."

I leaned my head onto her shoulder. "You're a good friend."

"I know," Val said, guiding me to Cutter's.

CHAPTER TWENTY-THREE

I FORCED A SMILE FOR AGENT TREVINO while stopped at check-in, and then I steered my Camry toward the parking garage. I was already in a foul mood from the weekend, and the fact that it was Monday wasn't helping matters.

Thomas was right. I did hate driving on the freeway, and that annoyed me as well. I found a parking space and pushed the gear forward into park. Then, I grabbed my purse and brown leather messenger bag. Shoving the door open, I stepped out to see Agent Grove struggling to get out of his blue sedan.

"Morning," I said.

He simply nodded, and we headed for the elevator bay. I pressed the button, trying not to tip him off that I was nervous to have him standing behind me.

He coughed into his hand, and I used that as an excuse to glance back.

My sleek ponytail whipped over my right shoulder as I did so. "Summer colds are the worst."

"Allergies," he grumbled, almost to himself.

The elevator opened, and I stepped on, followed by Grove. His pale-blue shirt and too-small tie made his expansive midsection look even more pronounced.

"How are the interviews going?" I asked.

Grove's wiry mustache twitched. "It's a little early to engage in chitchat, Agent Lindy."

I raised my eyebrows and then faced forward, holding my hands in front of me. The seventh floor chimed, and I stepped into the hallway. I glanced back at Grove, who glared at me until the doors slid shut.

Val merged with me as I approached the security doors. "Open the door, open the door, open the—"

"We're not finished," Marks said with a grimace.

Val instantly switched on a smile and turned around. "For now, we are."

"No, we're not," Marks said, his bright blue eyes flaming.

I pushed open the door, and Val took a step backward. "But we are...so we are." When the door closed in Marks's face, she turned back around and squeezed my arm. "Thank you."

"What was that about?"

She rolled her eyes and puffed out a breath. "He still wants me to move out of my condo."

"Well...I wouldn't like my boyfriend living with his wife either."

"Marks is not my boyfriend, and Sawyer is not my husband."

"Your status with Marks is debatable, but you are definitely still married to Sawyer. He hasn't signed the papers yet?"

We turned into my office, and Val shut the door before falling into a club chair.

"No! He came home from Cutter's one night, going on and on about how Davies was a mistake."

"Wait—Agent Davies?"

"Yes."

"But you..."

Val's nose wrinkled, and when recognition hit, she jumped out of the chair. "No! Ew! *Ew!* Even if I were a lesbian, I'd much prefer ChapStick to lipstick. Agent Davies looks like a reject from a Cher look-alike contest with all that"—she circled her face with her index finger—"stuff on her face."

"So, when you said you experienced both Sawyer and Davies, you meant because he'd cheated on you with her."

"Yes!" she said, still disgusted. She sat back in the chair, keeping her butt on the edge, while letting her shoulders fall back against the cushion.

"If you say that to anyone else, you might consider clarifying."

Val let that thought simmer, and then she closed her eyes, her shoulders sagging. "Shit."

"You're not going to forgive Sawyer?" I asked.

"God, no."

"What keeps you there, Val? I know it's your condo, but that can't be all there is to it."

She lifted her arms before letting them slap to her thighs. "That's it."

"Lie."

"Well, now," she said, sitting up and crossing her arms, "look who is honing her craft."

"More like common sense," I said. "Now, if you're going to be a bad friend, shoo. I have work to do." I shuffled papers, pretending to be disinterested.

"I can't forgive him," she said, her voice small. "I've tried. I could have forgiven anything else."

"Really?"

She nodded.

"Have you told him that?"

She picked at her nails. "Pretty much."

"You need to tell him, Val. He still thinks there's a chance."

"I'm dating Marks. Sawyer still thinks I'm hung up on him?"

"You are *married* to him."

Val sighed. "You're right. It's time. But I warn you, if I put down the hammer and he doesn't budge, you might have a new roommate."

I shrugged. "I'll help you pack."

Val left with a smile, and I opened my laptop, input the password, and began scrolling through my emails. Three from Constance marked *Urgent* caught my eye.

I directed the mouse to the first email and clicked.

AGENT LINDY,

ASAC MADDOX REQUESTS A MEETING AT 1000.
PLEASE CLEAR YOUR SCHEDULE, AND HAVE
YOUR CASE FILE IN HAND.

CONSTANCE

I opened the second.

AGENT LINDY,

ASAC MADDOX REQUESTS THE MEETING TO BE
MOVED TO 0900. PLEASE BE PROMPT, AND HAVE
YOUR CASE FILE IN HAND.

CONSTANCE

I opened the third.

AGENT LINDY,

ASAC MADDOX INSISTS THAT YOU REPORT TO
HIS OFFICE THE MOMENT YOU RECEIVE THIS
EMAIL. PLEASE HAVE YOUR CASE FILE IN HAND.

CONSTANCE

I looked at my watch. It was barely eight a.m. I grabbed the mouse and clicked through recent documents, printing the new intel I had accumulated. I grabbed the file folder, snatched the papers off the printer, and ran down the hall.

"Hi, Constance," I said, winded.

She looked up at me and smiled, batting her long black lashes. "He can see you now."

"Thank you," I breathed, walking past her.

Thomas was sitting with his back to me, staring at the gorgeous view outside of his corner office.

"Agent Maddox," I said, trying to sound normal. "I'm sorry. I just saw the email...s. I brought the case file. I have a few more—"

"Have a seat, Lindy."

I blinked and then did as he'd commanded. The three mysterious picture frames were still on his desk, but the center frame was lying on its face.

"I can't make them wait any longer," Thomas said. "The Office of the Inspector General wants an arrest."

"Travis?"

He turned. The skin under his eyes was purple. He looked like he'd lost weight. "No, no...Grove. Travis will start his training soon. If Grove hears from Benny or Tarou about Travis...well, we'll be dead in the water anyway.

"Constance will send everything you have to the US Attorney's office. They're going to stage an armed robbery at the gas station he frequents. He'll be shot. Witnesses will testify that he was killed.

"Then, Tarou and Benny will think they're shit out of luck instead of packing up and destroying evidence because Grove was busted and all roads lead to their criminal activity."

"Sounds like a home run, sir."

Thomas winced at my cold response and then sat behind his desk. We remained in awkward silence for a solid ten seconds, and then Thomas made the smallest gesture toward the door.

"Thank you, Agent Lindy. That will be all."

I nodded and stood up. I walked to the door, but I couldn't leave. Against my better judgment, I turned, holding my free hand in a fist and tightly gripping the file folder so that I wouldn't drop it.

He was reading the top page of a stack, holding a highlighter in one hand with the cap in the other.

"Are you taking care of yourself, sir?"

Thomas blanched. "Am I...excuse me?"

"Taking care of yourself. You seem tired."

"I'm fine, Lindy. That will be all."

I gritted my teeth and then took a step forward. "Because if you need to talk—"

He let both hands fall to his desk. "I don't need to talk, and even if I did, you would be the last person I would talk to."

I nodded once. "I'm sorry, sir."

"*Stop*...calling me that," he said, lowering his voice at the end.

I held my hands in front of me. "I feel it's no longer appropriate to call you Thomas."

"Agent Maddox or Maddox is fine." He looked down at his paper. "Now, please...please leave, Lindy."

"Why did you call me in here if you didn't want to see me? You could have just as easily had Constance take care of it."

"Because, once in a while, Liis, I just need to see your face. I need to hear your voice. Some days are tougher for me than others."

I swallowed and then walked toward his desk. He braced himself for what I might do next.

"Don't do that," I said. "Don't make me feel guilty. I tried not to...this is exactly what I didn't want."

"I know. I accept full responsibility."

"This isn't my fault."

"I just said that," he said, sounding exhausted.

"You all but asked for this. You wanted your feelings for me to replace your feelings for Camille. You needed someone closer to blame because you couldn't blame her. You have to get along because she's going to be family, and I'm just someone you work with…someone you knew would move on."

Thomas seemed too emotionally drained to argue. "Christ, Liis, do you really think I planned this? How many ways do I have to tell you? What I felt for you, what I still feel for you, makes my feelings for Camille insignificant."

I covered my face. "I feel like I sound like a broken record."

"You do," he said, his voice flat.

"You think this is easy for me?" I asked.

"It certainly seems that way."

"Well, it's not. I thought…not that it matters now, but that weekend, I hoped that I could change. I thought, for two wounded people, if we were invested enough, if we felt enough, then we could make it."

"We're not wounded, Liis. We're matching scars."

I blinked. "If we ran into unfamiliar territory, which is everything for me, we could adjust for variables, you know? But I can't throw away every plan I have for my future on the hope that, one day, you'll stop being sad because you're not with her." I felt tears burning my eyes. "If I were going to give you my future, I'd need you to move on from the past." I grabbed the flat frame and held it in Thomas's face, forcing him to look at it.

His eyes left mine, and when he scanned over the photograph beneath the glass, one side of his mouth turned up.

Incensed, I turned the picture around, and then my mouth fell open. Thomas and I were inside the frame together, a black-and-white snapshot, the one Falyn had taken of us in St. Thomas. He was squeezing me against him, kissing my cheek, and I was smiling like forever was real.

I picked up the other frame and looked at it. It was all five Maddox brothers. I picked up the last one to see his parents.

"I loved her first," Thomas said. "But you, Liis…you are the last woman I will ever love."

I stood there, speechless, and then retreated toward the door.

"Can I…have my pictures back?" he asked.

I realized then that I had left the file on his desk, and instead, I'd walked off with the pictures in my hands. I slowly walked over to him. He held out his hand, and I returned the frames.

"I'll just give this to Constance," I said, picking up the file, feeling disoriented. I turned on my heels and bolted.

"Liis," he called after me.

The moment I breached the door, I practically tossed the file at Constance.

"Have a good day, Agent Lindy," she said, her voice carrying throughout the squad room.

I withdrew to my office and sat down in my chair, putting my head in my hands. Seconds later, Val burst in from the hall, and Marks came in after her, slamming the door behind him.

I looked up.

Val pointed at him. "Stop! You can't chase me all over the building!"

"I'll stop following you when you start giving me straight answers!" he yelled.

"What the hell is wrong with everyone today? Has this entire office gone crazy?" I yelled.

"I've already given you an answer!" Val said, ignoring me. "I told you I would talk to him tonight!"

Sawyer popped his head in, knocking as he did so. "Boss?"

"Get out!" Marks, Val, and I yelled in unison.

"Okay then," Sawyer said, ducking out.

"And then what?" Marks asked.

"If he won't move out, I will," Val said as if the words had been punched out of her.

"Thank Christ!" Marks yelled to an invisible audience, pointing all his fingers in Val's general direction. "A straight fucking answer!"

Thomas blew in. "What the hell is with all the shouting?"

I covered my face again.

"Are you all right, Liis? What happened to her, Val? Is she all right?" Thomas asked.

Marks spoke first, "I'm sorry, sir. Are you…are you okay, Lindy?"

"I'm fine!" I shrieked. "I just need you toddlers to get the fuck out of my office!"

All three of them froze, staring at me in disbelief.

"Get out!"

Val and Marks left first, and then after some reluctance, Thomas left me alone, closing the door behind him.

The rest of Squad Five stared at me. I walked over to the glass wall, flipped them all both of my middle fingers, shot off several strong words in Japanese, and then pulled the blinds closed.

CHAPTER TWENTY-FOUR

I READJUSTED MY CELL PHONE, so it sat better between my cheek and my shoulder while I tried to cook. "Hang on, Mom. Just a sec," I said, resorting to setting the phone on the cabinet.

"You know I hate the speakerphone." Her voice wafted with the spices in the air. "Liis, take me off the speakerphone."

"I'm the only one here, Mom. No one else can hear you. I need both hands."

"At least you're cooking for yourself and not eating that processed poison every night. Have you gained any weight?"

"I've lost a few pounds actually," I said, smiling even though she couldn't see me.

"Not too much I hope," she grumbled.

I laughed. "Mom, you're never happy."

"I just miss you. When are you coming home? You're not going to wait until Christmas, are you? What are you cooking? Is it any good?"

I added broccoli, carrots, and water to the hot canola oil and then pushed them around the skillet as it sizzled. "I miss you, too. I don't know. I'll look at my schedule, chicken and vegetable stir-fry, and hopefully, it will be amazing."

"Have you mixed the sauce? You have to mix it first, you know, to let it blend and breathe."

"Yes, Mom. It's sitting on the counter next to me."

"Did you add anything extra? It's good just the way I make it."

I giggled. "No, Mom. It's your sauce."

"Why are you eating so late?"

"I'm on West Coast time."

"Still, it's nine there. You shouldn't eat so late."

"I work late," I said with a smile.

"They're not keeping you too busy at work, are they?"

"I'm keeping me too busy. I like it that way though. You know that."

"You're not walking alone at night, are you?"

"Yes!" I teased. "In just my underwear!"

"Liis!" she scolded.

I laughed out loud, and it felt good. It seemed as if I hadn't smiled in a long time.

"Liis?" she said, concern in her voice.

"I'm here."

"Are you homesick?"

"Just for you guys. Tell Daddy I say hi."

"Patrick? Patrick! Liis says hello."

I could hear my father from somewhere in the room. "Hi, baby! Miss you! Be good!"

"He started the fish oil pills this week. Gives him gas," she said.

I could hear the scowl in her voice, and I laughed again.

"I miss you both. Good-bye, Mom."

I pressed the End button with my pinkie, and then I added in the chicken and cabbage. Just before adding the pea pods and sauce, someone knocked on the door. I waited, thinking I'd imagined it, but the knocking happened again, louder this time.

"Oh no. Oh, crap," I said to myself, turning the heat almost all the way down.

I wiped my hands on a dish towel and jogged to the door. I peeked through the peephole, and then I scrambled to open the chain and bolt lock, grabbing at it like a madwoman.

"Thomas," I whispered, unable to hide my utter shock.

He was standing there in a plain white T-shirt and workout shorts. He hadn't even taken the time to put on shoes, gauging by his bare feet.

He began to speak but thought better of it.

"What are you doing here?" I asked.

"It smells good in there," he said, taking a whiff.

"Yeah." I turned toward the kitchen. "Stir-fry. I have plenty, if you're hungry."

"It's just you?" he asked, looking past me.

I chuckled. "Of course it's just me. Who else would be here?"

He stared at me for several seconds. "You're wearing my hoodie."

I looked down. "Oh. Do you want it back?"

He shook his head. "No. No way. I just didn't realize you still wore it."

"I wear it a lot. It makes me feel better sometimes."

"I, uh…needed to speak to you. The office is buzzing about your outburst."

"Just mine? I'm the emotional one because I'm a woman. Typical," I muttered.

"Liis, you spoke in Japanese at the office. Everyone knows."

I blanched. "I'm sorry. I was upset, and I…shit."

"The S.A.C. gave the green light to move forward with the plan to remove Grove."

"Good." I hugged my middle, feeling vulnerable.

"But they haven't found him."

"What? What about Sawyer? I thought he was the Master of Surveillance. Doesn't he keep tabs on Grove?"

"Sawyer's out there, looking for Grove now. Don't worry. Sawyer will find him. Do you…do you want me to stay with you?"

I looked at him. His expression was begging me to say yes. I wanted him here, but it would only mean long conversations that would lead to arguments, and we were both tired of fighting.

I shook my head. "No, I'll be okay."

The skin around his eyes softened. He took a step and reached up, cupping each side of my face. He gazed into my eyes, his inner conflict swirling in his twin hazel-green pools.

"Fuck it," he said. He leaned in and touched his lips to mine.

I dropped the dish towel and reached up to grip his T-shirt in my fists, but he was in no hurry to leave. He took his time tasting me, feeling the warmth of our mouths melding together. His lips were confident and commanding but giving way as my mouth pressed against them. Just when I thought he might pull away, he wrapped both arms around me.

Thomas kissed me as if he had needed me for ages, and at the same time, he kissed me good-bye. It was longing and sadness and anger, twisted but controlled, in a sweet soft kiss. When he finally released me, I felt myself leaning forward, needing more.

He blinked a few times. "I tried not to. I'm sorry."

Then, he walked away.

"No, it's…it's fine," I said to an empty hallway.

I closed the door and leaned against it, still tasting him. Where I stood still smelled like him. For the first time since I'd moved in, my apartment didn't feel like a sanctuary or the representation of my independence. It just felt lonely. The stir-fry didn't smell as good as it had minutes before. I looked over at the girls in the Takato painting, remembering that Thomas had helped me hang them—not even they could make me feel better.

I stomped over to the stovetop, switched it off, and grabbed my purse and keys.

The elevator seemed to be taking an extraordinary amount of time to reach the lobby, and I bounced in anticipation. I needed out of the building, out from under Thomas's condo. I needed to be sitting in front of Anthony with a Manhattan in my hand, forgetting about Grove and Thomas and what I'd refused to let myself have.

I looked both ways and crossed the street in wide strides, but just as I reached the sidewalk, a large hand encircled my arm, stopping me in my tracks.

"Where the hell are you going?" Thomas asked.

I yanked back my arm and shoved him away. He barely moved, but I still covered my mouth and then held my hands at my chest.

"Oh God! I'm sorry! It was a knee-jerk reaction."

Thomas frowned. "You can't just go walking around alone right now, Liis, not until we get a location on Grove."

A couple stood ten feet away on the corner, waiting for the light to change. Other than that, we were alone.

I puffed out a breath of relief, my heart still racing. "You can't just go around grabbing people like that. You're lucky you didn't end up like drunk Joe."

Thomas's smile slowly stretched across his face. "Sorry. I heard your door slam, and I was worried you'd risk going outside because of me."

"Possibly," I said, ashamed.

Thomas braced himself, already hurting over his next words. "I'm not trying to make you miserable. You'd think I could stay busy enough just doing that to myself."

My face fell. "I don't want you to be miserable. But that's what this is—miserable."

"Then"—he reached out for me—"let's go back. We can talk about this all night if you want. I'll explain it as many times as you want. We can lay down some ground rules. I pushed too hard before. I see that now. We can take it slow. We can compromise."

I had never wanted something so much in my life. "No."

"*No?*" he said, devastated. "Why?"

My eyes glossed over, and I looked down, forcing tears to spill down my cheeks. "Because I want it so bad, and that scares me so much."

The quick onset of emotion surprised me, but it set off something in Thomas.

"Baby, look at me," he said, using his thumb to gently lift my chin until our eyes met. "It can't be any worse together than it is apart."

"But we're at an impasse. We have the same argument over and over. We just have to get over it."

Thomas shook his head.

"You're still trying to get over Camille," I thought aloud, "and it might take a while, but it's possible. And no one gets everything they want, right?"

"I don't just want you, Liis. I need you. That doesn't go away."

He pinched the sides of my shirt and touched his forehead to mine. He smelled so good, musky and clean. Just the tiny touch of his fingers on my clothes made me want to melt into him.

I scanned his eyes, unable to respond.

"You want me to say that I'm over her? I'm over her," he said, his voice growing more desperate with every word.

I shook my head, glancing down the dark street. "I don't just want you to say it. I want it to be true."

"Liis." He waited until I looked up at him. "Please believe me. I did love someone before, but I have never loved anyone the way I love you."

I sank into him, letting him wrap his arms around me. I allowed myself to let go, to give control to whatever forces had brought us to that place. I had two choices. I could walk away from Thomas and somehow tolerate the heartache I felt every day from being without him. Or I could take a huge risk on just faith with no predictions, calculations, or certainty.

Thomas loved me. He needed me. Maybe I wasn't the first woman he'd loved, and maybe the kind of love a Maddox man felt lasted forever, but I needed him, too. I wasn't the first, but I would be the last. That didn't make me the second prize. It made me his forever.

A loud popping noise echoed from across the dim street. The brick behind me splintered into a hundred pieces in every direction.

I turned and looked up, seeing a small cloud of dust floating in the air above my left shoulder and a hole in the brick.

"What the hell?" Thomas asked. His eyes took in every window above us and then settled on the empty road between us and our building.

Grove strode across the street with his arm outstretched in front of him, holding a Bureau-issued pistol in his trembling hand. Thomas angled himself in a protective stance, covering my body with his.

He glowered at our assailant. "Put your sidearm on the ground, Grove, and I won't fucking kill you."

Grove halted, only twenty yards and a parallel-parked car between us. "I saw you sprinting out of your building to catch Agent Lindy—in your bare feet. I doubt you thought to grab your gun. Did you tuck it into your shorts before you left?"

For a greasy-looking, pudgy, short man, he was awfully condescending.

Grove's mustache twitched, and he smiled, revealing a mouthful of teeth well on their way to rotting. It was true. Evil ate people from the inside out.

"You sold me out, Lindy," Grove sneered.

"It was me," Thomas said, slowly bending his elbows to hold up his hands. "I brought her here because I was suspicious of your intel."

Two men walked around the corner and froze.

"Oh, shit!" one of them said before they spun around and ran back the way they'd come.

I slowly reached into my purse, using Thomas's body to hide my movement.

Grove's gun went off, and Thomas jerked. He looked down and held his hand to his lower right abdomen.

"Thomas?" I shrieked.

He grunted, but refused to move out of the way. "You're not walking away from this," Thomas said, his voice strained. "Those guys are calling the police right now. But you can flip, Grove. Give us the information you have on Yakuza."

Grove's eyes glossed over. "I'm dead anyway. Stupid bitch," he said, aiming his gun again.

I raised my hand between Thomas's arm and his torso, and fired my gun. Grove fell to his knees, a red circle darkening the front pocket of his white button-down. He fell onto his side, and then Thomas turned, grunting.

"How bad is it?" I asked, scrambling to pull up his shirt.

Blood was pouring from his wound, pushing out thick crimson with every beat of his heart.

"Fuck," Thomas said through his teeth.

I slid my gun into the back of my jeans while Thomas removed his T-shirt. He wadded it up and pressed it against his wound.

"You should lie down. It'll slow the bleeding," I said, dialing 911 on my cell phone.

The same two men from before peeked around the corner, and once they saw it was safe, they came out. "Are you okay, man?" one of them asked. "We called the cops. They're on their way."

I hung up the phone. "They got the call. They're coming."

As if on cue, sirens wailed from just a few short blocks away.

I smiled at Thomas. "You're going to be all right, okay?"

"Hell yes," he said, his voice strained. "I finally got you back. One bullet isn't going to fuck that up."

"Here," the other guy said, taking off his shirt. "You might go into shock, dude."

Thomas took a step, reaching for the shirt, and from the corner of my eye, I saw Grove raise his gun, pointing it directly at me.

"Shit!" one of the guys yelled.

Before I had time to react, Thomas leaped in front of me, shielding me with his body. We were facing each other when the pop went off, and Thomas jerked again.

"He's down again! I think he's dead!" one of the men said, pointing to Grove.

I looked around Thomas to see the two guys cautiously approach Grove, and then one kicked his gun away.

"He's not breathing!"

Thomas fell to his knees, a shocked look on his face, and then he dropped to his side. His head hit the sidewalk with a loud knock.

"Thomas?" I shrieked. "Thomas!" Tears blurred my vision as they welled up in my eyes.

My hands checked him over. He had a bullet wound on his lower back, three inches from his spine. Blood oozed up through the hole and spilled out onto the sidewalk.

Thomas whispered something, and I bent down to hear him.

"What?"

"Exit wound," he whispered.

I pulled him back to look at his front. He had matching gunshot wounds, one on each side of his lower abdomen. One was on his right side from the first time Grove had shot him, and another was on the opposite side.

"This one's clean," I said. "Went straight through."

I paused. *An exit wound.*

Pain blazed from my midsection, and I looked down. A red stain had spread on my shirt. The bullet had gone straight through Thomas and into me. Yanking at my shirt, I pulled it up to reveal blood oozing steadily from a small hole on my right lower chest, just beneath my ribs.

My blurry vision hadn't been from tears but from blood loss. I slumped next to Thomas, still keeping pressure on his wound with one hand and on mine with the other.

The sirens seemed farther away instead of closer. The neighborhood began to spin, and I collapsed onto my stomach.

"Liis," he said, turning onto his back to face me. His skin was pale and sweaty. "Stay with me, baby. They're coming."

The cold sidewalk felt good against my cheek. A heaviness came over me, an exhaustion unlike anything I'd ever felt before.

"I love you," I whispered with my last remaining strength.

A tear fell from the corner of my eye, crossed the bridge of my nose, and then dripped to our concrete bed, mixing with the red mess beneath us.

Thomas let go of the T-shirt, and with a weak hand, he reached for me, his eyes glossing over. "I love you."

I couldn't move, but I could feel his fingers touching mine, and they intertwined.

"Hang on," he said. He frowned. "Liis?"

I wanted to talk, to blink, to do anything to calm his fears, but nothing moved. I could see the panic in his eyes as life slipped away from me, but I was helpless.

"Liis!" he cried, a weak yell.

The corners of my vision darkened, and then it swallowed me whole. I sank into nothingness, a quiet loneliness where I could rest and be still.

Then, the world exploded—bright lights, commands, beeping in my ears, and pinches on my hands and arms.

Strange voices called my name.

I blinked. "Thomas?" My voice was muffled by the oxygen mask over my nose and mouth.

"She's back!" a woman said, standing over me.

The concrete bed beneath me was now a firm mattress. The room was white, making the spotlight overhead seem that much brighter.

I heard answers about my blood pressure, pulse, and oxygenation but none about my neighbor, my partner, the man I loved.

"Liis?" A woman stood over me, shielding the light from my eyes. She smiled. "Welcome back."

My lips struggled to form around the words I wanted to say.

The woman brushed my hair from my face, still squeezing the bag attached to my oxygen mask, the hissing noise next to my ear.

As if she could read my mind, she gestured with a nod behind her. "He's in surgery. He's doing great. The surgeon says he'll be just fine."

I closed my eyes, letting the tears fall down my temples into my ears.

"You have friends in the waiting room—Val, Charlie, and Joel."

I looked up at her and frowned. Finally, I realized Charlie and Joel were Sawyer and Marks.

"Susan just left to let them know you're stable. They can come back in a bit. Try to rest."

My muffled voice garbled my words.

"What?" she asked, lifting the mask.

"You don't call family, do you?" I said, surprised at how weak my own voice sounded.

"Not unless you request it."

I shook my head, and she reached across the bed before putting a lighter mask over my nose and mouth. A hissing came from inside.

"Deep breaths, please," she said, leaving my line of sight, as she adjusted the equipment surrounding me. "You're going to have to go upstairs later, but the doctor wants to get your stats up first."

I looked around, feeling groggy. My eyes blinked a few times, almost in slow motion. My body felt heavy again, and I drifted off for a moment before jerking awake.

"Whoa!" Val said, jumping up from her chair.

I was in a different room. This one had paintings of floral bouquets hanging on the walls.

"Where's Thomas?" I asked, my throat feeling like I'd swallowed gravel.

Val smiled and nodded up once. I looked over, seeing Thomas sleeping soundly. The rails had been lowered, and our hospital beds had been pushed together. Thomas's hand was covering mine.

"He had to pull some serious strings to make this happen," Val said. "Are you okay?"

I smiled at Val, but her face had darkened with worry.

"I don't know yet," I said, wincing.

Val picked up the call button and pressed it.

"How can I help you?" a nasally voice said.

The volume had been turned down so low that I could barely hear it.

Val raised the plastic remote closer to her mouth, so she could whisper, "She's awake."

"I'll let her nurse know."

Val gently patted my knee. "Stephanie will be in with your pain meds soon. She's been awesome. I think she's in love with Thomas."

"Isn't everyone?" Sawyer said from a dark corner.

"Hey, Charlie," I said, using the remote to sit up a bit.

He and Marks were sitting on opposite sides of the room.

Sawyer frowned. "You've already died once in the last twenty-four hours. Don't make me kill you again."

I giggled and then held my breath. "Damn, that hurts. I can't imagine what two feels like. Thomas probably won't be able to move when he wakes up." I looked over at him and squeezed his hand.

He blinked.

"Morning, sunshine," Marks said.

Thomas immediately looked to his left. His features softened, and a tired wide grin formed. "Hey." He pulled my hand to his mouth and kissed my knuckles. He relaxed his cheek against the pillow.

"Hey."

"Thought I'd lost you."

I wrinkled my nose. "Nah."

Sawyer stood. "I'm going to head out. Glad you're both all right. See you at work." He walked over to me, kissed my hair, and then strolled out.

"Bye," I said.

Val smiled. "He promised to sign the papers."

"He did?" I asked, surprised.

Marks snorted. "On the condition that he keeps the condo."

I looked to Val.

She shrugged. "I hope you were serious when you said you wanted a roommate."

"It's only temporary anyway," Marks said. "I'm going to talk her into moving in with me."

"Fuck off," she snapped. She smiled down at me. "You just worry about getting well. I'll take care of everything. It's perfect timing anyway. You'll need someone to help you cook and clean."

Marks looked at Thomas. "You're shit out of luck, buddy."

"Can I move in, too?" Thomas teased. He held his breath while he shifted to get comfortable.

Val motioned to Marks. "We should go. Let them rest."

Marks nodded, standing and patting Thomas's foot rail. "Hang in there, brother. We'll hold down the fort."

"I was afraid you'd say that," Thomas said.

Marks held out his hand to Val, she took it, and they walked into the hallway together.

"What about Grove?" I asked Thomas. "Any updates?"

He nodded. "Marks said they're taking care of it, keeping it along the same lines—a mugging gone wrong."

"What about the witnesses?"

"It's taken care of. Benny has no clue that Travis will be knocking on his door soon, and Tarou will just think he's lost his infiltration. The investigation can go on as planned."

I nodded. Thomas rubbed my thumb with his, and I looked down at our hands.

"I hope this is okay," he said.

"It's better than okay."

"You know what this means, don't you?" he asked.

I shook my head.

"Matching scars."

A wide grin stretched across my face.

Thomas held my hand against his cheek and then kissed my wrist. Slowly lowering our hands to the mattress, he settled in, relaxing, as he made sure he could see me until he fell asleep.

Thomas needed me. He made me happy and made me crazy, and he was right: only together did we make sense. I refused to ruminate on what would happen next, to analyze the probability or logistics of a successful relationship, to try to control whether I felt too much. I'd finally found the kind of love that was worth risking a broken heart.

We'd had to find each other to finally understand that love could not be controlled. Predictions, assumptions, and absolutes were illusions. My love for him was volatile, uncontrollable, and overpowering, but…that was love. Love was real.

EPILOGUE

E<small>VEN THOUGH YEARS HAD PASSED</small> since the last time I had half-unpacked boxes lying in every room, the organized chaos still made me smile. Memories of moving into my first condo in San Diego—even the first volatile months—were good ones, and they had carried me through the stress of training in my job as the newest Intelligence Analyst at the NCAVC in Quantico.

Just six months before, I had applied for my dream job. Three months later, I had been transferred. Now, I was wearing a robe and fuzzy socks, unpacking the sundresses I would be wearing if I were still in California. Instead, I had to promise myself not to adjust the thermostat—again—and I was sure to keep near the blazing fireplace in my bedroom.

I untied the belt of my robe, letting it fall open, and then lifted my heather-gray FBI hoodie, reaching down to feel the thick circular scar on my lower abdomen. The healed wound would always remind me of Thomas. It helped me to pretend he was close when he wasn't. Our matching scars were a little like the feeling of being under the same sky—but better.

A car engine grew louder as it pulled into the drive, and headlights raced over the walls before extinguishing. I walked across the living room and peeked out the curtains next to the front door.

The neighborhood was quiet. The only traffic was the car in my drive. Nearly all the windows in the neighboring houses were dark. I loved the new house and the new community. A lot of young families lived on my street, and although the door experienced regular knocking and I'd seemed to be fielding daily requests for chocolate or cheese sales from the local school kids, I felt more at home than ever before.

A dark figure stepped out of the vehicle and grabbed a duffel bag. Then, the headlights came on again, and the car backed out and drove away. I rubbed my sweaty palms on my hoodie as the shadow of a man slowly walked toward my porch. He wasn't supposed to be here yet. I wasn't ready.

He climbed the steps, but hesitated when he reached the door.

I turned the bolt lock and pulled the knob toward me. "It's over?"

"It's over," Thomas said, appearing exhausted.

I opened the door wide, and Thomas stepped inside, pulling me into his arms. He didn't speak. He barely breathed.

Since my transfer, we had lived on opposite sides of the country, and I had become accustomed to missing him. But when he'd left with Travis a few hours after supervising the delivery of the rest of his belongings to our new home in Quantico, I'd been worried. The assignment hadn't just been dangerous. Together, Thomas and Travis had raided Benny Carlisi's offices, and organized crime in Vegas would never be the same.

By the look on Thomas's face, it hadn't gone well.

"Have you been debriefed?" I asked.

He nodded. "But Travis refused. He went straight home. I'm worried about him."

"It's his and Abby's anniversary. Call him tomorrow. Make sure it's done."

Thomas sat on the couch, dug his elbows into his thighs, and looked down. "It wasn't supposed to go down like this." He breathed as if the wind had been knocked out of him.

"Do you feel like talking about it?" I asked.

"No."

I waited, knowing he always said that before he began a story.

"Trav's cover was blown. Benny and his men took him underground. I panicked at first, but Sawyer got a location on them. We listened while they beat Travis for a good hour."

"Jesus," I said, touching his shoulder.

"Travis got some good intel." He laughed once without humor. "Benny was making a grand speech and giving him everything, thinking Travis was about to die."

"And?" I asked.

"The stupid son of a bitch threatened Abby. He began detailing the torture she would endure after he killed Travis. It was pretty graphic."

"So, Benny's dead," I said, more of a statement than a question.

"Yeah," Thomas said with a sigh.

"Years of work, and Benny won't even see the inside of a courtroom."

Thomas frowned. "Travis said he was sorry. We still have a lot of work to do. Mick Abernathy has contacts with a lot of bosses besides Benny. We can work the case from that angle."

I raked my fingers gently through Thomas's hair. He didn't know that Abby and I had a secret. She would be handing the Bureau everything she had on her father in exchange for keeping her husband home and out of trouble. Abby had agreed to give it to Travis by their anniversary, and he would furnish that intel to Val, who had been promoted as the new ASAC in San Diego.

"I promised you I'd be finished unpacking by the time you got home," I said. "I feel bad."

"It's okay. I wanted to help," he said. His mind was elsewhere. "I'm sorry you couldn't be there. This was just as much your moment as it was mine." He looked up and touched the stretched fabric of my hoodie that covered my protruding belly—the second unplanned thing to ever happen to us. "But I'm glad you weren't."

I smiled. "I can't see my scar anymore."

Thomas stood and wrapped me in his solid arms. "Now that I'm finally here, you can just look at mine for the next eleven weeks—give or take a few days—until you can see yours again."

We walked, hand in hand, across our living room, and Thomas led me through our bedroom door. We sat together on the bed and watched the flickering fire and the dancing shadows on the stacks of cardboard holding picture frames and trinkets from our life together.

"You'd think we would have figured out a more efficient system for this by now," Thomas said, frowning at the boxes.

"You just don't like the unpacking part."

"No one likes to unpack, no matter how happy that person might be to move."

"Are you happy to move?" I asked.

"I'm happy you got this job. You've worked toward it for a long time."

I raised an eyebrow. "Did you doubt me?"

"Not for a second. But I was nervous about the ASAC position in DC. I was beginning to sweat getting settled before the baby arrived, and you didn't seem to be in a huge hurry for me to get here."

I wrinkled my nose. "I'm not thrilled about your hour commute though."

He shrugged. "Better than transcontinental. You dodged the part about not being in a hurry for the father of your child to be around."

"Just because I'm learning to allow for a few variables doesn't mean I've given up on having a master plan."

His eyebrows shot up. "So, this was the plan? For me to go crazy from missing you for three months? For me to take the red-eye to be here for every doctor's appointment? For me to worry that every phone call was bad news?"

"You're here now, and everything's perfect."

He frowned. "I knew you would apply for this position. I psyched myself up for the move. Nothing could have prepared me for you to tell me four weeks later that you were pregnant. Do you know what it did to me, watching my pregnant girlfriend move across the country—alone? You didn't even take everything with you. I was terrified."

I breathed out a laugh. "Why didn't you tell me all of this before?"

"I've been trying to be supportive."

"It all happened exactly the way I'd planned," I said with a smile, incredibly satisfied with that statement. "I got the job and took just enough with me to get by. You got the job, and now, we can unpack together."

"How about, when it involves our family, you plan with me?"

"When we try to make plans together, nothing happens the way it's supposed to," I teased, nudging him with my elbow.

He put his arm around me and pulled me close to his side, placing his free hand on my round stomach. He held me for a long time as we watched the fire and enjoyed the quiet, our new home, and the end of a case that we had both worked on for a few years shy of a decade.

"Don't you know by now?" Thomas said, touching his lips to my hair. "It's somewhere in the unforeseen when the best, most important moments of our lives seem to happen."

ACKNOWLEDGMENTS

Thank you to Kristy Weiberg, for not only being one of my biggest cheerleaders, but for also introducing me to Amy Thomure who is married to FBI Agent Andrew Thomure.

Andrew, I appreciate your patience as I asked what you probably thought were odd questions, but you never made me feel that way. Thank you for all your help!

As always, thank you to my incredible husband, Jeff. I couldn't list everything you do on a daily basis to keep the house running, to get the kids to various places they need to be—on time—and on top of everything else you do behind the scenes. You are my savior, and I would not be able to keep the hours I do without you.

Thank you to my children for understanding my strange hours and for their forgiveness when Mommy says for the hundredth time, "I can't. I'm working."

Thank you to Autumn Hull of Wordsmith Publicity, Jovana Shirley of Unforeseen Editing, Sarah Hansen of Okay Creations, and Deanna Pyles. You are all such valuable members of my team, and I appreciate the tremendous effort you put into helping me complete this novel.

To authors Teresa Mummert, Abbi Glines, and Colleen Hoover, who allow me to vent and celebrate, be random, and ask silly questions—You are my home base, and I would be lost in this life without you.

Thank you to Selena Lee, Amanda Medlock, and Kelli Smith for being a constant source of encouragement and laughter. Kelli, thanks for allowing me to borrow your husband's name! I can't wait until we're all together again. Your company (with Deanna) truly makes up some of the best days of my life.

Thank you BIG to Ellie of Love N. Books and Megan Davis of That's What She Said book blogs. Without their help in the last two months, I wouldn't have been able to concentrate on finishing this novel. Thank you for doing all the heavy lifting on the A Beautiful

Wedding Vegas Book Event, and thank you for stepping up to help without hesitation!

Last but never least, thank you Danielle Lagasse, Jessica Landers, Kelli Spears, and the awesome MacPack for the amazing support and for spreading the word about my work!

ABOUT THE AUTHOR

 JAMIE MCGUIRE was born in Tulsa, Oklahoma. She attended Northern Oklahoma College, the University of Central Oklahoma, and Autry Technology Center where she graduated with a degree in Radiography.

Jamie paved the way for the New Adult genre with the international bestseller *Beautiful Disaster*. Her follow-up novel, *Walking Disaster*, debuted at #1 on the *New York Times*, *USA Today*, and *Wall Street Journal* bestseller lists. *Beautiful Oblivion*, book one of the Maddox Brothers books, also topped the *New York Times* bestseller list, debuting at #1.

Novels also written by Jamie McGuire include: apocalyptic thriller, *Red Hill*; the *Providence* series, a young adult paranormal romance trilogy; *Apolonia*, a dark sci-fi romance; and several novellas, including *A Beautiful Wedding*, *Among Monsters: A Red Hill Novella*, and *Happenstance: A Novella Series*.

Jamie lives on a ranch just outside of Enid, Oklahoma with her husband, Jeff, and their three children. They share their thirty acres with cattle, six horses, three dogs, and a cat named Rooster.

Find Jamie at www.jamiemcguire.com or on Facebook, Twitter, Tsu, and Instagram.

happenstance

a novella series

Part Three

February 2, 2015

The sweet, heartfelt final installment of a story about
chance, choices, and change.

Pre-order Now